3

THE INFIDEL BOOKS

THE

MERCENARY'S DECEPTION

ANGELA R. WATTS

THE MERCENARY'S DECEPTION

THE INFIDEL BOOKS - 3

ANGELA R. WATTS

Contents

ALSO BY ANGELA

THE INFIDEL BOOKS

The Divided Nation, The Infidel Books #1

The Grim Alliance, The Infidel Books #2

The Mercenary's Deception, The Infidel Books #3

The Blood Republic, The Infidel Books #4

Emmanuel, an Infidel Books short story prequel

Lockdown, an Infidel Books short story prequel

REMNANT TRILOGY

Golgotha

Tabor

WHISPERS OF HEAVEN

Seek

ANTHOLOGIES

Run from the Dead

LIFE

The Depths We'll Go To

PRAISE FOR THE INFIDEL BOOKS

"Fresh, fast, and almost too timely for comfort, The Divided Nation is a gripping thriller from an authoritative new voice on the thriller scene. Angela Watts can really, really write." – Ryan Steck, The Real Book Spy

"Superior novel by the talented author Ms. Angela Watts. Action, adventure, general badassery? Oh yes!" – Lt Col USMC (Ret.) H. Rip Rawlings, New York Times and USA Today bestseller of RED METAL

"I highly recommend this book. It is packed with everything a good thriller should have - action, memorable characters, a plot that flies by, emotion, light & darkness, and more action." – Stuart Ashenbrenner, Best Thriller Books reviewer

To those who choose faith over fear,
Even when we shake,
May mountains move, as well.

GANGSTERS

George Johnston: United Nations politician, businessman, and ganglord of his own large army that controls large portions of the UN across the globe.

West Johnston: gangster son of George Johnston, the Johnston heir.

Kaleb Savage: ganglord and close ally of George Johnston. Father of Nate Savage and uncle of Jack Savage.

Jack Savage: gangster son of Hunter Savage.

Hunter Savage: ex-special operative, assassin that works for George.

Nate Savage: gangster son of Kaleb. Best friends with Simon.

Jordan Bucks: ganglord and close ally of George Johnston's. Father of Simon Bucks.

Simon Bucks: gangster son of Jordan Bucks.

Gideon Hochberg: close ally of George Johnston. Best friends with Alex Thompson.

Alex Thompson: gangster in George's gang. Comrade of Gideon Hochberg.

Percy & Preston Royal: brothers in Gideon's group.

Spencer Anderson: gangster in George's group. Friends with West and Jack. Older brother of Randy Anderson.

Ty Brooks: gangster in George's gang, close friend to West.

FISHER FAMILY

Burl Fisher and Kay Fisher: parents of the Fisher family and leaders of Springtown, Kentucky.

Rene' Fisher: daughter of the Fisher parents. Friends with Simon.

Lee Fisher: son of the Fisher parents.

Brian Jones: Union Army General. Husband and father. Birth son of Kay Fisher.

Terri Brewer and Howie (Henry) Brewer: daughter and son-in-law of the Fisher parents, and their five kids, Dax, Jaycee, Paisley, Lily, and Aiden.

OTHER

Keegan Black: a new ally to Springtown and Gideon Hochberg. In secret, he aids small townships by paying enemies to leave them alone. Brother of Brett Black.

Thomas Flannery: ganglord to the Falcons.

Chloe Downfield: a civilian of Springtown.

Philip & Danny Dunnham: brothers that fled George's group and abide in Springtown.

ANGELA R. WATTS

CHAPTER ONE

December 24th, 2027

THE FATE OF THE Second Civil War rested on Union leader Brian Jones. He had worked in secret for years, leading the Union to success, honored as he rose in the government's ranks. Once a soldier, always a soldier.

But no one said you had to fight for the same side forever.

The phone line was silent for one long moment before his eighteen-year-old baby sister spoke, "Brian?"

"Rene'... it's me. Listen closely." Brian licked his lips and glanced at the entrance of his tent. His men didn't need to hear this conversation. When he gave his oath to serve the Union, no matter the cost, part of his resolutions included leaving his family behind, too. That's why he hadn't rescued Rene' only months ago, when she had been held hostage by a bothersome enemy to gain his attention.

She swore sharply at him.

"Rene'—"

Rene' cut him off. "You haven't said a word to this family for over five damn years," she hissed. "You can't just call me after what you did—"

"You know of the failed Union attack in D.C.?" Brian continued, unfazed by Rene's jab. The past was history. Brian had dedicated his life to his career, to saving the nation he respected. He wouldn't allow regret for abandoning his family to blind him—especially not now.

"You failed."

"I did." His words were flat. "In case I don't get the chance to contact you again, Rene'—" He hesitated. How long had it been since he had breathed a single word to his parents, or siblings? "I need you to know that I will fix what I've done. For you, for our family, for the nation... I will end this war."

"So I've heard," Rene' said bitterly.

The line was as secure as he could make it, so long as he kept it brief, but he couldn't risk explaining anything to her. It wasn't worth the risk because she wouldn't listen or care. He had hurt her and there was no fixing that. But he could fix the nation so his family wouldn't be slaughtered.

"I know it doesn't mean shit but you'll soon see." Brian hung up. He sat on his cot, running a hand through his hair.

Brain couldn't shake the reality that Lee was sixteen now, old enough to fight in the war between brothers. And despite his efforts, Gideon Hochberg, the ruthless ganglord he had allied with, had gotten under his skin. *"One day, you'll shoot a rebel across enemy lines, and it will be Lee."* The words rang in Brian's head repeatedly.

If Brian didn't stop this nation's war, it would never end, and there would be nothing left of the USA before long. There wasn't much left of the old America, anyway. Most basic constitutional rights were gone or restricted. Still, every sorry soul was caught up in a war they'd tried to avoid.

Every American citizen had a place in the scheme of things, as warriors or cattle. Brian had played a key role in the evolving ideology of America. But now it was time to take it all back. Even if it killed him.

Considering the shit the government was working on in the underground lab, it probably would kill him. Truth be told, Brian was ready for that.

BRIAN'S CREW KEPT LOW, but the rats that called themselves Confederates lurked in every shadow. A group of the rebel soldiers ambushed the crew that night.

However, the enemies had bit off more than they could chew.

Brian, alongside his finest soldiers, picked them off one by one in the pale, thick snow. The men screamed and dropped into snow banks and the mud. Brian fired his rifle, hitting a civilian in the back of his head. The soldiers ceased fire, and the moans of the Confederate militia filled the silent forest.

Brian went over, gun aimed. There wasn't much use in asking for intel—they were obviously rookies, sent by no leader, only looking for a quick fight and fast ammo.

Brian fired and killed the man groaning in the snow, sending a blast of blood and brains into the white snow.

"General!"

Brian cast one last glance to ensure the attackers were all dead, turning to face his men. But his gaze fell to his close friend, Davy Wilson. The soldier with eyes like a hawk and a sniper's steady hand lay in the snow beside the Humvee.

"Davy." Brian's breath caught. He ran over, dropping beside his comrade and checking his injury. A gunshot had gone through Davy's neck—it wouldn't have penetrated if Davy had his helmet on but they'd removed them to sleep. Davy had hardly gotten out of his sleeping bag on the cold ground before he'd been shot down.

Davy didn't respond, eyes staring into the sky, gun in the snow beside him. Brian gripped Davy's gritty face. "Davy..." No pulse. No breathing. Of course not. His goddamn neck had been blown through.

Brian had seen worse before. He'd seen much worse dozens of times.

But it was Davy. It wasn't supposed to be Davy. Not now. Not like this.

The crew was silent in the eerie forest, heads lowered. Davy had balanced Brian's hostility, balanced his coldness —Davy was everything Brian hadn't been, including a good husband and father.

Brian took a slow breath. Someone will have to tell his family. *But I can't. Not now on the run. Let them think he'll come home... for now.*

Tears burned Brian's eyes. A part of his brain told him to get up, start burying his close friend into the cold dirt that would be hell to shovel. But he just sat there with Davy's hand in his own, stroking Davy's hair.

He'd always wanted to go rogue.

Now it's my turn to be the mercenary and betray my country for its own betterment. I'll do what Davy never could.

CHAPTER TWO

December 24th, 2027

CHRISTMAS EVE WAS MEANT for rejoicing and fellowship, even in post-apocalyptic America. But when Brian hung up, Rene' Fisher didn't feel like rejoicing. Her stomach jumbled into knots, memories flooding back as she sat on the back porch, fighting the tears pooling in her eyes. Brian had left her family long ago. When she'd been kidnapped and tortured, he had gotten the message and hadn't done a single thing.

How dare he talk to her like he hadn't done anything wrong? He hadn't even apologized for what he had done.

"Rene'?" Simon's voice broke into her thoughts. "I thought we agreed not to come back out here again, it's cold—" He stopped. "Why are you crying?" He sat beside her, and searched her face with wide eyes.

Rene' hesitated. Should she tell him? The night had been so perfect—everyone gathered inside, safe and cozy. Simon had kissed her for the first time, too. For once peace had settled in her heart, and now Brian had uprooted it again. "Brian called me."

Simon's expression darkened. "Brian called you just now?"

"Yeah."

"What did he say?"

Rene' told him everything. His face remained unreadable, eyes heavy with anger. "He didn't say anything about... about if he was sorry, did he?"

"No." Rene's chest tightened. She wouldn't cry in front of Simon again that night. "He didn't. He doesn't care about us, he never has. Not really. E-even if he did, he doesn't now. He made his choice. He chose his career. I get it." She wiped her eyes, steeling herself and allowing a cold anger to take over. Hurt and grief wouldn't drive a person to be strong, but logic and anger could. She'd be strong.

Simon took her hand and kissed it. "Well, to hell with Brian. If he fixes what he messed up, that'll help others, but it doesn't mean you have to do anything." A pause. "You don't have to talk to him again. You don't owe him anything, OK?"

But she wanted to fix Brian. She wanted him to love his family. She wanted him to come back, to apologize and set things right. It was a selfish thought however, especially if his change of heart would lead him to benefiting the entire nation.

Rene' shook her head. "How can he fix anything?"

"Well, he's some Army general or whatever, right?" Simon sighed. "He's got plenty of training. If he turned against the Union... He didn't mention that, so maybe that's not his goal, but no matter what he does, he could set a lot of stuff right. It'd just be hard."

"It'd be easier if more people did the same thing," Rene' mumbled bitterly.

"We are." Simon put his arms around her. "It will be OK, Rene'. No matter what." Only hours before, all had been perfect. Rene' had high hopes, and so much faith things would be fine despite it all.

How could she be so weak as to allow Brian to break her heart again?Rene' hugged Simon tightly, her body relaxing. "I-I hope he does fix things, Simon. Whatever he can fix, I hope he does."

Even if he never came home and never loved them, maybe he did have the power to end the war. That would change everything. People could have hope, could heal, could rebuild America like it had been created to be.

Simon kissed her cheek, arms strong around her as he rested his chin on her head. "Me too. But I'm still gonna kick his ass if I ever meet him."

"I won't stop you." Rene' chuckled weakly. "But... I should go tell Mom and Dad."

"Give it the night," he whispered. "You need some time to just relax... Please, don't let Brian ruin this for you. You've been so excited for this Christmas party."

She sank against him. "I'll tell them tomorrow."

"I'll tell them with you." Simon helped her stand. "For tonight... Let's wait for Santa Clause to climb his fat ass down the farmhouse chimney like we're ten-year-olds."

Rene' laughed and followed him inside her home. Her family and crew from George Johnston's gang gathered as one family. Even though they were George's finest men in the most powerful mafia in the US, Gideon Hochberg and Alex Thompson were eating their weight in gingerbread cookies at one corner of the living room while Graham played with Rene's youngest niece. Graham was a scrawny teen and a close friend of Simon and Nate's.

Nate, Simon's best friend, was talking with Rene's sister Terri and her husband, Howard. Everything was a bit loud, with the chatting, and the kids hyped up on sugar and excitement for tomorrow morning, but Rene' settled back down with Simon. It wasn't long after that the kids were rounded up by their parents and taken home.

The men all slept on pallets and cots, Alex being wounded so he got the couch in the Fisher's living room. They were still reserved and a little shy, but Rene' knew they were enjoying the aspect of a family holiday more than they let on. Her stomach twisted. Why did good things never last?

Or would good things even mean as much if hell didn't follow?

Rene' hugged Simon and her younger brother, Lee before going to bed. She didn't want to think about anything tonight except her first kiss with Simon. The fate of humanity would still be looming over her head in the morning.

———

ONCE RENE' WENT TO bed, Simon snuck out of the living room and caught Mr. Fisher in the hallway. Mr. Fisher was preparing for bed, eyes narrowing at Simon's interruption. "Is something wrong?" he asked, concern in his tone.

"N-no sir. No, sorry. I, uh, had a question." Simon gulped hard, palms sweating. He'd wanted to ask the question before, but there'd never been a right time. Tonight worked as well as any—if Mr. Fisher agreed.

"Go ahead." Mr. Fisher nodded. He was a good man, a good father, like Simon's Dad, Jordan. While the fathers had a lot in common—morals, strength, kindness—Mr. Fisher terrified Simon. At any moment, he could decide Simon wasn't good enough for Rene'.

And he'd be right.

Simon fought hard to keep his voice steady, chest tightening. *Just ask. Say it.* "I, um—" Another breath. "I want to start seeing Rene'."

Mr. Fisher raised one eyebrow, a thin smirk coming to his face. "You see her often, don't you?"

Simon flushed. "I-I mean I want to date your daughter, sir. Please." Was there a right way to ask? Simon didn't know. Maybe he should've asked Jordan how to do this properly.

Mr. Fisher cocked his head and studied Simon like he saw through his soul. He probably did. "Simon, you've proven time and time again that you love Rene' and you're willing to put your life on the line to protect her—you have before." He sighed. "I think it would make Rene' happy to date you. But..."

The breath rushed out of Simon in surprise but he still didn't dare speak, waiting for a final answer.

"This isn't normal life, Simon. If you date Rene', you understand what that means, right?"

Simon straightened. "I love Rene', sir. I'll die to protect her. I haven't asked her if she sees a future for us, but if she does, or even if she doesn't, I will protect her, no matter what. I love her more than anything." The words came quick and firm, straight from the fibers of his being.

"You both need to love God before all else." Mr. Fisher gave him a calm frown. "But you..." he chuckled softly, grasping Simon's shoulder. "You're doing just fine. You'll be less fine if you do anything—and I mean anything—to hurt my daughter or break her heart, but I don't have much doubt you two aren't meant for each other."

Simon gaped, deflating. "Y-you mean...?"

"If she wants to date you, you have my blessing."

Simon grinned, suppressing a whoop of excitement before hugging Mr. Fisher like a giddy kid. Mr. Fisher patted him on the back, grunting. "I'm not much of a hugger, kid."

Simon pulled away quickly. "Sorry—"

Mr. Fisher laughed and nudged his arm. "You'd best get used to the joking."

Simon's spirits soared. Home—he'd found a home. A place where he belonged, right at Rene's side. A family that loved him and joked with him. It was the opposite of the gang he'd grown up in.

Mr. Fisher went to bed, and Simon went into the living room again. Graham was curled up on a pallet, his thin shoulders shaking softly.

"Graham?" Simon whispered, stepping over. "Bud, are you crying?" He knelt beside Graham and touched his arm.

Graham flinched hard, his head shoving further under his pillow, words muffled, "Go to bed, Simon."

Simon sat down and gently prodded Graham out from his covers. "You are crying." He frowned. "Why? What's wrong? Do you feel OK?"

Sniffling, Graham wiped his red eyes, tears soaking his face. "I feel fine."

"Then why are you crying? You wanted to be here, right?" Simon wrapped a protective arm around him and sat against the couch. Graham had always been soft-hearted and timid, but after one of the gangsters in the group had assaulted him, he talked less and would never tell Simon what was truly bothering him.

Simon should've pushed more. The kid shouldn't be breaking down now—what had Simon done wrong?

"Y-yeah!" Graham forced quickly. "I-I love it here."

"What's got you upset, kid?" Simon asked softly. "You can talk to me, OK?"

Graham hesitated. "T-the Fishers are Christians."

"Yeah," Simon said. "So are we. What's up?"Graham took a shaky breath. "W-what if they hate me because... b-because of what happened?"

"Is this about what Brock did?" Simon's anger flared, but he hid it. He squeezed Graham and smiled weakly. "They're not like that, honest. They love you."

"If they found out what happened to me, they'll think I'm a freak. Or they'd be all grossed out and not want me around the babies—" Graham's face twisted in pain, but Simon cut him off.

"That's not gonna happen, Graham. They know. They don't see you any different." Simon smoothed Graham's unruly brown curls.

"They do?" Graham's expression crumbled, fear in his eyes. Simon held tight, wishing that he could take away Graham's pain and struggles—he'd tried for years and it only got worse.

"Yeah, kid, I-I told them when it happened. I wanted them to pray. I thought... thought that God could help us if He heard them praying," Simon said quietly. "And He did."

Graham fell quiet for a long moment, then, "I don't think He did."

"What makes you say that?"

"Because I think I'm gay. And God hates that. Right?"

Simon's heart fell to his feet at the bitterness and shame in Graham's voice. He pulled Graham close and Graham buried his face against Simon's chest. "He doesn't hate you, Graham. He loves you."

"If I was a good Believer I wouldn't be struggling, Si!" Graham sobbed.

Simon held tighter, voice firm, "Don't say that, G. Everyone struggles with something. God's not angry at you, OK?"

"The Bible says He is!"

Simon pulled away and cupped Graham's trembling chin in a hand. "Graham, I love you. We all love you. God loves you. Whatever you're struggling with is not your fault, and you're gonna be OK."

"No, I won't! M-my sister—" Graham stopped himself short, just like he always did when he almost spoke of his older sister who cared for him before he'd moved into the gang. Sometimes he still visited, always returning to Paradise a defeated mess. He never told them what she did or told him.

It couldn't have been anything good.

"I don't care what your sister or anyone else says," Simon said sharply. "Understand? You're gonna be fine, Graham. You've got us and we won't go anywhere, no matter what."

Graham sobbed against him. "A-are you mad, Si?"

"Mad?" Simon laughed tiredly, ruffling Graham's hair. "I've been a worried wreck, kid. I'm grateful you're talking again."

"B-but I'm messed up now."

"No, you're human. Like the rest of us." Simon pulled the cover around Graham carefully. "And we'll get through this, together, just like we always do."

Graham shuddered, eyes heavy with tears but he let go of Simon. "Y-you're sure God doesn't hate me for what I... what I'm thinking?"

"If He hates you, kid, then He'd have to hate me for the stuff I've done." Simon hesitated. "I've done stuff I don't like G, and it was wrong. All I can do is try to let it go and make better choices. Maybe this will be like that. I don't know honestly, but we'll find out together, OK? Just promise me you'll hang tight." Simon hadn't the slightest clue what to do. Graham was soft and he couldn't survive the gang much longer, but if the boy hated himself, what then? If Simon wasn't there, what if the kid did something stupid out of fear or guilt? It wasn't like Simon knew what God said about this either. He'd never cared to know.

Simon tucked Graham in. "Sleep kid; it'll be fine."

Graham closed his eyes and fell back asleep in a matter of moments. Simon sat on his pallet, heart in his throat, a tired voice breaking his thoughts, "I'll talk it over with Mr. Fisher," Nate whispered from the couch. Nate lifted his head, expression unreadable.

Simon nodded, biting his lip hard. "We both will. Maybe he'll know how to help." Simon knew plenty of gay men, and it never mattered to him, but he'd never known them to be broken. He didn't want Graham broken. Whatever it took, Simon would fix it. He'd help Graham.

I won't fail again. Could he be man enough to protect what he now cherished most? Or was he destined to be a gangster that died in a ditch like so many others?

CHAPTER THREE

December 25th, 2027

CHRISTMAS MORNING BROUGHT THE most joy Gideon Hochberg had ever seen in one room before. The children opened their gifts—few in number but adored in their eyes—and spread laughter, hugs, and silly shenanigans. Graham was practically glued to Rene's baby nephew who squealed in delight as his siblings played. Even the adults acted a bit childish; Alex, tired and sore, played with the kids happily.

Lee and Danny, the younger brother to Philip— George's finest sniper who had fled George thanks to Gideon's recent help—talked in the dining room while the women started breakfast. There had been a good amount of gifts but nothing crazy. The heart behind those little, simple gifts had meant the world to them all.

Gideon stared down at the homemade knife that Lee had gifted him, along with the small Bible that Mrs. Fisher had given him. Didn't these people know that he was a killer? A thief? A con artist? Why wouldn't they expect him to be a liar? He had helped Rene' be kidnapped, after all. Why would these people—the Fishers, the town of Springtown—open their doors for gangsters? Gangsters without homes, without redemption?

Officer Sean O'Malley sat beside him on the couch, offering him a mug of black coffee. Gideon took it and thanked him, tucking the gifts into the pockets of his pants.

"Stay in touch, Gideon," Sean said firmly, voice low. "I know what you wanna do. I wanna help."

Gideon set his jaw, watching Alex play with the kids beside the gleaming Christmas tree. Originally from Australia before his parents moved, Alex had then grown up in foster care after his parents died. He'd run and ended up in the Falcons, a cruel gang led by Thomas Flannery, but at seventeen or so, had gotten himself beaten nearly to death by Flannery and tossed for dead—but Gideon had saved him. The two hadn't looked back since, until Flannery attacked Springtown and kidnapped Alex and Simon, torturing them both for fun.

Gideon was going to hunt and kill Flannery. Sean O'Malley wanted in—but why? Sean had no personal attachment to the gangs.

Sean chuckled tiredly. "Springtown fought hard, Gideon. It's barely been over a month since we buried our dead." He took a long sip of his steaming black coffee. "I want Flannery to pay for killing my people too."

"That's not really what I heard you saying last night." Gideon frowned.

"I told you to let me know if you needed help."

Gideon eyed him. "You meant it, huh?"

Sean nodded.

"All right, Carrot Top. I'll let you know."

Sean smirked and stood, going to help Mrs. Fisher, Rene', and Terri with breakfast. Gideon watched the others, drinking his third coffee of the morning. Alex laughed and talked with the kids, their faces bright as stars. This was the sort of life Alex deserved. He deserved a wife, kids, a home in Springtown where he could be safe. He didn't deserve to be tortured and dragged around as a warrior.

When the kids were called to breakfast, Alex went over, sitting beside Gideon. Gideon smiled, Simon's words from a few days ago ringing in his head. *Be happy for Alex's sake.* "Having fun?"

"Not too much." Alex smiled. "But they're pretty good at not body slamming my injuries, so yay for me. Ready to eat?""Yeah, I'll be there in a second."

Alex studied him for a moment, blue eyes shining. "Thanks, Gid. I know this social thing isn't your gig."

"Don't thank me." Gideon shook his head. "I think I'm doing fine."

Alex laughed. "You haven't killed anyone, mate."

"I deserve something for that." Gideon teased and stood. "Don't I?""Absolutely." Alex rolled his eyes, following Gideon into the kitchen. "But... really. Thank you."

Gideon nodded, refusing to admit even to himself that this sort of life wasn't that bad for him either. But he was a fighter. This sort of life was out of reach for him. Besides, it would get boring after a while. Without his missions, Gideon wouldn't have anything to live for.

"And, uh," Alex started a bit more nervously. "Now's probably not the best time, but I invited Noah Gyles to come work with us."

Gideon groaned and headed to the coffee pot. "We'll discuss that later." He preferred it if Noah stayed behind with Philip and Danny, who'd be hunkering down in Springtown to help out, but Noah wouldn't make it long alone.

SPRINGTOWN AND KALEB HAD formed the Grim Alliance months prior. While no gangsters would live within the town's borders, Kaleb's men would offer assistance and supplies if the town ever needed it again. A blessing for Springtown, but Gideon wasn't sure how long it would last.

The gangsters left Springtown the day after Christmas, returning to their sanctuary a couple states away. Gideon kept his eyes on the road for any caravans or enemy groups, letting rock music play over the speakers. Alex slept in the passenger seat, leaving Gideon alone with his thoughts. The kid, Noah, slept in the backseat, nothing but a bag of bones and bruises.

The events of the past six months weighed heavily on Gideon, but the largest mistake he'd made was allowing his alliance with Brian Jones to dissolve. Brian hadn't had contact since their argument—Gideon had warned Brian not to play his role on the Union side, Brian had ignored him, and the Union had lost the capital.

Gideon ran a hand through his hair, shoulders sagging. The Second Civil War had gone on long enough. Hell, most of the United States didn't consider themselves at war with each other. Rich citizens or any middle-class civilian willing to obey the dictatorship's every command were allowed to live in bliss. They lived in housing, gated communities, safe and secure locations where the realities of war couldn't reach them.

It was hard to stop a war that didn't affect every civilian. Millions of Americans were complacent, not caring who was slaughtered a hundred miles away, so long as they got their government funding. After all, why would such Americans want the rebels to live? No matter what was done, the Confederates would lose.

When the patriots each breathed their last, it would be game over.

Truth be told, Gideon didn't care what happened to America. He was one man and couldn't fix the entire American government. The United States weren't even united anymore. There was a Union side, made of the original government, and a rebel side, governed by Confederate President Larry Simmons.

No, they could all choose their sides, get shot up, die with honor.

Gideon had different goals in mind.

He'd kill Flannery and kill George Johnston. The rest was up to the glory bastards.

CHAPTER FOUR

December 26th, 2027

WEST JOHNSTON HAD ONE mission—kill his father. All things considered, he wasn't doing a terrible job at being George's trusted right-hand man and confidant. He pulled off every job George gave him, and most importantly, he'd passed the legendary Test only a month or so before.

So why did he have a gut-feeling he was missing something?

West grabbed his duffel bag and got out of the bullet-proof vehicle. George had removed him from Alamo, Mexico, calling him back home to the family mansion in Michigan. He hadn't wanted to leave the Mexican border —the men there were good followers. West's leadership had strengthened them, and he had even smuggled kids to Jordan, saving them from the human trafficking ring.

But every bit of good he did had to stay hidden, or George would find out and ruin everything.

Bracing himself, West entered the mansion, greeting the two rottweilers in the grand foyer. George came into the room with a pleasant smile, hugging his son gently. "It's good to see you again, son. Your room is waiting as always."

West released him. "Thank you, Father." He still hated calling George by any endearment, but it was part of his role—if he wanted to kill George, he'd play the perfect son and all it entailed.

"Your mother will join you for dinner. I'm afraid I have some matters to tend to. It's nothing serious, just the men." The gang was George's pride and joy, but not his sole focus. George was a businessman, leeching off the politicians in high places, twisting things for his personal gain. There wasn't much he couldn't make happen. The world feared him.

"May I help?"

"Not this time," George said. "I'll return by morning, and we can begin the next part of our work."

West smiled and nodded. "Sounds good." He didn't try thinking what the next mission might be. Instead, he went to his room, put his bag on the floor, and sat on the bed.

Jack was West's best friend, but he had a new family, and it was up to West to ensure their future. If he failed his ultimate mission... What would happen for families all over the US? *They'll keep being slaughtered if they don't submit.*

A shudder ran down his spine, and he fell asleep, dreaming of the friends he had left behind when he'd chosen George's legacy.

WEST'S SECURE PHONE BUZZED in his pocket. Groaning, he rolled over, pulling it out and answering when he saw Hunter's number. Hunter Savage was Jack's father, and only years before, George had made him fake his death. He was back now, but as far as West knew, everyone else thought he was dead.

"Hello?" West asked, rubbing his eyes.

"West?" Hunter's voice was sharp. "Did you hear the news?"

"What news?"

"Brian Jones and his crew went AWOL."

West sat up, mind racing. "AWOL?""The Union is shitting themselves. They're trying to find them and nail them for treason, but have to find a new Union war general at the same time."

"Have they found one?""Yeah, but he's not as good as Brian."

"Where is Jones?"

"Dunno. I'll track the crew down, see what they're thinking." The ex-military veteran was the best man for the job. He'd done countless special ops, with the government and with George.

West's heart hammered. This was he and his mother's chance to take action—they could destroy the corrupt government from the inside. What better time to do so than when the Union Army was in limbo? "Understood. Keep me updated."

"Will do, boy." Hunter hung up.

If West could form an agreement with Brian, how much could they fix together?

And how much would go wrong because of it?

WEST AND HIS MOTHER drove her bulletproof SUV to her favorite spot in the Michigan woods beyond the mansion. Cindy smiled, parking the vehicle on the concrete lot overlooking the barren, winter scenery.

While West had been stationed in Alamo, Cindy had come and told him her secret intentions. For decades, Cindy had worked in the shadows—preparing for the day she could help save America from the clutches of men like her husband and George himself. West didn't entirely trust her, but they had agreed to work together to stop George. If West couldn't trust her now, when could he?"

"Mom?" he asked.

"Yes, dear?" As always, she wore prim and proper clothes, hair smooth and lipstick red. West missed when he'd been younger and she'd had shining eyes—eyes full of hope.

Those years were gone.

West told her how Brian was AWOL, but she merely nodded. "I know, I brought you out here to inform you."

"You knew already?" She smiled, eyes distant, watching a lost bird scurry around a tree. "Yes. I have many friends in many places." "Any idea where Brian went?" "Not yet."

He didn't tell her Hunter was searching. "Do you think he'll benefit from what we want to do?"

"Yes." She nodded, meeting his gaze. "Are you certain you want this, West?"

West hadn't told Cindy that he was going to kill his father. He'd only said he'd stop George and help America. "Of course."

"Then you deserve to know what happens next." Cindy took a slow breath. "Government officials in the UN—those within America—must be eliminated."

West's skin crawled, but he didn't speak.

"It will take effort to avert the attention of the media, and comfort the people of the US, but the wicked leaders..." Cindy sighed and paused, decades of hard work and exhaustion weighing her shoulders. "Some must be dealt with before restoration can come about."

"Who will handle them?" *Kill.* Why couldn't he say the word *kill*?"Not your concern," she said softly. "It is in the works now."

"The nation will riot..."

"It will, and we will be there to guide it. We must act now, while the Union Army is weak, while the officials are scrambling for control." Cindy clasped West's hand, squeezing firmly. "Lord willing, it will work, West. We must hope that America can reunite under God once more."

"That's why we're fighting." West held her hand but his mind was elsewhere. Everything rested on West's shoulders. If he failed to please George and turn on him efficiently, what then?

No, I can't think of failure. It can't happen.

CHAPTER FIVE

December 27th, 2027

GIDEON WATCHED THE MONITOR, eyes blurring, forcing more cold coffee down. Three government officials —with seats in what was left of the Senate—had been found dead the previous night. Hours later, the speaker of the House of Representatives had been found dead in his house. While news coverage went into a frenzy and the civilians would hear the reassuring side of the story, Gideon dug deeper.

He didn't like what he found. His hunches were right. Somebody had something going on.

"Gideon?" Alex came into the cabin's small kitchen, yawning. "It's 2 AM. What are you still doing up?"

An alert popped onto the news screen going in the living room: a congresswoman from North California had committed suicide. Alex stopped in his tracks, paling. "What the bloody—"

Gideon showed him the new body counts. "Something's going on, Al. I've contacted George and he said he has no idea who's killing these people, but that they can't find anyone. The media is claiming suicide or accidents when they can but..."

Alex sat down at the table, gaping at the TV. "T-they're all—"

"Bad people," Gideon said wryly. There was no humor in murder, but Gideon was a logical man. If a person deserved to die, he wouldn't mourn them, even if the way of death was without valor.

"We don't know who the killer is?" Alex asked quietly. "Seems like it'd have to be more than one person."

"I'd say so. They're all spaced around, different locations... Couldn't be one person, probably not one team. At least two teams, I'd say. But they're professionals." He got up, starting another pot of coffee. "*No one* caught them or knows who they are. No one in the government, even."

"Any word from Hunter?" Alex's voice was soft.

Gideon chuckled. "Nope. But George doesn't have me involved yet. My job is still to hunt Flannery." George wanted the leader of the Falcons caught and tortured before the year ended, but he'd have to give Gideon more time than that.

Alex didn't comment, just sat up and watched the news as the nation tried to hold onto the hope that the current strong government could maintain control—even without a solidified army and with beloved officials gone.

"THINK HE'LL SHOW?" PERCY took a sip of steaming black coffee from his thermos. The fight dome was a smaller one, tucked away in the boondocks someplace in Alabama. The parking lot was full of cars and trucks, none of them familiar. To cover their voices, just in case someone got too close to their small car, Gideon had a Hollywood Undead album playing, their old favorite.

"Would we be waiting if I didn't?" Gideon set his jaw and turned the music down.

Percy smirked. Gideon knew waiting up for Flannery at a location where he was usually spotted was a long shot. He didn't have any other leads, and George gave him a job. He'd run every possibility dry.

"We'll find him, Gid." Percy took a sip of his coffee again. "And we'll kill him." "I know."

"You gotta relax." Percy sighed. "Alex is getting worried about you, and honestly, so am I. You know better than anyone that a leader without rest is going to make mistakes."

"I'm fine."

"You're not fine," Percy argued.

"This isn't the time to talk about it, Royal."

"There's never a good time," Percy said. "You're either working or grabbing a few hours of sleep. Flannery will kick our asses if we keep this up."

"What should I do, then?"

"Sleep."

Gideon watched a truck pull up and frowned. "That's one of his guys."

Percy scoffed. The truck parked across the lot and a tall man got out, heading into the dome. Gideon smirked when he spotted the Falcon wing tattoo on the man's upper right arm. "We have ourselves a start, Royal."

"Let me do the talking," Percy said firmly.

"Fine." Gideon wouldn't snap. He needed information from the man, not the satisfaction of torturing him.

They got out, heading into the run-down dome reeking of cigars and bourbon. Gideon and Percy had taken countless jobs together, their styles crossing seamlessly, proving an unstoppable force. Where Alex balanced Gideon's cold ruthlessness, Percy took it all the way. Where Gideon would have a plan at all times, Percy would make a reckless choice for the sake of a win. They'd lost before, but not often.

Percy headed to the back where the man had slipped into the halls. If the man had seen them, he'd flee, but Gideon didn't think he had. Percy smiled at a guard who let them right by. He stopped in front of a door down the hall and pulled a small lock pick, casting Gideon a casual glance.

Gideon kept watch while Percy broke in. The hall clear, Percy shoved the door open carefully. A soft sob filled the tiny room, the putrid smells hitting Gideon once he stepped inside. Two little girls were naked and crying on a bed in the corner. The man was undressing, belt in hand.

Percy's eyes flashed, and for a brief moment, he froze.

Gideon lunged, gun in hand now, bashing the man upside the head.

The man dropped, and Gideon caught him so that the sound didn't alert anyone outside. Gideon lowered the man down, growling, "Percy, help."

Percy jerked into action and yanked the man off the floor. "We were supposed to escort him out subtly."

"Change of plans." Gideon threw open the small window in the wall to his left. The cool night air hit him like a welcome slap to the face. "Here. Climb out—I'll toss him to you."

Percy swore, but crawled out of the window and landed on his damned parkour trained feet. Gideon shoved the burly body through the window. A tight fit, almost too tight, but he didn't care if the man got gashed up in the window sill.

The man in Percy's grip, Gideon went and grabbed the girls. He took the stenching blanket off the bed and wrapped it around one, then took off his own coat and covered the second. "Keep quiet, we'll get you out." They trembled in his arms, but he sat them down and looked out. Percy reached up, taking each girl from Gideon's arms, and then Gideon climbed out. Landing less graceful than Percy's, Gideon ignored it and scooped up the girls.

Percy led them quickly, keeping the man over one shoulder, as subtle as he could make it. His muscles bulged as they walked, but he didn't show any other signs of exertion.

Men's voices came from the dome's entry. Percy weaved through some cars as cover till they reached the car. Gideon dropped the kids beside the door, opening it and pushing them in. "Stay down," he ordered sharply.

They did.

Percy tossed the man into the trunk. They'd stop a short bit away and tie the man up, but for now they had to get out of Dodge. Gideon cranked the car and Percy jumped in, a grin on his face. Once Gideon drove them out of the lot and toward the highway, Percy glanced into the backseat. "It'll be fine now," he told the kids firmly. "We'll getcha someplace safe. No more bad guys."

The girls fell asleep before Gideon pulled over. Percy got out and bound the man in the trunk, getting back in with a sigh. Gideon drove on for a while without a word.

No more bad guys.

Gideon and his team worked to eliminate the scum—no matter the cost. He glanced at Percy. "Royal?"

"Hm?"

"I'm hunting Flannery, even if it kills me. If it does, I need you to run the crew," Gideon said simply.

Percy blinked, expression flickering with rage. "No. It's your crew. You're not dying on us."

"Percy—"

"Drop it, Gideon." Percy cut him off.

It was as close to a yes as Gideon would get.

TWELVE HOURS OF TORTURE later and the man was an open book. It only took three finger nails and an electric shock—Percy's strength wasn't patience—for him to tell that Flannery was in Canada and his men were left in the USA. Besides that, he didn't know the political side of the plan, nor did he know Flannery's exact location. "He's probably in Ontario. That's all he told me!"

Gideon wiped blood from his hands and glanced at Percy. Percy set his jaw, nodding once. That settled, Gideon left the room to call Alex.

The small house in the woods was a private location of George's. Gideon stepped outside, taking a weary breath.

"Gid?" Alex answered. "How did it go? Did he talk?" "He told us what he knew."

"And the girls, did someone pick them up?"

"Yeah, they're someplace safe now."

"Are you coming home?"

Gideon sighed. "I'll be home by tonight."

"Are you going after Flannery?" "Not till tomorrow morning," Gideon said.

Alex hung up. Gideon went to the car and got in, turning the heater up. Percy came out, dumping the body with a small bullet hole through his skull, in the ditch out back, and tossing the dirt from the hole Gideon had dug hours earlier back in.

A shallow grave for a piece of shit.

"Ready?" Percy got in.

"We'll head out with the team tomorrow morning."

"What's this? Hochberg actually taking my advice on sleeping before important events?" Percy asked dryly.

"Don't push it." Gideon drove them to HQ, dropping Percy off before heading home.

———————

IN THE MORNING, GIDEON received a call from Keegan Black. He set his coffee down and answered wearily. Keegan had been aiding Springtown in hiding— paying off any threats so they didn't attack Springtown. He'd only failed twice, when Shane attacked the town to challenge Gideon, and Thomas attacked for the hell of it —and to kidnap Alex.

"Hey, Hochberg," Keegan said, exhaustion creeping into his voice. "I've taken it you've seen the news."

"I have."

"I-I heard about what happened at Springtown last month. Why didn't you tell me?" Keegan asked tightly.

"You had problems to solve. I solved that problem."

"We're supposed to be allies."

"You could not have sent help," Gideon replied flatly. "Telling you would not have helped anyone."

Keegan fell quiet for a moment. "You'll be hunting Flannery?"

Gideon bristled, making sure Alex was still outside tending the stray cat he'd found howling outside at 4 AM. "What's that to you, Black?"

"I'd like to help if I can."

"Why?"

Keegan hesitated. "One of my brother's joined Flannery's group. I'd like to make Flannery pay for that."

"You never struck me as the vengeful type." Gideon leaned back in his chair, interest piqued. Keegan was a soft-spoken man with nerves of steel, but he didn't start fights. He did all he could to eliminate such threats or help clean up the aftermath of eliminations.

"I am with him. Only him." Keegan's voice was dark.

"He's that sort of man," Gideon said, licking his lips. "He's hurt a lot of people."

"Can I help?"

"Right now, Black, George has given me full clearance to hunt Flannery down and bring him back. He called me this morning. He's been a bit behind schedule due to the state of the nation... but I've got my orders now."

"Oh," Keegan said, sighing. "That's better than having to sneak around."

Gideon scoffed. "I'll let you know if I need help."

"Wait, Gideon? Can I ask you something?" Keegan asked quickly. He sounded so normal. He had no military or law enforcement training. He was smart, but his way of speech was relaxed, even when speaking to one of the best assassins in the US.

Gideon sighed. "Sure. I can hang up if I don't want to answer." A dry tease, but Keegan didn't seem to grasp dry teasing. It's why Gideon kept doing it.

"There's sorta something I haven't told you."

Gideon frowned. "What would that be?""I-I was wondering if you could help me with something, too. Springtown was hit so hard again... I've been thinking about my community." Keegan mustered.

"Community?"

"I was raised in a pacifist community, Gideon." He sighed. "They're located just inside the Missouri border. They should be safe but... but if Flannery goes haywire again, I might not be able to keep them safe."

"You'd want my help protecting them if Flannery attacked. Why would he attack besides wanting supplies?"

"I wasn't worried because he didn't know we existed, but we harbor refugees—anyone who needs help or sanctuary, they're welcome. One of the people my community harbored was a spy from the Falcons." Keegan paused, sounding like he was choking on his own words before he pulled it together. "He hurt some of the women and ran. We think Flannery might come back, take supplies, people to sell, whatever. They don't have weapons, Gideon. I've tried to convince them to defend themselves but they won't."

"How many people?" Gideon asked, void of emotion.

"Right now probably only 75, give or take. Most of them left after a while."

Gideon worked his jaw. "Missouri's border?""Please, Gideon, I'll do anything. I'm never nearby to help or protect them. They're all I have." Keegan mustered. "I'll give you anything. Our pact won't be broken, just tell me what you need—"

"We have a pact," Gideon said calmly. "You have helped Springtown and other townships. I can afford to help yours. Just hope that George doesn't discover it."

"O-of course." Keegan exhaled deeply over the phone line. "Thank you. And I understand if you are unable to help them if they need it because of George—you can't blow your cover—but thank you."

"I'll keep my eyes on them. Warn me if you hear something first." Gideon watched Alex come through the front door, the black-and-white kitten meowing in his arms. "I've gotta go." He hung up.

"Who was that?" Alex shut the front door, taking the kitten over to the table.

"Keegan."

"Everything OK?" Alex glanced up, eyes heavy with worry.

"Yeah, just checking in." Gideon sighed and told him about the community in Missouri. It wasn't a big deal, but it might prove difficult to pull off if they needed help. 75 people without weapons—people entirely against violence in any fashion... Gideon couldn't force them to save themselves. He rubbed his aching head.

"Well..." Alex said slowly. "I'm sure God will help us figure it out, if it comes to that. Keegan's just covering his bases."

"We have enough to deal with," Gideon agreed. "Keeping up with Springtown, helping George figure out what's going on in the high places..." He didn't mention Flannery.

Alex stroked the mangy kitten's fur. "Yeah. We'll be fine." He glanced up. "I think it's finally about to end, Gid. All these years I've babbled about hope and pulling through and God fixing things..." He looked down, sighing. "I dunno. Just... desperate for it to be over maybe, but I have a good feeling."

Gideon didn't share the feeling. His gut screamed that things were just getting started. But he smiled, stood, and patted the shoulder of the best friend he considered a brother. "Yeah. It will be fine."

CHAPTER SIX

December 28th, 2027

SIMON DREAMT OF THE day he could live in Springtown with Rene', but today was not that day.

He watched the men of Paradise prepare for their first mission into uncharted territory—human trafficking rescue operations. Sure, Jordan was a pro at it, but Kaleb hadn't joined him in such endeavours. George wasn't supposed to find out Jordan was helping innocent lives, and he wouldn't now since they had to keep it on the low radar. Only a few men were prepping for the job ahead. The rest of the group consisted of Jordan's men, and they were waiting at another location.

Nate got into their truck, cranking the engine. "Ready?" he asked.

Simon glanced over. Nate had changed since he'd stood up to his father, Kaleb, before they'd all gone to war for Springtown. He acted older—or maybe his somberness was because of Ben's death, one of the veterans in AJ's group. AJ was like a father to Nate, and Ben had been a crazy uncle figure, until he'd been killed on a rescue mission. Nate had held him while he died. Simon didn't imagine for a second that his best friend was all right. "Uh... Yeah. I guess."

"The others will follow." Nate slammed the truck door shut. Simon climbed into the passenger side, quiet as Nate drove to the edge of the gang's HQ border. Nate sighed and turned on a rock CD.

Simon was silent for a few songs before turning it off. "Can we talk?"

Nate growled.

"Do you really wanna do this?"

"Do what?"

"The trafficking ops... Stuff my dad has always done but we rarely helped with."

"Sure."

Simon sighed, glancing out the window. "It's just not what we always planned on.""We planned on fooling Kaleb for our freedom. Well, we didn't fool him, and he's finally let us be our own people." Nate shrugged and smirked. "Plan changed but we're doing fine, right?""You're oddly optimistic about this." Simon ran a hand through his thick dark hair. Nate was usually cynical, and Simon was the hopeful one—why were the tables turned now, of all times?

"You've missed your dad a lot." Nate reasoned. "Seems fitting that you guys finally get a shot at working together to do some good."

"Do some good... yeah." Simon leaned back. It would be hellish work, saving kids, but it was better than the work Kaleb had had them doing. Simon didn't want to cause more chaos or destruction. He wanted to help people.

He wanted to protect Rene'.

He wanted a lot of things, but what if God started saying no?

The way she hugged me before I left... I want to hold her again. I don't want to have to let her go. Ever again. But I have to fight.

Simon worked his jaw, remembering Rene's smile, the way she laughed when the kids did something silly, the way she took care of others no matter what. He remembered what it had been like to kiss her. Would he be able to again?

"Si?" Nate frowned at him before directing his attention back to the road. "You've been acting weird."

Could say the same about you. "Just tired."

"Don't lie to me."

Simon worked his jaw. "Mr. Fisher agreed that I could date Rene' if she wanted to."

"And?"

"S-she said yes."

"No duh." Nate smirked. "What's wrong about that? Aren't you happy?""Yeah! Yeah, of course!" Simon shook his head. "But it just... scares me, Nate. I've failed Rene' before. I wasn't there to protect her when she got kidnapped... I just keep letting her down. She deserves better. What if I..." He looked away, heart aching like something was squeezing it with pronged clamps. "What if I can't be a better man, Nate? What if I can't be who Rene' deserves? On top of that, Graham... What Graham said, Nate, how am I supposed to help him?"

"Oh, for the love of—" Nate swore. "Come on, Simon! Don't be such a dimwit!"

"I mean it, Nate—"

"I mean it, Simon!" Nate cut him off. "Graham is staying with the Fisher family, and you know Mr. Fisher said he'd help Graham sort through his feelings, probably better than we could try to. Graham is broken, but he'll be OK. They can help him more than we could. And," he continued vehemently. "Mr. Fisher told you when it happened, it wasn't your freaking fault. You did everything you could—and you know what? You've saved

Rene', too. You saved her whole town with supplies! Mr. Fisher wouldn't have agreed to let you guys even be friends if he didn't think you could keep Rene' safe."

Simon's heart hammered. "What if I can't?"

He thought of his mother's death when he was younger —how much it had broken his father. Simon couldn't lose Rene'. He'd promised himself he wouldn't allow any more harm to befall her, but if God said no, and something happened, how could Simon accept that? Simon was trying to love God and do His will, but he couldn't shake the fear of losing his family.

"Then shit happens." Nate gripped the steering wheel tighter, knuckles going white. "And you deal with it, and if you trust God, then I guess faith would play into that. You were just telling me how a warrior fights for love, right? How love is worth not being safe?" He glanced over, eyes dark with anger. "Well, guess what, Si? Time for you to take your own advice. Whatever demons raging because you have a shot at Rene' now can just shut up. Got it?"

Simon gulped hard, shoulders sagging as he smiled weakly. "Thanks, Nate. I... I needed your weird way of pepping."

"Anytime." He nudged his shoulder. "Now, stop harping at me."

"No."

"Worth a shot." Nate grunted.

———————

THE FIRST HUMAN TRAFFICKING dome—and one of the largest—set in San Diego, South California. Kaleb wouldn't be there right away, since George needed him close by while chaos erupted in the government due to the deaths. But Jordan, his men—a group of Kaleb's finest —and Reese Burns would be working together on the first op.

Nate didn't mind the change of plans. Truth be told, he almost preferred the work to what he'd done as Kaleb's puppet. He didn't want to see kids messed up but saving them was something. It mattered. And Nate needed a reason to keep going. Unlike Simon, he didn't have a caring father, he didn't have a girl, and he barely had any friends—he wasn't kind like Simon.

Not that Nate wanted friends. He just needed a reason to keep fighting, what with the war possibly ending soon.

Even if the war ended, too much had changed. America would never be the same. Even human trafficking had gotten worse, if that was possible. The rings didn't even have to hide anymore—entire industries and domes were dedicated to selling and trading adults and children alike. Nate used to watch crime shows about human trafficking —kids being smuggled house to house, kids being exploited by relatives. The civil war had upped the ante, showing wicked deeds as nothing to be concerned over, and even as acceptable.

But if they could wipe the big domes out, save thousands of kids, maybe it'd help. Maybe.

They all gathered at a large warehouse outside of San Diego. While the men prepped their supplies and settled for the night, Reese poured over maps at a table in the main room. Nate watched from the doorway, the dimly lit rooms almost relaxing if he ignored the smells of sweaty men, stale foods, and dust.

If Reese noticed him, he didn't show it. He was a giant man, not an ounce of fat on his muscled body. He was one of the best fighters the domes had ever seen—and he was going back in with a vengeance. But what for?

Nate sighed, stepping over. "The maps haven't changed in the past hour."

Reese smirked without lifting his gaze. "We don't have much time to make this gig work, kid. These sort of operations take time—weeks, months—to properly formulate. They can go wrong very quickly. Men and the victims could be killed." He snapped his fingers. "Just like that. This isn't the battlefield or the slums. Innocent lives are at stake if we ruin this."

Nate crossed his arms and studied the detailed map of Southern California. "Why are you doing this?"

"Told you, I've got a group that needs saving."

"Are they here in San Diego?" Nate frowned.

Reese worked his jaw and straightened. "I think so."

"Think so?"

"The last I heard, yes." Reese rubbed his thick brown beard. "But fighters are moved all the time."

"They're all fighters?" Nate studied the man closely.

He'd fought in domes that Reese had fought in. Kaleb didn't like it when he did, but sometimes Nate needed the outlet. Reese was a terrifying fighter—but he was a safe one, all things considered. Other people enslaved weren't so lucky or valuable. They died in the domes, tortured, raped, fought till they collapsed.

But Reese hadn't ever crossed Nate as the empathetic or even honorable type.

"Yes." Reese met his gaze. "You have something to ask, kid, go ahead."

"Every time I see you, you're alone. But you're acting like this group means everything to you," Nate said testingly.

Reese laughed, shaking his head. "You're too much like your dad."Nate tensed, jutting his chin. "You're avoiding the truth."

"What truth?""You're holding onto false hope. Your group has been missing for a long time, haven't they? You don't know if they can be found—you just summoned

Kaleb for one last hoo-rah." Nate's tone grew bitter. He'd been raised to be a cold prick and it still came naturally. Better know the truth and someone's true colors the hard way, rather than pretend they were good at heart.

Reese's brown eyes narrowed, expression growing dangerous. "For a while, yes, they've been lost to me. But more is at stake than the group, Nate. The government is wiping out townships, kidnapping people from trafficking rings, all for experimentations or whatever the hell they've got going on. It has to stop."

"Destroying domes will stop the government from messing around?" Nate rolled his eyes.

"No, but it'll help us find answers on how to stop the government from hurting innocents." Reese looked at the map. "You don't believe me when I say the government is creating genetically mutated things, do you?""Not really. I'm sure if it's true, it'll show real soon, what with the Union being desperate." Nate leaned against the table. "Guess we'd better be ready, huh?"

"This isn't a game, Nate." Reese gave him a withering frown.

Nate smirked. "I know it's not." More than any of them knew.

Nate knew what was at stake. He knew the wicked controlling the world. But he wouldn't be afraid. Not anymore. "It's getting late... We should get some sleep."

Reese sighed softly. "Nate?"

"Yeah?"

"You're a good kid."

"I'm not a kid any more." Nate cut his eyes at him.

"Guess not. But thanks for coming to help with this.""My pleasure, Reese." For once, it was.

Ever since Nate had killed the man who raped Graham, something had awakened in him. If he got to kill more bad men and help lost kids while he was at it, remaining cold and in control while doing some good... it would be worth it.

SIMON WATCHED THE MEN ready for lights out, barely keeping his eyes open. The preparation for the rescue proved more intense than he expected. Not only did they have to efficiently infiltrate the dome by con men posing as buyers and interested clients, but plans had to be made for the children once they were rescued.

Jordan patted his shoulder, leaning back in his chair at the large wooden table. "Go on to bed, Simon."Simon sighed. "I'm fine."

"You've been up for twenty-four hours straight." Jordan's eyes pierced his, the same scolding frown that he'd given when Simon was little. "These ops can't be done with weary, broken men, Simon. We rotate members, keep everyone mentally evaluated—why do you think that is?"

"Your team is well put together?" Simon avoided the question.

"*Simon.*" Jordan drilled him.

"So their work isn't affected by their personal abilities."

"More or less." He nudged Simon's arm. "Bed. Now."

"Dad?" Simon leaned up but didn't stand. He'd been too busy to think much as of late, but he couldn't ignore things forever.

"Yes, son?" Jordan put his pen down onto the notebook in front of him.

"I... I'm dating Rene'." There, he'd said it. Finally.

"I know."

Simon blanched. "What? How? I didn't—"

"I thought you've been dating since I first met her?"

"We never went on a date!" Simon's cheeks flushed.

"Well, I don't know how teens do it nowadays." Jordan chuckled. "Or young adults, I should say. You're pretty striking for a twenty-year-old."

"Shut up!" Simon laughed and shoved his father's arm. "But... you're OK with us dating?"

"Why wouldn't I be?" Jordan blinked in surprise. "You two are perfect."

Perfect. Dad thinks we're meant to be together? A lump formed in Simon's throat and he looked away, fiddling with his phone on the table. "I... I don't know."

Jordan clasped his shoulder, squeezing softly. "I think you'd be great together. I think your mother would've loved her too." He smiled, a twinkle in his eyes. "I have her ring. I'll give it to you when we get back to my HQ, how's that?"

Tears burned Simon's eyes. "Dad..." Marrying Rene'... there was nothing in the world he wanted more. But he hadn't even asked yet.

"Is that a yes or no?" Jordan teased.

"It's a yes."

"Good. I think the diamond will look nice on Rene'." Jordan, voice growing thick with emotion, gathered his papers. "Good night, son."

"Dad?" Simon choked, grabbing his arm. Jordan stopped, meeting Simon's gaze with teary eyes. "I love you so much. I'm sorry I left; I'm sorry I never worked with you enough like I should've; I'm sorry I haven't been a good son." The words tumbled out before he could stop them. He'd spent years battling for Nate, trying to keep Nate safe despite his abusive father.

How much of his relationship with his own dad had he allowed to go dormant? He'd taken Jordan for granted.

Jordan wrapped his strong arms around Simon and held tight. "I love you, Simon. You've made me more proud than you could ever imagine." He rubbed Simon's hair.

"God's got you, son, and no matter what, He'll guide you. Just follow. Don't follow me, don't follow anyone, just keep your eyes on God."

Simon nodded, but didn't pull away from Jordan. Just for a moment, Simon didn't want to be strong. Just for a second, he wanted to be held by his dad like he was a little kid.

I'm grown, I'm becoming the protector of my family now. What if Dad never holds me like this again? Something snapped inside and he sobbed silently, body wracking as he held his father. "I love you."

"I love you, boy." Jordan held him there in the dark warehouse room with the bare bulbs flickering in and out.

It was enough. It had always been enough to just be held.

CHAPTER SEVEN

December 28th, 2027

GIDEON HEADED INTO HQ, coffee in hands, watching the calculated chaos unfold about him with a strange sense of relief. His team would be ready for the hunt in a few minutes, following him into every battle without doubt or complaint.

Percy greeted him at the door, eyes dark. "George has a jet waiting for us. Should get us to Ontario in a timely fashion," he said. He wore a black shirt and jeans just as Gideon did, only with far more supplies on his belt and a small knife on a chain around his neck.

Gideon nodded. "Let's head out."

Percy hesitated. "Any word on what's going on at the White House? And the deaths?"

"No, and it's not part of the job right now. Flannery probably ran because of it though, so we'll assume it's bad."

"Fair enough." Percy chuckled.

They alerted the team that they'd head to the airport in five. Preston, Percy's little brother, and Preston's boyfriend, Jacob, came over, both with weary faces and slumped shoulders.

"All set," Preston said. "Uh, Gideon?" "What?" Gideon studied him closely, doubting that they should come alone. They were still teens and the battles wore on them fast.

"Your shirt's on backwards, sir."

Gideon glanced down and Percy laughed, but a glare from Gideon cut him off. Gideon quickly fixed his shirt. "Pretend that didn't happen."

"Busy night?" Preston teased.

"You should nap on the way," Jacob spoke up firmly. "You look like crap." "You two are just rising on my list of favorite people." Gideon headed to the trucks with a growl. They loaded up and headed to the airport.

If Flannery is in Ontario, we'll catch him by surprise. We'll kill him.

AS THE TEAM POURED into the airport, the jet waiting for them at the ready courtesy of George, something tugged at Gideon's gut.

"Percy?" Gideon asked quietly as the men unloaded from the trucks.

"Yeah?"

"Does something feel off to you?""Off?" Percy frowned deeply. "What do you mean?"

"We're not getting on the jet." Gideon turned, calling his men back over. As the men exchanged concerned glances and headed back over, the jet went up in flames.

Preston and Jacob ducked behind the truck, and Gideon swore. The men dropped once the bomb went off, but it was far enough away it didn't hit them.

If they'd gone any closer, it would've.

If they'd been on the jet...

Gideon dialed George's number, fuming. "Move out!" he shouted at the men. "Now!"

CHAPTER EIGHT

December 30th, 2027

WEST SAT SILENTLY AT the dinner table, feeling as insignificant as he had when he'd been a child. George and Cindy spoke vehemently over the murders in the government and the media coverage, George's anger dripping into each word.

"The people of this nation are fools, Cindy. You can't expect them to ignore the obvious for much longer, and when they discover the media has lied to them—"

"They will do nothing and justify it in their own minds," Cindy said gently. "You have seen it before. They have been conditioned not to rally together against the government, George. They won't start now."

"And if they do?" George shook his head. "We're where we are today because of playing the game better than anyone. One slip up and we'd be found and killed."

"You can't silence the nation, media, or citizens." Cindy patted George's hand. Meanwhile, she'd done the opposite —it was Cindy aiding the news to reveal tiny truths and questions unallowed by the media corps.

"They're saying the wrong things," he growled. "You've seen them. Their tone is shifting, they're saying things that haven't passed corporate. They're going against the government in little jabs and sources. It not only endangers the government, but it will get them killed."

"We have faced worse." She smiled tiredly. "Have we not?"

"That's not the point—"

"The government will regain control soon." Cindy smoothed George's hair, holding his gaze. George melted a little at her touch and sighed. "Just give them time. We'll be safe so long as we avoid the spotlight."

George kissed her hand before turning to West. "Are you packed for your next mission?" He started his breakfast once more.

West's stomach twisted but he nodded. "Yessir." It was West's job to be diplomatic and ruthless all at once— diplomatic so the government accepted him, and ruthless so no thug thought they had a chance at ruining the Johnston legacy.

"Good," George said. "You fly out tonight. Spencer, Bo, and Nabeel will join you. I don't expect you to have any trouble?"

West smiled. "Of course not."

But he didn't want the job. He didn't want to assassinate the Confederate Vice President while he was trying to get out of Georgia and into Alabama where he was needed. The Confederates were brave but few in number. They were hunted like rats and now, and West was one of the hunters. He had plenty of experience in this sort of job, but it didn't get easier.

"That's my boy." George chuckled. "I'm proud of you, West."

Five words West had fought to hear ever since he'd been a young child. Why did they sound meaningless now? What had West ruined to hear them? His gimmick might have the end goal of killing George, but was that justified by what he had to do along the way?

THE SNIPER RIFLE SET up in front of West was in perfect shape—it had been rarely used. West wanted to keep it that way. He waited from a building top, covered by the night.

The previous night, the Confederate Vice President had arrived with his small militia. The place had been bombed and ransacked. West's inside sources had confirmed this was where the group would bunk safely for the night before crossing the border into Alabama tomorrow.

But no place was safe in post-apocalyptic America.

The vehicles were parked outside of the warehouse where the rebel VP also slept tonight. The building stood strong, unlike many in the small town, with boarded windows. Soldiers stood outside as guards, bulletproof vests showing beneath their thick shirts.

New shirts.

Strange detail, considering the Confederates got little to no funding. Those who funded were small, useless leaders throughout the US who got booted from their positions or killed. Maybe the Confederates had taken to ransacking and thievery like the news said, hitting any township they could break into for supplies.

West watched the soldiers for a moment. In the wee hours of the morning, when his target came outside to head out, he would pull the trigger on him. This would send the Confederates into disarray, same as the Union was now. That was George's intentions, anyway.

West gritted his teeth, closing his eyes briefly. He had killed before— bad men who deserved to die—but he'd also killed men who hadn't deserved death. It was part of the job.

The men on the job with him had killed before too.

Spencer and Bo weren't exactly special ops, but Nabeel had done far darker things than West ever had. Nabeel was one of George's favorites, but the black giant of a man rarely showed himself. West hadn't heard him even speak.

The acid in his stomach threatened to rise into his throat. The four of them had accepted the job as they had others in the past, but this was different. He couldn't quite describe how it was, but he couldn't pull the trigger on Smith. He couldn't kill a man who was trying to help his people. He couldn't kill a man with little kids waiting at home.

Not again.

He wouldn't kill like this again.

But he had to, didn't he? That was his job. Simple as that. Plenty of men did plenty of hellish things just to keep things moving, just to keep things in order. It didn't matter if it hurt—the mission mattered most.

Wasn't that true?

West didn't know. The voices in his head clashed like a tsunami on a shore. Why couldn't he come to terms with this part of his new life? Good men could be assassins, he knew that. His friend Ed had been the best sniper the gang had before George had him killed to teach West a lesson.

But what about the other good men? The good men who backed away from careers when they couldn't do as much good as they wanted to? Those who changed their missions so they didn't have to overlook—or take part in —so much evil?

Spencer's voice came over the comm. "You about ready to switch off, big man?"

West set his jaw. "Not yet." He kept his crosshairs on the soldiers. Why was he even struggling with the question? Hadn't he made up his mind when he agreed to join George? He'd do whatever it took to kill George.

The means justified the end. He didn't have the luxury of finding another way around the wicked path before him. If the VP left the township alive, George would find out, and West would be out of the game.

"You've been acting kinda weird, West." Spencer sighed. "We can't mess this up."

"Don't intend to." West couldn't call his brothers for help and lock the VP up either. George would still get word the man was taken captive and it wasn't his orders. West might convince George that letting the man live was wiser, however...

But what if it was too risky and George erupted?

Spencer dropped it. "Still the same guards?"

West watched the men at the door. The soldiers talked quietly, and one of them laughed. They were large men, probably ex-military by the looks and hyper alert, but they hadn't seen West. The droll idea of allowing the enemy side to capture him crossed West's mind, but he doubted it would help more than harm. George would kill him for shaming the Johston legacy, if West ever returned.

"Yeah, still the same guards. They must not have a lot of guys to spare for security detail."

The brief idea kept tossing around in his head. Surrendering probably wouldn't give the Confederates much leverage.

Would it?

West licked his lips, letting the thought bounce around in his head. Entering enemy lines with ulterior motives was risky business—too risky. The Union and Confederates both had lost dozens of spies to the opposing side. West had everything at stake too. His plans with his mother, his goal to kill George, and with West complying to George's wishes, his brothers were also kept safe.

"Well, I'm ready to switch off," Spencer continued. "What's the hold up?"

West didn't answer. *Besides keeping my brothers somewhat safe and getting close enough to George to kill him, what am I doing?* Cindy was leading the big guns and having the government officials killed. She was coercing the media. She'd prepared for the war for decades, and this was the outcome she was ready to work with.

Where did West fit into that? She could do fine without him right beside her.

A cool breeze hit the mask on West's face. What was he thinking? He couldn't just hand himself over to the enemy. The government wouldn't give a damn if he was kidnapped—they had bigger fish to fry at the moment.

But it would stall George.

"Hey, Spencer?" West cut his friend off mid-sentence as the Yankee started talking.

"Are you listening to me?"

"Shut up. Bo, Nabeel, are you guys on?"

"We are," Bo said, voice muffled. "What's cookin' inside that head of yours, blondie?"

"Hmm." If West played it right, he could give the Confederates a small upper hand, make George falter, and not have to kill a good man, all with one very reckless stone.

God-willing, Cindy might even take the chance at having George killed before West returned. *If I make it out.*

God, let this work.

"And?" Spencer asked.

"None of us really want to take this target out, right?"

"Of course not, but—" Spencer started.

West stopped him. "I've got an idea." West took a deep breath. Well, here went everything he'd worked for.

He checked once more to see if the rifle was still loaded. Then he called out, voice carrying across the still night atmosphere like a bullet, "Don't shoot! I wanna make an offer!"

CHAPTER NINE

December 30th, 2027

THE FIGHT DOME IN San Diego was less busy than usual according to Reese. "Things have gone a bit quiet since big wigs started getting killed off," he muttered. "But it'll do. There's a large group within the dome that's stationary, so we'll get them first."

Simon watched the large group of men prepare for the raid. It was only a couple hours away. They were almost completely set to go. Jordan had done these sorts of operations hundreds of times before, and he had polished up the group fast, but Simon was still worried.

What if they missed something? What if something got out of hand and someone was hurt—or killed? What if the dome was better defended than they thought? Simon watched Jordan for a moment. What if Simon couldn't match his dad's abilities?

He shook the doubts from his mind. He needed to be strong for everyone. He didn't have time to fear anything —he only had time to do the best he could do. Steeling himself, Simon went to help Jordan load up.

The drive to the dome was uneventful but well calculated. The small militia had to get just close enough to the dome to get there fast, but remain unnoticed—and they had to have the dome's location surrounded.

When they pulled that off, Jordan sent in the spies.

Three men had been sent into the dome, each having a different role. One man pretended to be a buyer, one man pretended to have kids to sell, and the third was there to place high bets on the best fighters. No one had been caught or scrutinized—they were Jordan's finest, and they knew how to play a job well without pushing too hard.

Still, there had been the risk of moving too fast, but it hadn't bitten them yet.

Once the three men were in the location, that's when things could go terribly wrong. There would be no turning back once the infiltration started.

Simon took a steady breath and glanced at Nate. "You ready?"

"Hell yeah."

AFTER ALL OPTIONS WERE considered, the ambush was the best option. The veterans of the task force went in first—men trained for such operations—and the dome was hit full-force. Over forty men rushed in during the cover of the night.

Simon wasn't with them, but he could hear the chaos ensue over the comms. Some of them had cameras on their helmets, and Nate watched the footage, too. The dome wasn't overflowing with newcomers but a few fights were going on, a small crowd fleeing from the first floor when the men burst inside.

Nate watched with cold eyes. None of them dared speak. It didn't feel right to Simon, just sitting there, waiting till he could go in without being a hindrance. The gunshots echoed and rang in his ears, but he just focused on breathing and staying calm. Jordan said such situations usually didn't last very long.

But with numbers like this, on such short notice, the expectation of something going wrong lingered in the air like smoke.

The group moved through the fight dome. Simon heard the cries of at least two of their own drop, but the rest of the team didn't stop. A medic team grabbed a vehicle and headed toward the frenzy.

The rest was a blur. Simon was one of the first heading out after the agonizing wait when Jordan contacted them for backup. He was one of the first inside the giant building.

The first thing that hit him was the stench, then the images of bodies littering the ground, blood splattering the walls, and the cries of kids filled his ears.

Immediately, his body took over and he knew what to do, all emotion aside. He went to the cells downstairs and began unlocking them. Jordan was already doing the same, guiding teenage victims to the stairs, a young boy in his arms. Jordan tried to tell the children to not look at the bodies, but there wasn't much use in that. The kids had seen worse, no doubt.

Simon went into a cell and picked up a boy no older than fifteen. He was black and blue, like he had barely survived a fight and they'd tossed him into a cell to die. The boy barely woke when Simon grabbed him.

"It's gonna be fine, kid," Simon said, straining to be heard over the ruckus around him. He hadn't gotten a good count of the amount of victims they had to retrieve.

The boy moaned but couldn't open his swollen eyes. Simon carried him outside, keeping his head covered the whole time protectively. "It'll be fine. You're safe now— we'll get you someplace safe and warm."

The vehicles full of medics and supplies were parked outside now. Simon got the boy to one of the medics and ran back inside without looking back. Men carried kids outside and ushered groups of children toward the vans. Some kids were pretty young, or looked like it, but most of the victims were teenage boys and girls. Simon didn't let his mind go to any thoughts or realizations—he just worked.

The cells filled the downstairs rooms, reeking of urine, sweat, and blood. It almost made Simon wretch but he held it together.

The men opened the cells that contained victims—most in the cells were fighters, slaves used to earn money off fights. The main floor was the arenas where they'd dropped a good crowd of bodies, leaving the room like a giant slaughterhouse. The floor above had rooms where most of the predators took their victims to rape them. That floor was bloody too by what Simon heard from a man over the comms, but all of the victims upstairs were being removed as they spoke.

Simon wished he could turn the comms off. Too many sounds. Too many screams and cries.

Simon broke into a cell, pushing all the chaos aside. Focus on the task at hand. That was his job.

A man—not much older than Simon himself—lay on the cot in the cramped, dark cell. His clothes were tattered and dark with blood stains. He had a long gash that'd cut through his pectoral muscle.

Simon swore softly. Bleeding out was a hell of a way to die—and the man had died alone. What for? What had he done—got slashed in a fight? Murdered by his handler?

Simon checked for a pulse but of course there was none. He ran out of the cell, heart pounding so hard his ribs felt like they might shatter.

He helped Jordan get the victims out of the large building and to the vehicles where they could be cared for. They couldn't stay any longer than necessary. A quick roll-out would be crucial, and they'd head for a refuge spot immediately after.

The bodies of the sellers, traders, and predators were left inside. Once a group of men searched the place top to bottom, gathering any intel and ensuring no living were inside, they torched the place.

Simon slammed the door shut to a medic van, gaping a little as the building was set ablaze. Jordan gripped his shoulder firmly, voice weary. "Let's go, son. We have a long night of driving ahead of us."

Simon steeled himself and followed the others to load up. They'd saved forty children total. He didn't know the amount of men they'd killed. Picturing the body of the man in his cell, thin as a rail, in a pool of his own blood, Simon knew they hadn't killed enough.

THE LARGE TRUCK BUMPED along the road quickly. It wasn't safe passing through San Diego, and while each truck had a shooter up front and a guard in the back with the kids, Nate still doubted they escaped scathe free.

Nate lifted his head, fighting off a pounding headache. Reese sat nearby with a teenage boy leaning against his shoulder—Ezekiel Prosner, a boy with bleach-white hair, black bruises on almost every inch of exposed skin, and a curt attitude. Reese had bandaged him up during the drive but the boy, apparently he went by EZ, had repeated the same thing: "We have to find J. We have to find the others."

Nate hadn't asked who J was, or who the others were, but judging by the pained expression Reese bore, he probably knew. Once EZ had passed out when the painkillers took a toll, Nate decided to test the waters.

"So... that's the kid you were searching for?"

Reese grunted.

"What's he talking about, *others*?" Nate frowned. "You said you were after a group—you said you thought they were all here."

"I thought they were." Reese's voice was tight. "I was obviously wrong."

"Who took them? Who even are they?""Can it, Nate."

"No. We just lost two good men of our own. We deserve to know what we're actually hunting," Nate snapped.

"We're hunting the bastards who hurt these kids. We're saving the victims. We're gathering intel from the domes. Is that not enough for you?" Reese asked sharply, grip tightening on EZ's shoulder.

Nate gritted his teeth. "Just because EZ told you off doesn't mean you can take it out on me."

Reese's scowl diminished and he looked away, large shoulders sagging in defeat. "Sorry, Nate."

"Who is the group?" Nate didn't want his guilt or hurt feelings. He wanted to know what the whole team had ahead of them.

"Some old friends of mine." Reese rubbed his forehead that was coated with sweat and some blood. "J, Markus, a few others... We worked together as fighters one time, EZ was there with us. I was moved first... haven't seen any of them since."

"Well, if they're anything like you, they're probably fine. We'll find them." Nate tried to be encouraging like Simon, but he didn't know if it helped. He wasn't as naturally comforting as his best friend.

Reese nodded, eyes absent as he rubbed one of the tattoos on EZ's arm. "Yeah... I'm sure they are."

Nate studied the tattoo of a crow and sighed. They both knew neither of them had a clue what they were saying. The world wasn't a place for vain hope.

CHAPTER TEN

December 30th, 2027

RENE' FINISHED HER WORK at the courthouse stockpiles early, grabbing a mug of coffee in the break room downstairs. Usually, she worked the same shift as her best friend, Bethany, or their friend, Chloe—a few years their senior—from before the war began. But today she'd needed some space, and both women had other matters calling first.

Rene' sat down at the break room table. She hadn't realized till she did how shaky her legs were. A glance at the time on her phone made her groan: she'd worked a full four hours nonstop at the stockpile, not to mention a bad night of sleep, the full day of ranch chores, and babysitting her nieces and nephews to give Terri a break.

And no texts from Simon for a full 24 hours.

"Hey, lass," Sean said, voice cheerful, peeking into the room. "Mind if I join you?"

"Not at all." She leaned onto the table and sipped her coffee. Sean had become the closest thing she had to a big brother. Spencer Anderson was probably a close second, since he'd helped save her from being held captive.

He got a cup of coffee and sat beside her. "Are you all right?""Yeah," she said. "You?"

Sean ran a hand through his shaggy red curls. "Same old, same old." He studied her. "What's this I heard about you dating Simon?"

"I haven't told you before?" Rene' moaned. "I'm sorry."

"I was told, but I haven't heard it from you." He chuckled and downed some coffee. "What do you think?"

"What do I think?" Rene's heart swelled, cheeks burning. Between Simon asking her to "go steady" as the old timers said and Brian calling out of the blue, Rene' hadn't much time to think about anything else. "I'm thrilled."

"Thrilled?" Sean smirked.

"I know I sound like a dumb teenager in love but—"

He held up a hand. "Don't even bother, lass. I know you two. It's not like that and you know it, so don't bother caring what others might think."

Rene' beamed. "He's coming back in a month. We'll have our first official date then. We just haven't planned details. No pizza place to visit with the end of the world and all," she said wryly.

Sean cocked his head. "Hmm. I'll fix that."

"Huh?" "Nothing." He leaned forward, sipping his coffee carefully. "You sure there's nothing else you wanna talk about?"

Rene' had talked with her dad and mom and Bethany, but the hurt was still there. Talking didn't help. "Not really."

"I'm sorry, Rene'."

Rene' bit her lip, shrugging weakly. "Not your fault. I just hope he works something out... Does some good for once."

"He shouldn't have called you." Sean sighed.

"Nobody else would've listened." Rene' rubbed the mug, shivering. Lee hated Brian, Terri wouldn't answer the unknown contact, and her parents... well, she didn't know why Brian hadn't tried contacting them first. It didn't matter. They had taken the news pretty harshly.

"Still." Sean shrugged. "I don't like seeing you upset. Your dad talked to me a bit about what happened."

Rene' forced a chuckle. "Everyone gets upset." But if she was honest, if it weren't for Sean continually reminding her it was all right if she was hurting, she would be worse off. Her parents were furious at Brian—and while Rene' was too, she wished she hadn't told them about the call. It didn't help or solve anything. All it'd done was remind her parents that their eldest had harmed their youngest daughter.

A few of the other officers came in, chatting tiredly and grabbing coffee. Rene' stood, gave Sean a quick side hug, and headed outside. The chilly winter breeze bit at her cheeks, and she pulled her thick coat tighter. Only months before, her town had feared the oncoming winter—now, thanks to the gang members bringing supplies, they were ready for a harsh season. Rene' gulped hard, heading towards her mare at the hitching post.

Quinn, one of the teenage boys constantly giving Lee's militia group trouble, came over quietly. Rene' eyed him with a frown. "Hey... can I help you?" The last time they'd talked, he'd bullied her into giving up the fight. He hadn't shown his face around the courthouse much since.

"How's the family?" he asked curtly.

Rene' undid her mare's lead rope from the post. "Fine."

"Word from yesterday's shipment says your brother went AWOL." Quinn smirked. "Think he'll join the rebels?"

"Probably not." Rene' set her jaw. "Did you need something? I'm late."

"You need to watch your back, Rene'."

"You keep saying that." Rene' glared at him. "What for?"

"You're gonna get hurt again." Quinn snapped.

"Like you care? And why would I get hurt—"

He gestured to the courthouse. "You people have no idea what'll happen to us if we don't surrender!"

"Surrender to who, Quinn? The Union?"

"The government!" Quinn stepped closer. Rene' clenched her fists, ready to strike him. "And you, Rene', you..." He stopped.

"What about me?" she asked tautly. "Do I scare you, Quinn? You give Lee so much shit, and you know I'll kill you if you tried anything—is that why you want me cowered at home? What the hell are you up to?" Anger burned in her chest, and she didn't try containing it.

Quinn's green eyes flashed with rage. "Don't act like I'm the bad guy! You guys are all screwed, and it'll be up to guys like me to fix it!"

"Guys like you?" Rene' snarled. "So you can stab us all in the back and save yourself?"

"Some of us want peace, Rene'!" Quinn said sharply. "And the cost of peace is worth it, no matter what."

Rene' sucked in a sharp breath. "Maybe it's not, Quinn. Maybe it's not peace if the wicked rule."

"It's better than death!" Quinn shook his head, breathing hard. "You know what? Forget it. I've tried to warn you. None of you people will listen!" He stormed off toward mainstreet.

Rene' mounted and pushed her horse toward the road, but her stomach twisted into knots. What was Quinn trying to warn her about? This had been the second time he'd confronted her, but he was still cryptic. What was he up to?

Rene' chewed her lip. Maybe she'd go find him again and ask—later, after she finished her evening chores.

RENE' DIDN'T GO FIND Quinn that day, but she finished chores, helped make dinner, and by the time she hit her bed, was almost too tired to keep her eyes open.

However, when her phone buzzed, she answered the call quickly. "Si?"

"Hey, Rene'."

"Hey. Are you OK?"

"Yeah, sorry for disappearing for a bit." Simon's voice was quiet and heavy. Rene' tensed, worry flooding her.

"Si? You sound rough... Is everything OK?"

A long pause. "I guess so."

"You can talk to me," Rene' said softly. "Please. I can listen."

"We infiltrated a dome earlier tonight." Simon paused. "I should still be helping, but Dad said they had it covered."

"Oh, Si..."

"We shut it down, we got the victims out, but... but I don't know. It's not any easier seeing the aftermath." The phone went muffled for a second, then, "Rene', honey, I'm sorry but I've gotta call you back."

"I love you," she said quickly.

"Love you, too." The line went dead. Rene's throat tightened, and she ran a hand over her face, trying to breathe.

Simon would be all right—he was strong, he had faith. But the evilness he had to face wasn't something that ought to exist. The men trying to fix it and save the victims would no doubt be broken. *God, please, give them strength and wisdom.* Rene' prayed for the victims and the rescue team before drifting off to sleep.

And as usual, she dreamt about Jed and his knife against her legs.

CHAPTER ELEVEN

December 31st, 2027

"WHY WOULD WEST JOHNSTON, George's only son, offer this?" Rebel Vice President Darius Smith spoke calmly, but disbelief shined in his pale gray eyes.

The warehouse they had camped in for the night was cozy and secure. West sat at a table with his arms tied in front of him. He worked through his options quickly. He had to make them trust him. They'd taken his weapons and his ear comm at the door, so he didn't have to hear his team's nagging voices in his ear, but he imagined they were pissed.

Now it was up to West to make the new plan work.

What better way to get the enemy of your father to trust you, than tell them the truth about your father?

"I'm the heir to the Johnston legacy," West said quietly. "And I don't want it, sir. I've watched George slaughter innocents for years. I've watched him rise into a position of power that no man should have."

Darius' expression grew hard. "Is this a trap, boy? Your father tells you to infiltrate us from within, act as a spy?"

"No. My orders tonight were to kill you." West shook his head. "The Union wants you in as much a frenzy as they are since General Brian Jones went AWOL."

"What do you know about General Brian?" Darius sat across from him with a weary groan. He was showing some exhaustion and frustration—that was a good sign.

"Not much, yet." West shrugged. "But I know that he's got something up his sleeve. He's dedicated too much of his life to the government to back out without a good reason."

"We can't seem to figure what that reason is." Darius rubbed his face, chuckling. "We've overcome a Union-run capital in Pennsylvania. News didn't cover it, did they?"

"No sir, but we've got inside sources. We knew." West leaned forward, jaw tightening. "Sir, I'm risking my life and the lives of my friends. I swore to myself I would never endanger my brothers' lives but... but this seemed like the best option. I trusted my gut. But now I have to trust you. You can use me, Darius. You have a leverage no one else has ever had in this war."

Darius met his gaze, silent for a long moment. His dark skin was littered in scars and burns. "I can't be certain this isn't a trap. Why else would you—"

"Because I want your side to win," West snapped. "I hate this nation, Darius. I hate it. I hate the government, the officials, the puppeteers in hiding who act like we're nothing. I don't want that. I want freedom. I won't get it, but if I can help your people, if I can help restore America to something similar to what it was, maybe my brothers can have freedom. One day, somehow, maybe it'll happen. But it won't happen if I follow my father's orders." West's shoulders sagged. "So use me."

"How?" Darius asked, voice challenging.

"The government won't save me, but George will," West said firmly. "We let George know the deal."

Darius was silent for a moment. "West... You didn't hear, did you?"

"Hear what?"

"The President of the Union was assassinated. Not too long ago. They say Confeds did it, but Larry and I... we never gave any orders, boy. Whoever killed the President and is in the House right now... We didn't send them."

The air rushed from West's lungs. "The White House is being taken over?"

"Yes." Darius nodded.

"Then use me!" West said quickly. "Contact George, tell him if he doesn't tell the Union to keep away, you'll kill me. If we can give those guys in the White House time to take over, you can send more troops."

Darius studied him in surprise. "George would care enough to stop a war for you?"

West's heart dropped to his feet. *No.* But what choice did he have now? "I think so, sir. He sent me to kill you and I couldn't. If you have any way you can use me, I'll do whatever it takes. But this could be our last chance. The government is weakened by the deaths and now, the loss of the White House." If more action wasn't taken now, everything would be lost.

Darius sighed. "We can try the hostage idea... Or we could send you back as a spy."

"A spy?"

"You can send us direct intel, West. Show us when to move, and how, and we keep going forward." Darius smirked. "That way George can't just let you die and our team has a fighting chance."

West grinned slightly. "I could pull that off, sir. George won't know what hit him."

"I'll give you ways to contact us. Any intel West, can be used. We need all we can get—irepower, anything." Darius stood, undoing the binds on West's wrists. "And if you get word about General Brian... let me know. I'd like to welcome him on our side."

CHAPTER TWELVE

January 1st, 2028

THE MEN LOUNGED AT the HQ warehouse in efforts not to show boredom that drove them up the walls. A few played pool, some gambled in the lounge area, and others worked out in the gym room. Their voices, laughter, and shouts mingled in the air, creating an atmosphere Gideon had long grown used to.

Since the bombing of the jet, George had told them to head out with vehicles the next day. The state of the political world and the assassinations of the leaders had George spooked, but he still wanted his men to, as safely as possible, eliminate Flannery.

Gideon stepped into the kitchen area wearily. Percy was reclining at the table, metal music playing on an old CD player. He turned it down and leaned forward, expression soft. "Hey... everything all right? You weren't supposed to be here till morning."

"Had some work to finalize before we head out." Gideon poured a cup of coffee from the pot.

"How's Al doing?"

"Healing."

"I meant up here." Percy tapped his head.

Gideon sighed. "Haven't asked. He won't talk much right now."

"He doesn't like the mission. I can't blame him; it's dangerous."

"They're all dangerous." Gideon sat across from him and sipped his steaming coffee.

"You know what I mean." Percy rolled his eyes.

"Doesn't change that it has to be done."

"We'll take care of it." Percy leaned back again. "I'll see to it."

Gideon nodded silently. "Thanks, Percy."

He smiled. "Don't mention it. That's what family is for, right?"

"Right." Gideon finished his coffee. "Percy?"

"Hm?" "Back at the dome...you hesitated. You haven't hesitated since..." Gideon trailed off. "Why?"

Percy's expression tightened and he looked away, eyes heavy. "Just memories." "Your grandpa?"

"Yeah."

"You did fine," Gideon said firmly. "The memories will leave eventually." A lie, but it made Percy smile.

"Sure." Percy scoffed, straightening again. "I won't hesitate again.""Twice in almost a decade isn't a shabby record." Gideon sipped his coffee. "We all have moments."

"You don't." Percy leaned against the table.

"I do." Gideon shrugged.

"Do you ever doubt any of this, Gideon?" Percy glanced toward the door but they were still alone.

"Which part?" Gideon asked dryly. "Myself? My men? The government? George?"

"All of it," Percy said, working his jaw. "Do you ever fear it's all worthless? That what we do will just... be for nothing. Like we shouldn't have fought at all."

"No. Why?" Gideon never doubted the fight. It was all they had, all they could do. Fighting was the one human instinct that mattered. Gideon's father had instilled the importance of fighting and never backing down from an early age. It'd stuck.

"I guess I do, sometimes." Percy licked his lips. "It's scary to think it could be for nothing."

"It isn't."

"I know. And I don't think about it much. But sometimes it feels hopeless." Percy paused, laughing bitterly. "I know it sounds stupid."

Gideon finished his coffee, frowning. "Not stupid. Just human."

"You sound like Alex." Percy smirked.

"Well, sometimes he says things that make sense when he's not rambling about technology."

Percy was quiet for a moment before studying Gideon closely. "You still think the war is ending soon?""It doesn't have a choice. Foreign aid will fail soon and the USA, or what's left of it, can't handle a war without supplies and funding from beyond borders."

"Then make me a promise, Gideon." Percy's tone grew hard.

"What?" Gideon held his gaze, unphased by his friend's sudden cold change of exterior. Percy was laid-back until he was in a fight or about to be in one.

"Promise me that we'll stick together, no matter what. We're a good team, the lot of us. If George tries to split us, promise me we'll ignore him."

"We usually do," Gideon said with a chuckle. "Don't worry, Percy. We're close to finishing this. George won't know what hit him." With George dead, Gideon could recruit an even larger team and restore some order in the US. Percy would be by his side, as usual.

"You've just seemed to get sidetracked." Percy sighed. "What with Springtown..."

"It's my job to help, Percy, but I haven't forgotten our end game." Gideon frowned. "You think I would?""No. I trust you."

"Good."

"We'll kill Flannery, and we'll restore some order to the world as a team... But what else do you really want, Gideon?" Percy asked quietly, studying Gideon's face as if seeking some great secret.

"What?"

"Al wants a wife and kids. What do you want when this is all over?"

"I don't think it'll be over," Gideon admitted.

"Then what do you want through it all?"

"Haven't thought about it," Gideon said. "Just focusing on keeping my team alive." And oftentimes, failing.

"Right," Percy said quietly. "Guess we're the same, then."

"Guess so." Dreaming and yearning for any sort of normalcy had been smothered from Gideon's soul years ago. Percy knew that. They'd killed their dreams early on. As teens, they'd talk it over—how Alex held onto hope while they accepted the fact they'd die young because of their job.

Would that ever change?

Would they ever choose hope?

Gideon thought of Alex's injured, burnt body and how Flannery had escaped once again. Gideon saw the man in the torture room while George had given him the branding.

Hope doesn't push me.

Rage does.

CHAPTER THIRTEEN

January 1st, 2028

SIMON WOULD'VE TRADED A kidney to spend New Year's Eve how a normal person did—kissing the person they loved. Instead of being with Rene', he was stuck on the road with a whole trail of rescues and special op men, headed to safety, and after the victims were safe, they would head to Oklahoma for another mission.

His life was nothing but chaos.

In a way, his current predicament held hope. The victims could find a new life as they were given care and helped in the brutish world before them.

But the hope of the situation didn't stick with Simon. The boy he'd carried to safety had passed away only hours before. A few other victims had died during the drive—

they were simply too exhausted to respond to the proper medicine or treatments.

Still, all the chaos lingering around him melted away as he watched the new year ring in with a surprise he'd never expected.

Union President Kaden was murdered in the White House.

The news feed kept replaying the same choppy message by different newscasters—the White House had been taken over by a group of unidentified terrorists. The President was reported dead. Over 50 hostages—the exact number was uncertain—were within the White House. No men could enter the House unless they risked hostages being killed, so no actions were being taken.

Simon kept the news on but muted it, fighting down the bile in his throat. The newscasters blamed the Confederates for the attack, but that didn't make sense to Simon. Why not murder the man sooner if they could? Besides, if it'd been planned on the rebel's end, where was President Larry making the triumphant announcement that they'd won the USA?

This wasn't the rebels. This was someone else— someone more skilled than the news wanted to let on.

Then who was it? Who had just disrupted the entire nation worse than it already was?

Simon rubbed his face and called Rene'. It was only 3 AM, but he needed to let them know what was going on.

"Hello?" Rene's voice was thick with sleep.

"Babe, I need you to go get your dad," Simon mustered.

"What? What's wrong? Are you OK?" Immediately alert now, Rene's breath caught.

"I'm fine sweetie, but you guys need to know what's going on. Please wake your dad up." Simon couldn't take the chance of not telling them and something catching them off guard because of it. Once Rene' got her parents, Simon told them what had happened.

Mr. Fisher sighed heavily. "Do you know who it was, son?"

"No, sir. The news won't say, but they're acting like it's Confeds."

"God, help us," Mrs. Fisher whispered.

"We'll stay alert." Mr. Fisher's voice grew tight. "Thanks for the call, Simon. Watch your back. If you need to come back sooner than planned, you're always welcome here."

"Thank you, sir. I'm on a job right now, but I'll keep you posted." He paused, waiting to hear Rene' say—

"I love you," came the gentle words.

He closed his eyes briefly. "I love you, too. See you guys." He hung up and buried his head into his hands.

The Union President was dead. So why didn't Simon feel relief?

The man had been wicked. A man with three wives and an obsession with children who had always been open about it. But had he deserved murder? Was it murder, or was that the closest to solid justice the US government was capable of now?

What happened now? Would whoever had broken into the White House escape, or would they be caught? Would the Confeds take over? Would they even make it if they tried?

Simon raked his hands through his thick black hair. *God, if You're listening, we need You. I don't understand what's happening. Please... help us. Show us what to do to make this right.*

THE SUPPLY DROP THAT night was eerily quiet. Rene' helped the men bring in the supplies that Tyler Brooks and his friend drove in for the town. Word about the assassination rang heavy over the group. The townsfolk wanted to know what was going on, but Ty didn't have much to tell them.

Rene' quietly slipped away and went to the break room again. Rubbing her fingers together to try to warm them, she sat at the table. The voices from the hall faded as the group went to stock the supplies and discuss the news that had rocked the nation.

Rene' didn't want to think about the war. She didn't want to think about the assassination. She didn't want to think about her town's future. She didn't want to think about the horrors that Simon was seeing while he took his new role.

Tears burned her eyes as she rubbed her thighs, pushing away the memories of Jed. She'd been helpless then, tied to a table and all alone. And she was helpless now, only she wasn't tied up, and she had a whole town alongside her. Why did she feel so weak, then? Why did things suddenly seem lost? The Confederates had gained ground—why couldn't Rene' rejoice?

Brian's voice filled her head again. He'd sounded older, but he was still her brother—the same brother that had taught her how to cross creeks, and the same brother that had taught her how to draw.

Why had he called? Rene' still didn't understand the meaning of his words. But was it a coincidence that he'd gone AWOL and the war switched to the rebels favor? It couldn't be, considering how good Brian had proven to be at war.

Her hands grew warm as she rubbed her jeans, and she took a shaky breath. So what if Brian had betrayed the

Union? *They could kill him for treason. He could get killed as a rebel as easily as he was a Union General.*

But that was the life of a warrior, period. Their family never knew if they were breathing or dead someplace on a bloody piece of ground. People easily forgot the hell the family members experienced.

Rene' shook herself. This wasn't the time to panic. If the war was shifting, it would take townships like Springtown to help restore the nation—or so the others had said. Springtown had been through battles before with the help of the gangsters. Whatever lay ahead, they could hold their own, even in the cold winter. They were prepared, united, and strong.

But that could easily change. War was a living, breathing thing, with a rhythm that sometimes fell off course. Anything could happen. Like soldiers attacking townships as they'd done to many towns.

Lee came in, boots dragging. "Hey, loser."

"Hey." Rene' didn't look up.

Lee slowed and put a hand on her shoulder. Even though he was two years her junior, he towered over her. "You OK?"

"Yep."

"It isn't Christian-like to lie," he said sarcastically.

"Just tired."

"Tired or upset?"

"Which are *you*?"

Lee sat beside her. "Both, I guess." A pause. "I hate Brian, Rene', but if this is him... what do we do?"

"What do you mean?" Rene' frowned.

"All shit can hit the fan, and it probably will. We just got settled down for the long haul. Now the war is gonna blow back up. What if it doesn't end? What if the Union takes over, once and for all?" Lee stared down at the table, picking at a scab on his hand.

Rene' gently hugged him, sighing. "It'll be fine, Lee. We're all tough. We've got the Grim Alliance going. God will help us through."

"If we get attacked... if the gang can't get here in time..." Lee's shoulders sagged. The weight of the world should never rest on a teen boy's shoulders, but Rene' couldn't seem to lighten the load.

"We'll fight and we'll win," Rene' said firmly. "All of us can fight, Lee. And besides, you've got a whole militia going on who will follow you into anything, if you're worried about that."

Lee rolled his eyes. "That's got me worried too. What if I mess up? Mo and I have been arguing all the time lately. Xander's getting cold feet after tonight. He just told me he's not sure we've got much chance."

Rene's blood boiled. She gripped Lee's hand, looking him in the eye. "You do have a chance—we all do."

Quinn's voice nagged at her mind. "We'll make it, Lee. Whether Xander or anyone else likes it, they'll have to pull their weight too."

Lee hesitated before giving a tired smirk. "All of that applies to you too, worry Nellie."

"It's *nervous* Nellie." Rene' sighed. "And I know."

CHAPTER FOURTEEN

January 2nd, 2028

"I DIDN'T THINK LIFE could get worse after 2020, but this is absolute bull—" Spencer started to swear, but the giant hulk of an assassin, Nabeel, eyed him. "It sucks, OK?"

Bo laughed and took a long swig of beer. "Could be worse. You could be ugly, like Nab."

Nabeel gave him a dark look, but Bo just gave a cheeky grin. "Bite me, pretty boy," Bo challenged. "Or should I say—"

Nabeel slapped him on the back of the head, and Bo yelled at him, smoothing his brown hair quickly.

The bar at Paradise wasn't ideal for a meet up location, but George had stressed that it was one of the safest places to meet up. Kaleb was out of town and on a job, George told them, so they should lie low till George arrived that evening.

In the span of two hours during their wait, Bo was nearly plastered, and Spencer had taken to loudly complaining that "a bar should have women, even if the HQ was no-women allowed".

West rubbed his temples and forced some beer down. The mission hadn't been a long one, and he was past his wit's end. *This is why I liked taking jobs with Jack. He shut up sometimes.*

"I'm just saying," Spencer continued, grabbing another drink. "That we're total dead meat."

"Shut up!" Bo hissed, glancing around even though the bar was empty, besides a few teens playing pool in the back. Then he winced at his own loud voice and downed the rest of his Jack Daniel's.

West rolled his eyes. "As far as George is concerned, they never arrived at the destination and we never crossed paths. We were late for the check-in report because we ran into a caravan of extremists."

They had been over the cover story a dozen times since leaving the rebel VP at the border. The men were good at their jobs, but Bo was a loose-lip when he was drunk, and if Spencer got nervous, West wasn't sure he'd outgrown his childish behavior from years prior. "Bo, when George gets here—"

"Go away so he doesn't think I'm some stupid hick, yada yada yada. I know." Bo scoffed, reaching for West's beer. "At least I don't have to face Georgie."

Spencer chuckled, nervousness leaking into his usually laid-back exterior. "Yeah. Lucky."

"You guys sound like schoolboys," West said sharply. But he couldn't really disagree with their uncertainty.

George had hired them all to do things they regretted. He held power and control over their lives and the lives of their loved ones. The slightest mishap could end them up like Ed Brooks—dead. A mess up like they'd done— meeting with the enemy vice president, formulating to work against George as a team... it was treason.

George had killed over treason. Thomas Flannery had passed George's test and left him, and now George had his finest hunting the bastard down. Gideon would make that death slow and painful.

But for them? If they found out, who would kill them? What would the price be if anyone discovered the coup they'd formed?

It can't happen, simple as that.

Bo cursed at him and went into a back room to sleep it off. West sighed and got up when the door to the bar opened. George smirked and strode over, smoothing his dark hair back. "Hey, son. What's this I hear about the job falling through?" Despite his smirk, his tone was ice.

Nabeel and Spencer watched silently, but the weight of the lying was on West. "They were gone by the time we got there. Backup was waiting at the border." George had told them not to make a scene, and pursuit would have caused one.

"Hmm." George rubbed his clean-shaven chin. "They went straight through?"

"Yessir."

"Well, next time, I suppose." George clasped West's shoulder. "I'm afraid we have bigger fish to fry. The rebel VP was low game anyway. It would have been a nice touch, but with what's going on now, we need to take it further, and the UN agrees." He smiled at them and patted West's broad shoulder. "Next, you boys will hunt Confederate President Larry."

West's heart pounded, but he didn't react. "What did you have in mind?"

"If he's dead, the VP will be in a weak spot. After President Kaden's death, the nation needs to see that we are still in control... Tit for tat." George picked up a drink from the wooden countertop. "You're the Johnston heir—you can handle this assassination. But you have a week to cover it, with some of my best men, and after that, if things go wrong, we're running."

"Running?"George eyed Spencer and Nabeel, leaning in closer to West. "Yes. You, Cindy, and I will go into Canada." They had a safe house in the Yukon. West had never been to it before, but he'd been told about it.

West nodded. "You think the nation will revolt?"

"A bit more than that, son. I did not expect things to fall like this. We don't have much time, but I'll explain everything tonight at the mansion. Your mother and I disagree on how these events will unfold, but my way goes. Let's go." George straightened and beamed at Nabeel and Spencer. "Well done, boys. You got back in one piece and next time, you'll handle it, won't you?"

Nabeel gave a silent, somber nod but Spencer gave a sloppy salute. "Yessir."

"Enjoy your night of bliss." George rolled his eyes and led West outside.

West's mind raced as he got into the armoured SUV with his father. What had happened that had George on edge? What had happened that had changed everything?

And would West, now a spy for the rebels, be able to pull his mission off?

CHAPTER FIFTEEN

January 4th, 2028

SIMON LISTENED AS HIS father went over the plan one last time. The team was well skilled and prepared, with only a few newbies on the job—Simon, Nate, and Spencer, who had joined because he was a fair sniper and they needed another set of hands. Kaleb had insisted on dragging Spencer into it, saying, "Randy's already knee-deep, his brother may as well be too."

Randy had proven his worth, but mostly at aftercare—he had a way with the victims that helped immensely. Despite his stoic attitude, Simon knew that the work was breaking Randy, fast and quite quickly. Randy wasn't cut out for seeing so much pain.

Is anyone?

As the men left the room, footsteps echoing in the warehouse hall, to begin packing up for the infiltration, Simon went over to Jordan. Jordan had worked this sort of gig for years behind George's back, never getting caught and never slowing down. He'd done the impossible.

But a voice in Simon's gut whispered, *for how much longer?*

What if Simon messed it all up? He messed everything up.

Jordan turned and smiled, pulling Simon into a brief, tight hug. "Hey, son. Ready to go?" "Y-yeah, Dad, I just wanted to tell you something." Simon steeled himself and straightened. He wouldn't act like a bumbling little kid anymore. He was a man, and Jordan deserved to know he'd done a good job at raising him.

Hopefully.

"What is it?" Jordan studied him with a frown.

"I know this isn't the time to get mushy or anything but we've been so busy, and I needed to say—"

"Spit it out, Si." He smiled.

"I wanted to tell you that I'm proud of you, Dad," Simon said quietly. "We haven't always been super tight. It was my fault. Nate always ran and rebelled against Kaleb, and I just... I let my relationship with you go up and down.

"A part of me thought you'd always be there, and the other part thought you'd eventually treat me the way

Kaleb treated Nate. I-I know that's stupid. But since we started doing these jobs..." Simon shook his head, clenching his jaw briefly. "I never realized how much of a hero you are. I don't say that lightly, Dad—I mean it. You've helped more people than I could've ever imagined, and I'm... I'm grateful I could do it with you." He took a shaky breath. "I'm sorry if I failed you, Dad. You deserve better."

Everyone deserved better than what Simon had to offer.

Jordan frowned and clasped the side of Simon's face firmly, eyes dark. "You could never disappoint me, Simon. Never. You're the best thing I've ever done, and even then I messed up, time and time again. But you're strong. Smart. You always pulled through even when I didn't know what to do." He paused and smiled softly. "I'll always be here, son. Always. You got that part right."

Simon wrapped his arms tightly around Jordan and didn't let go, insides shaking like his chest was being constricted. "I'm sorry, Dad."

"Sorry for what?" Jordan held him close. "You've done well, as far as I know."

"I should've been a better son. A better brother, a better man for Rene'—"

Jordan cut him off firmly. "Don't believe those lies, Simon. Never let those voices lead you."

Simon clamped his eyes shut and buried his face against Jordan's neck. "I want to fix it all, Dad."

"But you can't," Jordan said, voice thick. "That's life, son. War or no war, there will always be things a man just can't fix. And those are the times where you have to understand God's holding it together."

Simon nodded weakly. "I-I know He is."

"Doesn't always make it easier, huh?"

"Not always."

"That's life too, son." Jordan pulled away and smiled at Simon, brown eyes shining with tears. "I'm proud of you, Si. I don't say it enough, never have, but I am. You're doing just fine. I know you'll become a better man than I ever was. It's what I want."

Simon took a slow breath and then squeezed his father's shoulders, hands shaky but firm. "I'll try, Dad."

Jordan chuckled and slapped him on the back. "Let's go."

AT ONE POINT, ARKANSAS had probably been a pretty place, but it gave Simon the heebie jeebies now. Or maybe just the area around the dome was heaped with creepy vibes. Simon didn't understand it, but his skin kept crawling, and it felt like an elephant was on his chest even though he wasn't having a panic attack.

They'd been staking out for a bit now, the time for the infiltration growing closer, and he couldn't allow his head to override his mission.

Even if it was a strange feeling.

This dome was large in size, the building smack dab in what had once been a busy city. For months now, Jordan had a few spies inside the dome, working to gain intel and trust with some of the traffickers. Now it was time to not only save victims, but destroy what was left of the dome.

To do so, Kaleb insisted on having greater numbers, on top of Jordan's calm and collected sneak approach. With time to work such jobs running out due to George panicking about the White House situation, they had to finish the dome by the end of the night.

Nate and Randy were arguing in the back of the camera van. Simon shushed them sharply, crawling into the back. "Can you guys shut up for five minutes?" "Yes," they both snapped in unison.

Simon sighed, watching the cameras. They'd been left behind, a mile away from the dome site, just as a safety measure, with a whole group of teammates. Once security was sniped and fought down, they'd go in for rescue.

"Almost ready," Nate said quietly. He set his jaw and watched the cams again. "They're about done."

Simon turned away, unable to stomach the sights any longer. The war might be close to a victory, but the real war wouldn't end. The Second Civil War between the Union and Confederates might end, but what about the wars and battles that followed to stabilize the states afterward?

Saving these victims is part of the bigger picture. I'm doing my part.

I can't mess this up.

The comms lit up with the word for backup to haul in, and Simon's nagging doubt was put to rest.

THE DOME WAS FLOODING with victims of all ages and ethnicities. Nate didn't get very far into the building itself, facing the outpouring of victims as the special ops team retrieved them first and foremost, once the dangers were eliminated. Nate helped the best he could but once the others took over, he dug deeper into the corridors. Most of the cells were packed with kids and adults, all injured, malnourished, and even a few looked deceased.

Nate kept going. The intel they'd found at the last dome had been hinting at something more—and if this dome held vital intelligence about the Union government, they needed to find it. The job had to be quick before anyone realized what was going on—the surrounding area might have hidden moles ready to send out alerts.

Time was of the essence.

Each floor had a top-notch security system that just got stronger as it went. Lucky for them, their team was also top notch, and had malfunctioned the building's system before entering. All Nate had to do was use some doo-dad Simon had equipped him with and go through each door that was marked "PRIVATE" or "RESTRICTED".

Simple enough.

Nate ran over the scattered bloodied bodies of the dead the team had killed. Nate didn't look too closely. The crew didn't do half-ass jobs, so none of the men would still be alive, and Nate didn't want to waste time wondering what monsters looked like.

One floor up and Nate found everything the nation needed to implode on itself. He quickly spoke into his comm. "Simon, Kaleb, get up here now."

SIMON STUMBLED A BIT over the bodies littering the dark corridor. All electricity had been wiped out so the place was dark, eerily quiet besides children screaming and men giving orders. Nate was upstairs, away from the deep underground levels packed with victims, away from the aftermath of the bloodbath, and away from the horrors of the human trafficking ring.

Simon swallowed the bile in his mouth and kept going till he reached the door. "Nate?"

"Here." Nate's voice was muffled, and he shoved his mask down a little. "Look at this."

Kaleb came in behind Simon, going over to where his son was looking over computer files, some old, some newer and more technologically advanced. But they were untouched—the bastards hadn't had time to swipe anything before being killed.

"What is this?" Simon asked, watching Nate go through file after file, email after email. The computers were stacked full of intel by the looks of it—but what kind?

Nate showed them one of the pages. "It's plans for the vics, that's what. Experiments going on in the Union labs, trades between the gov and the traffickers, all sorts of ugly shit. Actual proof—more than the last dome had. We have a freaking case." He glanced at Kaleb. "We can actually do something, Kaleb! We can show the nation what the hell is going on! We can save these victims and stop the rings—"

"Back up, Nate," Kaleb said. "Si, can you start downloading? I'll get backup." He turned away and contacted the others so the professionals could come get to work and wrap it up.

Simon blinked at the documents and started to download them on his own drives from his pack. Hundreds of victims had been trafficked into the government's labs. What for?

If what Reese said is really happening... if they're performing genetic shit on people... what does that mean for the war? For the nation?

CHAPTER SIXTEEN

January 5th, 2028

THE TRIP TO ONTARIO had been a bust.

Gideon slammed the truck door and headed into his cabin in the woods. Protected by acres of forest, heavy artillery, and well-placed booby traps, the place was as safe as he could've made it set with security systems, but he intended to find a trained K9 to protect Alex and Noah while Gideon was out hunting Flannery.

The cabin was quiet, the porch light left on for Gideon. He dropped his bag in the foyer and locked the door back. Silence greeted him—everyone was asleep for once. He had time to hit the bag in the basement, shower, eat—

"Gid?"

Gideon looked over at the hallway, hanging his coat on the wall hook. "You should be in bed, Al."

"Did you find anything?" Alex asked quietly.

Gideon took a slow breath and headed to the kitchen. "Not yet."

Flannery had completely vanished off the map, just like he had before attacking Springtown and kidnapping Alex out of the blue. Gideon wouldn't stop till the man was dead, but the hunt was slow going. He'd been in Ontario but somehow, word got out that the man had been tortured for intel, so Flannery had fled again.

It was just the beginning.

Alex followed him, chewing his lip. "Oh."

"Noah asleep?" Gideon poured himself a cup of hot coffee waiting in the pot just for him, courtesy of Alex. Some old habits die hard.

"Yeah. He's struggling pretty bad with PTSD." Alex studied Gideon for a moment.

"You'll help him." Gideon turned away, going into the basement with his mug of coffee. "You're good at helping people." *And I'm good at hunting them, at destroying their lives, at killing them. And the one time I've wanted to kill someone more than anything, he's gone.*

Alex stepped down the stairs. "Gideon, if something's bothering you, you can talk to me. I'm good at helping people, remember?" His voice was weary, almost hesitant, like he worried Gideon might bring up Flannery.

"Just thinking, Al." He drank some coffee and sat the mug on the table near the door. He wrapped his hands without looking over.

"About?"

"The war."

"Oh." A pause. "What about it?""Just getting tired of it, Al. All of it. All of the work we've done... what's it been for? What good has it really done?" Gideon set his jaw, finishing the wrappings and stepping to the bag.

Alex frowned, eyebrows furrowing. "What are you talking about?"

Gideon took a slow breath. He didn't need to let doubts or emotions cloud his judgment. The fact was every route he planned, every mission he took behind George's back, where was it getting him? Was it helping anyone, was it helping the war? Every step forward equaled another seven backward. He couldn't outwit George, he couldn't stop the thousands of men and women in high places, he couldn't change the heart of a nation.

"We're playing a losing game, Alex." Gideon looked over. "I know you think this is it, this is the end of the war, this is the next step to God's ultimate plan—but I think we're just screwed."

Alex laughed softly, bitterness inching into his voice. "You think it's easy for me to find hope, Gideon?"

Gideon tensed. "What?"

"You think it's easy for me to wake up every day and choose God? To choose hope for this bloody nation? To decide I'll fight the good fight when all along, there's a good damn chance I'm as bad as the men we wanna kill?" Alex stepped closer, scarred hands clenched into fists. "It bloody isn't, Gideon!"

"Then why?" Gideon snapped. "Why choose God? Why choose a God that let all of this happen—for what? Punishment? Payment for the sins of our fathers?" Anger boiled in his blood. There was no cause for any of this. No reason for countless innocents to die. No reason for a nation to kill itself.

"You blame God for this?" Alex demanded, green eyes flashing.

"Yes!"

"God didn't do this, Gideon. Men like George, like Flannery—the people doing what Satan wants? They created that, not God!" Alex said firmly.

"Your God isn't stopping a damn thing!" Gideon snarled. "We watched families burn alive, Al! And you prayed and prayed like it changed something."

Tears burned Alex's eyes. "Maybe God is punishing America, Gideon. I don't know. Maybe He's punishing the wicked ones, and maybe He's protecting the righteous, like the people in Springtown. Or maybe bad shit happens and good people just have to deal with it. Because I don't know where I am in God's eyes."

"Then where are we, Al?" Gideon forced out, shoulders sagging. "What is all this for? We fight the good fight for a God that thinks we deserve hell?"

Alex gently gripped Gideon's shoulder. "That's not what these wars are about, Gideon. It's not about how much we deserve hell."

Gideon pulled away. "Yes, it is. Even you're terrified you don't do enough to please God. You're the best man I know, Al. Honorable and kind and loyal. If you fear for your soul, what hope do the rest of us have?"

What was the point of the fighting? Of the bloodshed? Of saving people from death? Gideon didn't need a God to judge him. He didn't need a God to save him during a war that Gideon had survived for years.

So why had he seen a man with pierced hands and feet when George had been digging into Gideon's back? Why did Alex insist on holding onto faith? And the girl, Rene', why did she still believe in God after He'd let her be kidnapped, cut into, and left for dead?

Alex shook his head softly but didn't touch Gideon again. "I don't have all of the answers, Gideon. Neither do you. No one does. But I never doubt what we do is right. I might doubt if I do enough to please God, but that's my own bloody demon to fight. And as for being tired..." he laughed again, a weak laugh, heavy with grief. "You've got no idea. I was tortured for hours, Gideon. Simon was, too. And I didn't know what God was gonna do. I didn't know if I was strong enough to stand against Flannery— and I wasn't. But God was with me and I managed." He gulped hard, Adam's apple bobbing. "So... so maybe we don't make a difference. Maybe the war is lost. Maybe we are screwed. But... I don't believe that."

Gideon worked his jaw, struggling to maintain control. "You struggle to believe the opposite."

Alex thought for a moment. "Just because we struggle to understand and grasp the truth doesn't make it less true. You could explain gravity to a person who doesn't understand English, and they wouldn't understand you, but gravity is still very real." He smirked tiredly. "That's... how Clint used to put it, anyway." He looked away, the memory of their deceased roommate still raw.

Gideon looked back at the punching bag. "I know what I saw in the torture room, Al, but I still don't trust your God." They'd been over the theology and logistics. It didn't mean much to Gideon. Not when he woke every day to face a hell he hadn't created, yet had to conquer. What sort of God forced the sins of the fathers upon their children? And what kind of loving God allowed harm to those who adored Him?

"God's the only reason you found me in the ditch. I prayed for hours, Gideon," Alex's voice caught. "I begged God not to let me die. I was sixteen, for cripe's sake. I didn't wanna die. And God let you find me. So it might look like God lets all the bad happen, Gid, but really... God fights for the good to happen. He fights for us, Gideon. He fought for you. He fought for me... And it's over." He closed his eyes briefly. "And every war has to end."

Gideon laughed softly. "Are you sure about that one?"

He didn't let himself dwell on Alex's words. God hadn't saved Alex that night. Gideon had. One story, one miracle, didn't make God some hero.

Alex met his gaze and smirked, eyes heavy. "With men like you fighting, yeah. I'm sure."

Gideon looked away. "The tiredness... it'll go away." Always did. Gideon just locked it away and moved on. Dwelling on doubts helped no one. But the shift of the war had challenged him—it had changed Alex. In a small way, after the Union's failure and Flannery's torture fiasco, Alex's faith had grown even more.

Where did that leave Gideon? Tired and broken and driven by rage and hatred.

Compared to Alex, he was a hollow shell.

And it scared him, but he wouldn't turn to a God that was unpredictable and cruel.

"I love you, Gideon. And maybe my faith just annoys you, but I do think we'll make it through this. God's will might look like hell, but it'll work out." Alex headed upstairs and left Gideon alone with his thoughts.

Luckily Gideon was good at shutting away unnecessary thoughts, and he started at the bag.

GIDEON CONTACTED GEORGE EARLY the next morning and updated him about the hunt for Flannery. They briefly discussed the state of the nation, but George had to go abruptly, so Gideon made breakfast for Alex and Noah.

"Morning," Alex said through a yawn, coming into the kitchen. He was still in pajamas and hadn't smoothed his unkempt blond hair.

Gideon set his plate of eggs and toast onto the plate. "Noah all right?"

"Bad night, but he'll sleep in for a few hours, I think." Alex sat down groggily. Gideon gave him a mug of coffee. "Thanks."

"Talked with George. He's pretty angry about the government's lack of progress."

"Union still losing?"

"Everything's at a strange stand-still, the eye of the storm." Gideon sat down with his own plate. "George has West and a team hunting down the Confederate President.""Larry?"

"How many Confederate Presidents are there?"

Alex growled and drank some coffee. "How's that going?""West is keeping it close to his chest, so George didn't say. But they're keeping low, letting the Union screw itself over. With Kaden dead, it's all in an uproar, and the media is trying to keep that quiet. George is spooked."

"Weird..." Alex winced. "Not like George."

"Not at all. He's got something up his sleeve, or the Union does. There's no way they're lying down this easily. George is trying to cover bases which means keeping himself a small target... I think he's just trying to suck up to the leaders right now, keep his top members away from him. He's giving us jobs that all add up to a bigger picture, I think."

"So you think they have a trick?"

"Probably." Gideon shrugged. "I mean, the Confederates taking a turn for the win was unexpected, so if they have a plan, I doubt it's foolproof. The rebels could still pull it off, depending on the surprise the Union has."

Alex lifted a hand. "I haven't had enough coffee for the rest of this conversation, mate."

CHAPTER SEVENTEEN

January 5th, 2028

BY 1 AM, THE crew had over 75 victims and were fleeing the city. Simon was in a van running over the evidence and intel. He couldn't offer much help to the victims, who mostly needed medical care. As they got out of Arkansas and crept into Missouri, where a small location awaited half of the victims, Simon started thinking.

Too much.

The evidence was bomb proof. The Union government had been experimenting on citizens for decades, and since the war began, the research had nearly doubled with solidified funding. The human trafficking rings and domes had supplied the government with the people. Like sheep headed to slaughter, the emails, contacts, and money transfers, pointed to a reality darker than Simon had ever imagined.

People were being sent to the labs. For what? The emails didn't say what for, at least not blatantly, not that Simon could find. He recognized some of the codes, the ones that showed some of the people and children being sold as sex slaves, not just lab rats.

If Reese had been right, the labs were meant for hybrids, DNA and genetic testing. For a sci-fi movie, sure, that made sense. But the United States wasn't in a sci-fi movie —they were in the middle of a brother's war. Why would the government want that sort of testing to be a main focus during a shitfest?

Simon stared at one of the emails, rubbing his temples. The back of the van was full of men trying to decipher the emails, codes, and new intel that could help them save more victims.

But Simon couldn't help but think he was missing something.

The government also targeted smaller townships, places that couldn't defend themselves, wouldn't be missed, and most often, were rebel civilian ships who offered the rebels aid. They tested the woman and children and usually sent the men to war in the Union troops. That's why Simon started these jobs, to ensure no one got a hold on Springtown, but what if there was more to it?

What if they could change the government? They could do more than just destroy domes. They could throw off the Union's plot.

Simon glanced at the other men silently, chewing his lip. If men that were loyal to George turned, and if they all followed Kaleb, Jordan, and even if Gideon's group switched, would they stand a chance?

Or would George and his truly loyal goons take them out first?

Rene' and her family deserved a future. Rene' deserved to be happy, to follow what God had in store for her. They didn't deserve any more pain, or fear, or destruction. If Simon could fight for that, he'd do it, even if it looked and sounded impossible.

———

THE FIRST DROP OFF was a success. Nate helped unload half of the victims, which roughly equalled all of the victims who needed immediate medical attention or couldn't be moved any further. The location was a small ranch at the border of Missouri and was run by a few old friends of Jordan's. They took the victims into a large metal barn, and once the drop off was finished, the crew took off again.

Nate rode in a truck with Jordan, mostly because he still didn't want to spend any more time with Kaleb than he had to. Jordan was cool and collected, even if the job had been huge, and things had gone a bit off track. Jordan said that's how it went, and you handled it accordingly—so long as the victims were all saved, a few mishaps and fights didn't matter.

Nate tried to keep quiet but as the hour passed, Jordan got a call. It was short, brief, and Nate got the gist that the people at their next stop had called it off.

"What was that?" Nate asked sharply once Jordan hung up.

"Cabins were ambushed just a couple hours ago. We lost a few, but most of them got out—but we can't get the vics there in Tennessee." Jordan dialed another number.

"What are you doing? What do we do with these people?" Nate hissed. "George will find out what we did if we don't get back—"

Jordan shushed him and answered the call. Nate shut up, listening as Jordan talked calmly to a man named Ted. After a few minutes, Jordan hung up. "All right, change of plans. We're going to a little place in Missouri.""What does that mean?" Nate scowled.

"It means I'm taking a course of action I said I'd never take, but I don't have a choice. George contacted me this morning—I'll need to report back, and I can't do that with kids and women hanging in the balance. So, we're dropping them off at a pacifist group." Jordan changed directions on the road, the trail of vehicles behind him following quickly.

"A what?"

"A—"

"You're kidding, right?"

"No." Jordan frowned. "I helped their leader years ago. He said if I ever needed a favor to call."

"That was Ted?"

"No." Jordan took a slow breath. "The man I helped was killed recently. Murdered. Ted is a friend of the guy's son; he said we could come seek refuge. They've got the room." He didn't say much else but dispatched the change of plans to his men and Kaleb.

Nate rubbed his jaw, uncomfortable with Jordan's silence. He had questions—how safe was this place? It couldn't be safe. Why drag helpless victims to an unsafe place? *We don't have a choice. The White House fiasco has knocked George off his rocker—we need to get back to reality.*

After a half-hour drive, Nate started to relax enough to fall asleep just as the sound of gunfire hitting the back of the truck jerked him awake.

CHAPTER EIGHTEEN

January 5th, 2028

THE NATION CRUMBLED DURING the night.

By 6 AM, West couldn't deny it—the war had only grown. Civilians from safe government housing and civilians from rebel townships had banded together to attack multiple nearby Union camps. Despite the media bragging about the Union Army's secure funding, Union soldiers ransacked townships that night like never before —desperate and dying for necessities the government had failed to deliver.

The Confederates had also gained foreign friends. Caravans of Middle Easterns, Mexicans, Canadians, and other groups of immigrants, had joined the Confederate forces during the previous week.

West was only hearing about the breakthroughs now. None of this had made the news. The government didn't want the people to learn their mistakes, or learn that their plans might not be bulletproof.

More than that however, the government still controlled the truth through the media. And last night had proven a defeat for the Union. They couldn't showcase their failure to their sheep.

He took a tired breath and curled up tighter in his sleeping bag. Three days had passed since George forewarned West what was coming. Since President Kaden's death, the nation fell into careless tumult, the majority blindly following the vice president as he claimed presidency, but a large portion of people had been alerted to the greater truths.

They chose truth.

The giver of the truth had been Cindy and her big secret web of people dispersing the right info and the right evidence, at just the right time and place.

Bit by bit, some of the people were finding out the truth. Die-hard patriots were rising from the ashes. The truth behind the assassinations of the government officials, the truth behind the foreign deals, and the truth behind the war itself.

The war was far from over. With the good guys causing havoc in the shadows, the nation could swing either way in the end.

Especially if the Union unleashed their lab experiments. Super soldiers with keen strength, speed, and even enhanced senses, according to George. West wasn't sure he would've believed his father a few years prior, but George had shown ample evidence that the experiments hadn't all been silly or failures. The Union had soldiers built for war.

What ragtag rebel army stood a chance against super soldiers?

None.

Maybe the truth being revealed to the American people wouldn't matter if they were silenced into submission by fear.

West rubbed his head and sat up. Three days had passed since he and his small crew had gotten instructions to take out the rebel vice president. They were close to the end goal now. Bo and Nabeel proved effective, and the other men in the group were ex-military. The plan was solid.

Yet, the feeling in West's gut wouldn't subside.

Brian was in the White House with some of the nation's finest warriors.

If the super soldiers were sent in, what would happen?

And why could West do nothing to change it? He had sent the rebel vice president every bit of info he knew, including warning him about the super soldiers. If West was caught, he'd be killed for treason.

Bo snored from his bag nearby. Somewhere in the Alabama forest, an owl called. Only miles away from the rebel camp, they didn't have to worry about much besides getting caught—and they were well hidden.

Besides, the soldiers were not sending out scouts, and hadn't in a few days. Too many risks of losing men, and they were down to low numbers already. Relying on drones was their last resort. For now, hidden by foliage and wearing clothes that easily blended in their surroundings, West's group could hold on.

After all, they'd made it this far, and tomorrow morning was the kill date.

It's too easy. It was unfair to sneak into a camp and assassinate the leader. War wasn't fair of course, and the terrorists in the White House threatened to kill the new President if battles broke out with the Confederate camps located throughout the USA.

The battles had broken out, but what happened in the House? Did Brian pull the trigger? Did he have a plan?

Had West's warnings gotten to the rebel VP in time? Would President Larry still be in the camp, or would he have had time to get out without anyone finding out? West wouldn't know till he slipped in.

He couldn't turn away from this. He had failed once. He hadn't killed the rebel VP, and George wouldn't allow for a second failure as large as this. If West wanted to remain in his father's graces, if he wanted to stay close enough to kill George, he couldn't let this slip. At least, not if the president was there. If he was gone, West would have a better cover story.

But if it came to it, he wouldn't be able to walk away from the president in his tent without leaving a body behind.

His phone vibrated, and he pulled it from his pocket, rubbing his eyes. A message from George glowed on the screen. "*The beast awakens.*"

The blood left West's face and ran cold through his body.

They were too late.

The super soldiers had been sent inside the White House to regain the Union's control.

West woke the others quickly. "We do this now. Move!"

CHAPTER NINETEEN

January 5th, 2028

"THIS IS FANTASTIC," BRIAN muttered. "They're sending the soldiers underground." He watched the monitors on the large holographic screens, jaw tightening. It had been almost five days of sabotage, and he wasn't about to lose the fate of the nation because a bunch of jacked-up hero boys wanted a swing at glory.

Especially not blond ones that looked like Captain America wannabes. "Amir, grab a group and watch these cams. I'll go check the floor."

"It's clear, Jones," Amir Kader said simply. "This place is on total lockdown. It can't be infiltrated from above, from around, from within, or from below. What are you scared of?"

"These super soldiers are some bad shit, Kader," Fernando snapped. "There's two dozen of the bastards headed our way underground, and you're not concerned?"

"We can take them." Amir shrugged. He was a large man and could put his money where his mouth was, but jumped the gun too often. "We have enough men and weapons, and we're in the White House on lockdown."

"The hostages still have to be guarded," Bosch spoke up. "That's a group of men preoccupied. We don't need needless losses, Kader."

Brian waved for Bosch and Fernando to follow. "Let's check the tunnels again. We're taking these mothers out before they get in."

"How?" Bosch followed. They hurried through the corridors of the White House, which were eerily silent with all of the hostages in a main room upstairs. The security system had been overridden, so the outside world had no idea what was happening behind the closed doors. They didn't know anything that Brian didn't tell them.

He wasn't telling them much.

"We'll try the gas first."

"If that doesn't work?" Bosch asked, ever the optimist.

"We seal the tunnels off and detonate the bombs."

Bosch sighed, following him through the corridors and down the flights of stairs. "Y'know, *just bomb the tunnels*, no big deal."

"Got a better idea?"

"I didn't say I did, merc man."

Brian led him through the basement tunnels until they reached the security room. The place smelled of concrete and dirt but was fairly clean, if not a bit cobwebbed.

The White House had over 100 people inside during the take-over, including the new President and his security. They also had the speaker of the House in their hostage room, a nice addition Brian hadn't expected. All things considered, they had two chess pieces they could use— threaten their lives and get control.

The super soldiers could change the plan, but Brian had expected it. They'd prepared for it, but things could always change.

The monitors in the secure room showed a small armada of soldiers heading deeper into the underground tunnels. Brian smirked. "Just as terrifying as they told us they'd be."

"Don't joke about this shit," Bosch snapped. "These are some effed up things."

"Things," Brian mused.

The government prided themselves on creating war machines *immune to feelings*, said the articles the government soldiers had been forced to read. Brian studied every ounce of intel on the super soldier creations he could get. The outcome was unnerving. He knew more about the tin-soldiers than he wanted to, but it might not matter in the end. They were built for war with qualities normal humans couldn't reach.

It was hard to betray a government that outsmarted you at every turn. Deception came naturally to Brian, but on the opposing side, it was growing tiresome. Still, his role wasn't finished. He'd deceive the Union and ensure his comrades' deaths weren't for naught—he'd bring back a nation of order.

Even if it looked different than it ever had before. A small price to pay for a group who had to do things their damn selves.

Bosch scoffed. "We gonna gas 'em?"Brian touched his comm. "Lavi, you in ops?"

"Ready to release the fumes," Lavi said easily. "If you boys are finished gossiping." Her dry teasing was normal for her—intense ops rarely phased her.

"Hit 'em." Brian watched the cameras.

In a matter of seconds, the tunnels where the two dozen soldiers were traipsing through was filled with invisible gas. Brian watched, working his jaw as the gas took a few seconds to sink in. Three soldiers immediately dropped.

But ten seconds in, the others kept working forward.

"This doesn't make sense," Bosch growled. "This shit is specifically made to kill them!" As a backup precaution, warfare products had been created for instances of treason

—if any super soldier got out of control or went haywire, they'd take them out.

"Lavi?" Brian asked. "Did you get the right case?"

"Of course I—"

Bosch gestured to the monitors. "They've gotta have masks we just can't see, Brian. Some see-through shit."

"They're moving closer. Plan B?" Lavi asked calmly. "If they have masks Brian, that means they're prepped for any back-up the White House is prepped for."

"Plan B. Let's surprise the bastards." Brian swore under his breath and left the room. "Lavi, Fernando, let's get the bombs ready."

"If it doesn't work, do we get to shoot them?" Amir asked, satisfaction seeping into his voice over the comms.

"We get to shoot whoever survives the blast, if they do." Brian replied, flipping a switch in his brain. He'd flipped it hundreds of times. It just got easier with time.

But this time could be his last.

CHAPTER TWENTY

January 5th, 2028

GIDEON DIDN'T HAVE A lead.

George gave him one mission: find and kill Flannery. The man was still off maps. George knew it too, and he warned Gideon that he would be up to something. "Catch him before he catches us off guard," George had said. "He'll have something in mind. He'll want to humiliate me and wipe out my good men. Don't let that happen. I've got enough to handle in the big leagues without worrying about a traitor."

Gideon finished his meal as he read through George's debriefing from earlier.

George did have a lot to handle, what with the President being replaced and currently held hostage, the

White House in the rebels' clutches, and the nation at a bloody war against itself with more zeal than ever before. Hundreds of people had died in the past few days alone during the civilian and soldiers' squirmishes. George had to calm the UN leaders, show his worth when dealing with the politics and battles, and somehow not get sniped out by the enemy.

More than this however, Gideon knew something else. He knew George was teetering on the edge of taking over the entire government. The leaders and the Union officials being assassinated could very easily be George himself, Gideon just didn't know for sure. Just because George didn't have Gideon taking out the big wigs, didn't mean George still wasn't the puppeteer taking out the competition.

Gideon doubted it, though. George liked to flaunt his success with his close friends, and Gideon was one of them. If George was up to killing people sooner than he planned, Gideon would be in on it, and he wasn't.

So who else was causing havoc in the government?

Gideon's phone rang and he sighed, standing from the table. "Hello?"

"Hochberg!" Keegan's voice skipped through any security talk. "Are you there?" "I am."

"It's my home, Hochberg, they need help." Keegan spoke quickly. "I got word from a source that they saw the

Falcons headed their way this morning. I can't reach them in time, and I can't contact them to warn them."

"You're sure it was the Falcons?" Gideon frowned.

"I'm sure. Flannery has sent spies into the place recently, they killed my dad and left. The place has been without leadership, and they're defenseless, Hochberg. I can't reach them. I'll do whatever it takes to pay you back but I have no other option—"

"Flannery sent men before?"

"My dad made the community years before the war started and it was off the maps, but some thugs discovered it a few months ago."

"That seems suspiciously simple."

Keegan hesitated.

"You can't expect me to fight for them and hide truth from me, Black."

"My dad knew things before the war started, Hochberg. He did the best he could with what he had after he left the government force."

"What did he know?"

A brief pause. "My dad was on the team of scientists trying to create those superhumans come to fruition. He didn't like what he saw so he ran," Keegan forced out. "If he knew things he didn't tell us, I-I guess Flannery wanted him dead for it."

"Regardless of the details, we'll head over to fight. I can't guarantee anything, Keegan. If it's a community of pacifists, I doubt they'll last more than a few minutes during a battle."

"Then let them run," Black mustered.

"While my men drop behind them?"

"I-I didn't mean—"

"Keep in touch. Send me the location." Gideon hung up and waited for the coordinations. Alex stepped into the kitchen, and Gideon quickly told him what was going on.

"I'm going." Alex went to the hallway but Gideon grabbed his arm.

"You're staying here with Noah."

"No. You'll need someone on drones." Alex pulled away, eyes flashing. "I'm not ditching you just because of Thomas!"

Gideon gritted his teeth but went to grab his gear without another word.

CHAPTER TWENTY-ONE

January 5th, 2028

THE FIRST ROUND OF gunfire hit the vehicles, but it was poor fire. Seconds after, Nate saw a vehicle in the woods to his left, followed immediately by a loud explosion. The flames flashed in his rear view mirror, and he swore.

The RPG took out one of the unarmored vans in a large fury. Per Kaleb's instructions, each vehicle had a good length between each vehicle, so that if it was taken out, the blast wouldn't take anyone else down unless the shrapnel did.

Nate's chest seized up. "Jordan!" The flames kept going. Despite the catastrophe only four trucks behind them, Jordan didn't slow down. "Jordan, stop! Stop!"

Jordan floored it as the gunfire continued. He went over the radios, speaking sharply. "Keep moving! Jaxson, we need cover, now." Jaxson was a special ops leader with a small platoon a mile behind them as backup, if they needed a counter attack for a situation such as this.

But Jordan hadn't explained what they'd actually do in an ambush. Why weren't they stopping?

Nate couldn't breathe, struggling to see behind. He couldn't tell if it had been a van that Simon was in. His head wouldn't work. "Si—"

"Not his van."

In the following moment, another blast went off—at the far end of the group's trail of vehicles. The very last vehicle was hit by what Nate assumed was another RPG. The remaining vehicles kept pushing forward, but the last few struggled to get around the debris of the last van.

"Jordan! There could be survivors! We have to stop!" Nate snapped, slamming the dashboard of the truck. "Go back! What the hell are you doing?"

Jaxson came over the radios, "Coming in hot, J. We've got your six. Over."

"Keep moving, team," Jordan spoke into the comms again, and he didn't let up on the gas. Nate stared in the rearview mirror, heart ringing in his ears as he watched the smoke and aftermath of the detonated vehicles.

Dead.

How many dead?

Who?

Survivors, there'd be survivors, people survived sometimes—didn't they? Nate's mind raced. Was an RPG to a truck the same as an IED to a man?

The gunfire ceased from the enemy hiding in the woods, and the trail of vehicles continued down the beaten down road. Nate tried to see backup arrive, but by the time the soldiers came to finalize the battle, the victims were being taken far out of sight.

Nate tried to text Simon, but he didn't get a response. He tried the comms even though he didn't know if they were linked still. "Si?"

"Nate? You OK?" Simon's voice came quietly.

"Fine." Nate gulped hard. "Is Kaleb still with you?"

"Yeah, we're fine." A pause. "W-who was in those vans?""I don't know." Nate clenched his jaw, glancing over at Jordan, but Jordan's face was completely unreadable.

They'd just lost a few valuable members. They'd just lost victims they'd promised they'd saved.

Gone. Just like that. Forever.

Nate closed his eyes and took his comm out, fighting a panic attack. But in the moving truck, with victims in the back being tended by a doc and driven by a deathly silent Jordan, no one could see Nate cry.

THE PACIFIST COMMUNITY WAS hidden in a miles-long stretch of forest in Missouri. It really wasn't much and not terribly difficult to find—if you looked for it. But if you weren't searching, you'd have no reason to stumble upon the place, and Simon couldn't believe they hadn't been wiped out sooner. He hadn't had time to ask his dad a thing about the place or who was there.

The victims needed immediate attention, and that's where his focus was until they stopped the vehicles at the edge of the woods. Simon stepped out the back of a van, wincing as he saw the sun lowering behind the horizon.

How long had they traveled?

"Let's go," Kaleb said tightly, glancing over. Most of the crew was bloodied now—by tending to victims or fighting the ambush or suffering a few minor wounds. Simon wasn't sure where the blood on Kaleb's SOG pants and black t-shirt came from, but he seemed unharmed. Simon glanced down at his own clothes and hands.

Red. Dark red. Light red. Most of the blood was dried but not all. He frowned a little, wondering how he'd get the stains out of the shirt Mrs. Fisher gifted him just weeks prior for Christmas.

But I'm not cringing. I used to get sick at the sight of blood.

He pushed the thought aside and went over to the armored truck. "Nate? Dad?" He took a shaky breath, trying to keep it together. He still didn't know who they'd lost. The men had been talking about it on the radio. It was obvious to the crew who was missing.

Simon blocked it all out. Every detail. He didn't let himself think about it. He knew some of the men they'd just watched get blown away. One of them had even gotten Simon coffee one morning in the warehouse when Simon had overslept. He knew their names.

They were dead now. No one had been found alive when Jaxson's back up crew came along. Simon didn't find satisfaction in the fact Jaxon's team had demolished the enemy—a platoon of Union soldiers, desperate for supplies by the looks of them. All dead now.

But after the damage they'd done, did it matter?

Jordan and Nate stepped out from behind their armored truck, shoulders sagging, faces pale as ghosts. Jordan quickly yanked Simon into a tight but brief hug. "You all right?"

"Yeah. Fine. Where's the group?" Simon asked Jordan quietly. He didn't want to ask about the losses. If he ignored it, he could focus on the tasks at hand, and there were many. *Save these victims. Stop the government from hurting anyone else with their lab testings. Protect Springtown, keep Rene' safe.*

Jordan glanced at the surviving crew and the mess of victims. They'd lost two dozen victims, two drivers, and three medics. "The community is about two miles into this forest and a vehicle can't get through. The leader, Brett Black, will meet us a mile away from the location. We carry the vics in on stretchers, most injured first, the rest will hide in the woods with Jaxson's team, till we come back. It'll take about two or three trips."

Simon set his jaw. "Let's get started." He went to help carry a couple of smaller kids, their expressions frozen, like they hadn't snapped out of shock. He ignored how tense their frail bodies were and held them tightly. "It's all right, we're gonna get you guys someplace safe and warm soon."

The temperature was quickly dropping, and the overcast sky loomed heavy. They didn't have much time before the weather caused issues, even with the protection of the vans and trucks, mini portable heaters, and blankets.

Jordan and Kaleb led the crew, each able-bodied person carrying a victim or helping man a stretcher. Jordan led the way into the thick forest as the chilly wind bit at Simon's uncovered face. They were close to the end now, the rescues would be safe and tended to, and Simon could keep working. He could take the intel they discovered and raise hell.

He pulled the kids closer and followed Jordan, not allowing himself to think about what'd happen just hours before.

———

ASK ANYONE IN GEORGE'S gang about Spencer Anderson, and they'd reply with, "He's a dumbass."

Spencer wouldn't argue with that. Ever. Especially not tonight.

He hesitated, watching the group begin to carry the victims into the creepy woods. Then he grabbed his phone and texted the number with cold, slow fingers. *Please come. Please come.*

I'm not even sure why they need to come, but they need to come. I can feel it in my gut. We need help.

We need help.

Not words Spencer liked to think. He never liked being helpless or failing missions. This had been his first "good" job, first time joining the traitors in their little Robin Hood-esque escapade. For once, he was a part of something good, instead of hurting or killing anyone.

We lost men and we lost victims.

But we need more help than what we've got. Who else did they have to turn to for this sort of situation?

He sent another text, shoved the phone into his cargo pants pocket, and went to help move people.

A few months prior, when Rene' had been taken by West, Jack, and Gideon, Spencer had helped get her out. In the aftermath, he'd challenged Jack and Nate to believe in God. Right now, though, he really prayed God actually heard their prayers.

MR. FISHER TOLD THE group at the courthouse that the plan and arrangements had been made immediately. A group of twenty men and ten women would make their way to the location Spencer had sent Mr. Fisher. They'd help aid the victims, and if needed bring some of the children to shelter in Springtown.

Rene' and Lee exchanged brief glances before thrusting themselves into the middle of the ruckus. "Dad, I can take my guys, too," Lee said quickly. "We're just as trained as the others." Half true—they were equal to some of the men, but the town also had vets, and few topped their skills though it wasn't mentioned. The town needed everyone they had, seasoned or not.

"All right." Mr. Fisher hesitated. "Get your guys."

Lee scurried off to gather his friends.

"I'm coming, too." Rene' gently gripped her dad's arm. Before he could open his mouth to disagree, she spoke. "You said able-bodied women could go help with the kids and I am. Please, Dad."

He set his jaw. "Your mom and your sister need you here."

"Those kids need me, too. Mom and Terri will be fine; they've got Jack and Mels to help." She insisted quietly.

Her chest tightened with fear. What if he said no? Could she sneak onto one of the trucks unnoticed? She wasn't staying here. Simon and those kids needed her help. She remembered the faces of the children they'd saved the first time. If she could do that just once more, she would.

Mr. Fisher's face darkened, his strong jaw clenching in anger. Was it anger toward Rene'? She grimaced. "Dad—"

"You've been hurt enough, Rene'." His voice was low, and he gripped her shoulder, his grasp like iron. "I can't let you risk your life again."

She hugged him, burying her face against his chest, not caring if they were in front of anyone else in the lobby. "I love you Dad, but I can't hide away forever. Please. God's helped us before, He won't stop now, but following Him is never safe. Please let me do it anyway." Her voice was tight, on the edge of cracking though she fought it. She needed to be strong. Like her parents, like her siblings, like her friends.

Mr. Fisher's strong arms held her close before he slowly pulled her away, cupping her chin. "You stay with me and Lee." His voice almost broke. Almost. "Promise."

"I promise," she said firmly. "I'll tell Mom what's going on."

"No, I will. You get packed." Mr. Fisher left the building in a rush, leaving Rene' to pack supplies and find the other women who were going too.

Bethany was staying behind, but Chloe, one of the town's survivors who had found her way home, was going. She stuck by Rene' protectively, whispering as they loaded the boxes of supplies. "You can stay, Rene'."

Rene' shook her head. She'd obeyed God once before. She'd gotten tortured, but she'd helped kids, and if she could do that again, why not? She wouldn't be afraid of getting hurt. Such a fear had suffocated her ever since she got home. No more. "I'm not changing my mind."

I'm listening to You, God, even if it terrifies me. Even if I'm not sure I can do what You're asking. I'm going.

CHAPTER TWENTY-TWO

January 5th, 2028

WEST AND HIS SMALL crew of men surrendered at the front of the rebel campsite. The soldiers, at a commander's word, kept their guns poised but didn't act. In the dark of the night, the only light came from the soldiers' headlamps.

Bo and Nabeel kept quiet right at West's sides, putting their lives in West's hands without any reason to trust that the rebels wouldn't blow their heads off. They had stripped all tech and most weapons off themselves, leaving only one pistol on their hips, clear to see.

West took a slow breath and watched the commander step out of the crowd of soldiers. "Sir," he said. "Is—"

"Darius told us about you." The man smirked. "Did you come to ambush us?"

"The White House is being infiltrated by government enhanced soldiers, and this is your president's chance to go in while the terrorists have control." West held his hands up where they could all see. "I need to talk to—"

Vice President Smith ran out from a great green tent. "Lower your arms!" he called. "Let them in!"

The commander obeyed and West rushed over to Darius. "I warned your lot to move out," West said, voice tight.

Darius' expression flickered. "I had to bury my son." His voice didn't waver. "He wanted to be buried in his home state, so that's what he got. If you had followed your orders and killed Larry... that would've been your problem —Larry said so himself."

"I'm... sorry for your loss." West flinched and relayed the new updates as calmly as he could. "If the rebels hold the House sir, you can go in and take control."

"Who is holding the Union President hostage?" Darius asked.

West hesitated. "We don't know yet, sir. George doesn't even know, as far as I'm aware, but I think it's Brian Jones."

Darius' eyebrows rose. "Brian? Did you get in touch with him, let him know we wanted his help?""No. As far as I know, he hasn't contacted anyone either, but I think it's him. When the President was assassinated we got word the VP is being held hostage too. If it is him... he's got a plan," West said. "But I wanted to tell you this would be your chance to go in, even if Brian doesn't contact us, it won't do any damage to pounce on the chance."

Darius nodded. "Can you contact Brian?""Not yet, but I know someone who might be able to." West tensed when a tent flap opened and President Larry stepped out, expression dark as he came over.

"Johnston," President Larry said coolly. "I got word from the terrorist in the White House just now."

West controlled his reaction. "Is it Brian Jones?"

"It is. He personally invited us to the White House." President Larry flashed a weary smile. "Said the Oval Office had a chair with my name on it. What do you boys say we go end this war?"

West's chest tightened and his breath caught. *Was the end close? Or was the beginning of the end just in the crosshairs? For now, it's a start.*

Darius eyed West's two friends with a chuckle. "You three and your team in the woods better head out... and stay low. George will be pissed if you fail another assassination."

Bo stepped up. "Could we come with y'all?"Darius blinked. West wondered if it was because of Bo's strong

Southern accent or his stupid question.

President Larry studied West for a moment, weighing the options and risks. "Sure. You lot come with us."

It was spoken casually, but West heard the threat behind it. He squared his shoulders. "I'll tell George we handled the assassination and we're headed back," he said, shaking his head. "I'll say Bo and Nabeel departed and we did the job. That way they won't suspect anything."

"He'll want proof of my death," President Larry said, frowning.

"He'll trust my word—long enough for you guys to get to D.C., anyway."

President Larry laughed. "It'll take us a few days to reach the White House, Johnston, even in our trucks without being stopped along the way."

"Exactly," West said. "Bo and Nabeel can go with you for backup—they're good at their job. I'll go to George and buy you guys time to at least get there. Brian can only hold the place down alone for so long. He'll need your soldiers."

President Larry and Darius exchanged glances, but Darius sighed softly. "All right, Johnston, I trust you. Tell George what you gotta, gain us some time... but ain't that gonna risk you? He'll kill you once he realizes you're a mole."

West laughed, voice bitter, "Yeah, but I'll kill him before he gets the chance."

Bo tensed beside him. "Sounds like a plan to me," he said quickly. "Let's move out? President and... sirs?"

West sighed and glanced at his friend in dismay. "Don't get killed, Brewer."

KALEB SENT THE WORD privately but it wasn't news to West—by the next night, Brian had taken the White House over, winning against the super soldiers.

Since then, the line had gone dead on the government's end. Brian and his men, somehow, had won. The news and government were shitting themselves to cover the truth—they needed the nation to be palpable and obey the big wigs. Something like this—the rebels winning the capitol—would throw the nation into a frenzy.

Which was why Cindy was leaking the intel to the nation's civilians.

West focused on the road ahead of him, flurries of snow covering the back road and clinging to his windshield. He had taken a jet from Tennessee to Michigan, leaving Bo and Nabeel in the ranks of rebels. He had contacted George briefly to alert him he was almost home, and that he had killed President Larry, but George hadn't been in contact.

West upped the windshield wiper speed and pushed on, mind racing.

Brian had won.

The rebels were taking the capitol.

His mother was telling the nation the truth.

What would stem from the truth being told? How many would turn away, stay in their government housing, and trust the Union to return order? How many would realize they'd been lied to, mistreated, and how many would take a stand?

How many will die? How many will be test subjects? How many are so brainwashed by the government they won't think anything of this tyranny?

Is this war hopeless? Both sides are full of good men, men fighting for what they believe is right.

If one side triumphs, will they truly be the winner? Will either future be worth the bloodshed? Which side is even right? They both have men with good intentions.

But one side is fighting for freedom. Even if I don't know who is good and who is a monster like me, I can at least fight for the choice to not be a machine.

West kept his eyes on the road but felt a sharp stabbing pain stem from the back of his head. The nerve pain was fairly constant since the Test. He popped too many painkillers, but sometimes those didn't soothe the discomfort.

He kept a hand on the wheel, slowing slightly, using his left hand to rub the back of his neck. The snow was picking up.

George didn't know they were actively sabotaging the government—and the Johnston legacy—but he could easily find out. It'd be game over then.

Tonight, George was with the Union leaders trying to smooth the chaos over in the big house and comfort them with Larry's death. Hours prior, Kaleb messaged West with evidence that the government labs were real, just like West had been told by George.

West already knew the government was experimenting on innocent people and creating hellshow beings. Kaleb had known some of it too, but the gangs hadn't gotten involved or shown interest in that side of the chaos. It was far-fetched, hard to digest, and no one wanted to think it'd bother them if they followed the rules and obeyed George.

But it was real.

It was no longer like it used to be. West couldn't go back to a wannabe normal teenager. He knew what happened in the shadows and had no choice but to fight it and win.

Another sharp jab of pain shot through West's skull. He winced. He'd just taken painkillers. They'd kick in soon enough. He focused on driving as the snow fell faster, the placid calmness stirring in the forest around him.

Another sharp throb like someone hit him in the back of the head with a baseball bat, but this time the pain shot through his head and down his spine. He swore, vision blurring. *What's wrong with me?* The nerve pain had been a steady side effect of the Test, but not like this.

The pain came again and West jerked hard. He lost control of his limbs, mind blacking as he felt pressure on his head. The shrieking sound of tires filled his ears before everything vanished.

———

THE SOFT SOUND OF a fussing baby filled West's head as he stirred. His head ached and his back felt twisted, but he couldn't feel any obviously broken bones. He was engulfed in warmth too.

The car. The snow. My head.

West shot upward, body tense, immediately shooting a hand to his side where he kept his Baretta. A thin blanket covered his body, and he almost got tangled up in it.

"Easy," a male voice said calmly. West looked up to face a man about his age with short brown hair and a tense expression. "Relax Johnston, you're safe."

"Who the hell are you?" West snapped.

In the flickering light of a small campfire, West made out the large warehouse room and a woman peering from across the small fire. She was sitting cross-legged with a bundle in her arms, nose wrinkled as she watched the two men stand-off.

"My name is Josh Hayse." The man frowned, eyeing the gun on West's side. "I left your weapons alone. Don't make me regret that decision."

West tried to stand but tensed in pain. The man gripped his shoulder tightly. "Look, we found you in rough shape. You crashed into a tree. I wouldn't be so quick to move around."

"Don't touch me." West pulled away but sat still, controlling his breathing.

The man stepped back, hands up, eyes narrow. "We helped you. Don't do anything stupid." He eyed West's gun again, standing in front of the fire as if to protect the woman and whatever she was holding.

"I won't." West set his jaw. "What happened?"

"I just told you—"

"Where are we?"

He sighed. "Old warehouse; used to be part of the farm, I think. We made up camp. I didn't know what else to do with you."

West's mind raced and throbbed. "Ah."

"You're Johnston's kid, right?" Josh asked, crossing his arms. "Big warlord Johnston?"

"What's it to you?" West ran a hand across his face. He felt a gash on the top of his forehead but no dried blood, like someone had cleaned it up.

Josh shrugged. "Just curious. I heard you guys lived close to here. Didn't think you'd be out and about all alone."

West scoffed and glanced at the woman. "What exactly are you two doing out here? You'll freeze."

"Running." Josh smirked. "Like you?"

"I'm not running." West sighed. "I'm working."

"Sure." Josh squatted in front of him, eyes narrowing. "We saved your life, you know. It wouldn't hurt to repay us."

"Repay you?" West didn't bat an eye. "What did you have in mind?"

"Money and a place to stay," Josh replied.

But the woman sighed. "Stop, Josh. He needs to rest." She pulled the bundle closer to her chest, but it fussed again—a baby. She had a baby.

He frowned at her but then rubbed his temples. "He's fine. I'll give you two what you need. Least I can do."

They couldn't be trusted, but all things considered, if they were enemies, they would've done a better job at taking him. They had no supplies, thin clothes, and the man looked skinny—they probably weren't spies or enemies. Most likely two siblings who didn't have a place to turn to. It wasn't uncommon.

Josh's eyes widened for a split moment, but then he smirked. "I'm holding you to your word." He cast a subtle glance to his own hip where a gun protruded from underneath his shirt and jacket.

West chuckled. It wasn't the worst threat he'd ever faced. "I'm a man of my word, unlike George."

The woman studied him for a moment. "Come sit down, Josh. He's not going to hurt us."

Josh didn't budge.

West rolled his eyes. "Why would I hurt either of you? You did save my life." George had a different MO, of course. Cruel, heartless, unpredictable. It was near impossible for people to trust the son of such a man.

"I know what George has done," Josh said.

"Then let's move." West shrugged. "I'll give you cash and get you a ride in town, you guys can go to a safe place. Let's do it now."

"Can't." Josh sighed.

"Why not?"

"There's some... men after us right now." Josh glanced to the door of the warehouse, which was barricaded shut in a shabby but determined style, with some supplies and boards.

West blinked at the blockage and glanced at Josh. "Who's after you?"

"None of your business."

"Fine. I'll call some friends to come get us. They'll be loaded. Shouldn't be a problem if we have to fight." West got to his feet, knees buckling but he held fast.

The woman snapped at him. "Sit down right now! You have a concussion! You can't be moving around." She shot a look at Josh. "Josh—can it. Now."

Josh clamped his jaw shut, heeding her words, but West frowned at her. "We can't stay here if you're being hunted. A sitting duck is a dead duck."

"The group after us is rough." Josh spoke quietly. "Thugs. Bad ones."

"What do you think I am?" West asked, voice dry.

"I mean, they want to kill us," Josh spat. "So if you drag us into the woods, we have less of a chance to survive than we do here. In the snow they won't see the smoke the fire's giving, so we have a few hours of rest. We've walked all day."

West shook his head, instincts kicking in. "Absolutely not. We need to move. You've got me now, so you'll be fine, but we need to get out of here. How close are these guys?"

"We lost them about a day ago." Josh stepped over to shield the woman.

"Not long enough; they could've found you by now. You need to tell me what's going on and who they are— but tell me as we're moving." West stepped over, anger rising. He didn't have time for this delay, but he couldn't leave them behind.

"We can't go back out there," Josh insisted. "The baby is already sick!"

West growled. "How sick?" He eyed the bundle crossly. The woman held the bundle closer, jutting her chin.

"I-if we have to move I can—" she started but West cut in.

"We have to leave." He took off his coat and shoved it toward Josh. "Keep it warm but we gotta move."

Josh glanced between the woman and West, but he took the coat to her. She wrapped the baby up again and followed Josh toward the doors after he put out the fire. West helped undo the barricade, nerves aching along his spine and neck, but he ignored it.

As soon as they escaped the warehouse, West texted a few friends their location and situation. West could at least get the two strangers closer to town via a shortcut in the woods he knew of. If help came in time, perfect.

If not, he'd make do. "Tell me who's after you."

"J-just some thugs," the woman muttered. "Um, my ex, he's... trying to find me. He's hunted us for a few weeks now."

West didn't look back, pushing through the falling snow, pulling the toboggan down lower on his head. "Is the baby his?"

"No!" Josh said sharply. "Felicity is mine. This is my sister—"

"You named your kid Felicity?" West muttered under his breath.

"What was that?"

"Nothing, keep walking. We're gonna stop a few miles outta town and wait for my guys."

"Won't they find us sooner?" The woman asked, worry heavy in her voice.

"Hopefully, but we might not be able to count on them, and we don't have time to waste if these guys are out for blood." West pushed onward. Domestic situations were often messier than anything. They were hard to gauge, so he had to be prepared for anything. The situation was already bad, but it could get worse a hundred different ways too.

The woman fell silent, and Josh helped her along in the snow that thickened beneath their feet. West prayed that his text was received and he didn't have to face thugs in the snowy woods, but there was a first time for everything, including fighting thugs alone in the snow.

CHAPTER TWENTY-THREE

January 5th, 2028

THE SECURE TUNNELS WEREN'T easy to get through when they ended underneath the White House. The entry to the underground was six feet of concrete, and the ways in were guarded with steel doors meant to withstand blasts, lasers, and more. The White House, from underground, was almost impenetrable.

Almost.

The gas that was designed to wipe out the government-created soldiers proved mostly ineffective. Bosch would no doubt have theories as to why before the night ended, but for now all that mattered was the soldiers were taken out by whatever means necessary.

Confederate President Larry had sent the message about ten minutes too late, but Bosch spoke over the comms and gave the word. "Hotcake is heading for the pan." *Hotcake* being President Larry and *pan* being the White House.

Amir chuckled from beside Brian. He climbed down the stairs into the underground tunnels that met up with the outside ones, where the soldiers were marching. "The plot thickens."

"He better get his ass here fast. We can't hold this place alone forever." Brian led Amir and Lavi into the great room that led the outside and inside tunnels together through a large, thick steel door. State of the art security wouldn't be much against super soldiers if they had super strength on their side. Nineteen super soldiers might not break through, but if they didn't handle the problem, the government had more where that came from, and backup would show up.

That was a situation Brian preferred avoiding.

"He'll come," Amir said. "And his VP."

"Never took you to be so gung-ho about this rebel nonsense." Brian watched the security cameras. The soldiers only had a mile left to go, and they'd picked up speed once the gas hit them.

"That's rich coming from you."

Brian ignored the comment. "All right. Lavi, keep hold of the security, we need this door kept shut. Amir and I will set the bombs off. Everyone hold tight—it shouldn't damage the structure of the building, underground, or upstairs, but let's be cautious. Fernando, Bosch, leave the others with the hostages if I give the signal that we need more shooters. These soldiers are supposed to be vulnerable in their head—if a fire blast gets 'em, it should do the trick, but we'll be prepared for survivors."

They each answered quickly to confirm the plan.

Nineteen soldiers. Enhanced strength, sight, and keen hearing. If these are the DNA enhanced soldiers, we have a good chance at sniping them out as they go through, along with Manny watching the booby traps from control.

But if they were the bio-soldiers, that'd be a hell of a lot trickier to triumph over. While the bio-soldiers had not been cleared at the government level, they were being worked on. Brian had never been briefed on their final capabilities, since they were not finished being enhanced, but he had gotten the rundown. Crazy bastards that resembled machines more than they did humans in almost every way.

Brian didn't doubt science and technology was there, but he hoped they hadn't gotten there just yet. If they were fighting infrared-shooters with the inability to feel pain... that'd be a different end.

Amir prepped the security in the room where the defense plans were ready to go. In a few seconds they could launch the bomb, which resembled more of a fire-launcher but larger and more forceful. It'd fill the tunnel leading to the entry with a lethal blast enough to take out dozens of men.

Would it hold up against super soldiers?

Brian reined his thoughts in. His job was to be prepared for any obstacle and mishap. They were as prepared as they could be, given the circumstances. They'd gone rogue with limited members and supplies, they'd broken into the White House and sabotaged every person present— including the President—and had cracked in the security and defenses. They had a good chance at killing the super soldiers, but anything could go wrong.

"Ready," Lavi said firmly. "They're in proximity."

"Everyone in location?"

Confirmations chimed in unison, and Brian set his jaw. "Now, Lavi."

The detonation worked. The underground tunnels rumbled ever so slightly, but the sound was heard through the thick walls. Brian half-expected the tunnels to concave but they held fast, built for such action.

Brian set his jaw, watching the monitors. The cameras were built to withstand the blasts, but the feed crackled and struggled to hold up. Once the fire and smoke died down, the tunnel just outside the secured door lay littered with scorching bodies.

Brian counted the ones left standing. "They're all still standing."

"How the hell did they survive being blown up?" Bosch asked over the comms.

"Suits are made for it," Brian snipped. "They've been equipped to withstand everything this place has got to offer. Hard to beat the enemy when they own the field."

"So the gov is just messing with us?" Amir came over to eye the cameras. "Or do they have a surprise card we don't know of?"

"This place is set up for far more damage than this," Lavi spoke up. "We can handle worse."

"They'll be able to withstand the defenses because the defenses are built to take out humans and the test subjects." Brian shook his head, taking his automatic rifle from his back. "Only thing that'll kill them now is a bullet to the skull, like the debriefings said. If they're wearing helmets, we'll have to get them off first."

Amir grinned. "We let a few in at a time and take them out here?"

"Can't think of a better option at the moment. We're running out of time, and if more come we'll need to be ready." Brian took a breath. "Lavi, secure the doors so this floor is the only one open. Let a few soldiers in at a time.

"Bosch, Fernando, if you ladies want to get down here, the help would be great." He named off four more soldiers. "Go around through the tunnels to the west wing. It'll take you a few minutes to get here, but corner them from behind and take out the rest on my command."

The crew confirmed without complaint.

"Is this the best plan we've got?" Fernando sighed. "I mean, this is crazy reckless and stupid, even for us."

"If you want to grab your purse and go home to mommy, we won't stop you," Brian replied.

"Jack off."

"We're on our way," Bosch piped up. "Save the big guys for me, Jones."

Brian watched the super soldiers stop at the entry door. One of them pulled out a large laser from the pack on his shoulders. They'd try frying their way into the wall—it was simpler and faster than breaking or drilling through.

Brian rushed over to the back of the room behind one of the custom-built hides, a large slab of bullet-proof material acting as a mini wall in the center of the defense room. It wasn't much, but it was a place to shelter behind during a gunfight. "They're trying to enter. Lavi, open the door."

The secured, thick door opened with surprising ease and quickness, considering how thick it was. Immediately, three super soldiers poured in, and by the time the door shut again, four were in the defense room.

Amir and Brian took fire. Two soldiers dropped simultaneously, and the two rebel soldiers continued the shots till the super soldiers lay only feet from them. The super soldiers' guns dropped to the floor.

Amir eyed the bullet holes all around them, hunkering closer to the thick block. "Next round, Lavi."

The next round wasn't as easy. Six soldiers jumped in, bullets firing before they even made it past the entry. The flash of the laser and Brian snarled as it hit the block. "Amir!"

Amir rolled to the left and Brian fired, hitting the super soldier in the head. The laser dropped, the clean line it had cut through the block burning red-hot. Amir swore and quickly fired at the remaining soldiers, dropping a couple as they ran at him, their motions quick, but their intent to kill resembling a starving animal.

A bullet hit Brian's left shoulder but he kept moving, and the remaining super soldier dropped his guns. He tackled Brian to the ground, the force behind the fall enough to snap bone. The super soldier reached to snap Brian's neck before tumbling forward. Hot blood splattered across Brian's face, and he shoved the corpse off.

Brian jumped up, staring at the corpses. "That was... different."

Amir licked his lips and loaded his pistol. "They're not all machine-like."

"Those are easier to fight. The way they've been programmed, we know how to fight it, how to overcome their programming." Brian blinked at the men who'd acted like hungry monsters. "Those are more unpredictable."

"Next round?" Lavi asked calmly.

"We're here; let us in," Bosch's voice came through the comms and the door behind Brian opened. The two soldiers rushed in and Fernando whistled, eyeing the bloody bodies.

"Guess we all bleed the same, half-machine or not." Fernando picked up the laser gun. "My son will not believe this when I tell him." He gave a goofy grin. "Check this out!"

"Use it," Brian said. "They're just as dangerous as we were told." He ignored the blood soaking his shirt, deciding it wasn't lethal.

The four soldiers readied at the back of the room but waited. Lavi reported that another soldier outside was lasering his way in, but the four going through the tunnels confirmed they were close enough to be back-up.

Brian glanced at Amir and Fernando, who flashed brief smirks before the four soldiers set their aim toward the entry. "Open up, Lavi."

CHAPTER TWENTY-FOUR

January 6th, 2028

THE PACIFIST COMMUNITY LAY nestled in the thick strip of woods, a tall steel wall built around it like something in a thriller movie. It was acres long and wide, containing housing, areas for food plots and crops, and pastures for animals outside of the walls. It wasn't as large as Simon quite expected, but it was large enough considering what it was and where it was. He never expected a community to survive alone during a war—it didn't make sense—but he didn't have time to ask questions.

The victims were moved into the community's med house, a large house where a doctor lived. It took hours to get them situated before Simon was free to slip out.

He ignored the blood staining his hands, shirt, and pants, wandering away from the house full of crying and sleeping injured. The crew of rescuers were scattered, some camping outside that house, some taking shelter in the communities' homes. Simon didn't want to sleep in a stranger's house. He didn't want to sleep in a tent on the ground.

He didn't want to sleep at all.

He couldn't get the explosions out of his head.

Two vehicles. All it had taken was two RPG blasts.

How many dead?

He didn't have a number, but the gaping hole the loss left stung deep. Simon wasn't a stranger to death. But it didn't get easier to be surrounded by it.

It could've been Dad and Nate. I can't live without them. I need them.

It could've been Spencer. He's my friend. I care about him.

It could've been me.

If I was dead, I wouldn't have that life I want with Rene'. I'd be gone, and she'd be left here. Who would protect her? Who would love her?

Simon shuddered and picked up his pace. He didn't know where he was going. Outside of the walls was a good option. He needed the constricting tension around his ribcage to ease off.

Simon found his way past the wall, ignoring Jaxson's sentries at the gate, and found a thick tree. He sat at the bottom of it and pulled his jacket tight.

I'm safe here. I'm away from the crying and screaming kids and the girls. I'm away from the injured teammates bleeding all over. I'm away from my teammates with dead eyes because they lost their friends. I'm away from Dad because I can't face him again tonight because I'm weak. I'm—

"Si?" Nate's soft voice came from behind him.

Simon jerked.

"Sorry," Nate said, sitting beside him, legs giving out. He shuddered and licked his lips. "Couldn't stay in there either, huh?"

Simon leaned back against the trunk. "Not for a while."

"You've helped nonstop, Si. You've gotta be exhausted." "So have you."

"Si?"

"I don't want to talk right now, Nate."

"We're going to win this."

"So what?" Simon asked tightly. "We win one war, and there'll be three left waiting for us."

Nate sighed. "That's life. But... we saved a lot of lives, right? We were a part of that. That counts."

"I mean the big picture, Nate."

"So do I."

Nate's quiet words took Simon back, and he dropped his head in his bloodied hands. "Nate... I-I thought it had been you and Dad. God, I thought I lost you—" His voice broke and a sob choked him.

Nate wrapped an arm around Simon's shoulders, holding tight. "I thought I'd lost you too, but we didn't. Hear me? We're alright. And we'll do the fallen proud. Got that? We'll make them proud."

Hot tears ran down Simon's stubbled cheeks as he nodded. "Yeah. We will."

"No moping around." Nate leaned his head against Simon's tiredly, like they used to do when they'd been little kids, scared of the world that awaited them.

The world they faced was worse than they'd ever imagined, but they'd make it. They always had.

SPENCER WATCHED JORDAN AND Kaleb, along with some men he didn't recognize, gather in the house's small kitchen. They nursed cups of coffee, and only one light from the ceiling illuminated the room. Spencer kept close to the door, waiting, listening. After hours, the victims were situated and resting, and Mr. Fisher had messaged that they were on their way, too.

That would be hard news to break to Simon, but Spencer couldn't shake the feeling the group needed to come. First, Jordan and Kaleb's team was exhausted, every single member worn to a frazzle from the events of the past three days of nonstop work and adrenaline.

Second, the pacifist community only had fifty members, and thirty more children, so not many capable helpers for the sick, injured, or mentally impaired—especially when they avoided the gangsters and veterans like the plague. Third, well, Spencer knew Rene' was good with the kids in despair, and there were so many... He didn't want to see them alone like this.

But Simon would see it differently. He'd kill Spencer for dragging the Springtown group into the fray.

Spencer didn't blame him. He didn't want the Fishers in danger.

Was my gut wrong, God? I've tried to pray and listen to You, but am I just listening to my stupid head? If I messed up...

"Anderson?" A sharp voice broke through his thoughts. Spencer jerked his head up, tensing.

Jordan sighed. "Anderson..." He offered a cup of coffee, and Spencer took it.

"Sorry. Thanks." Spencer cleared his throat.

Jordan sat beside Kaleb at the table, sighing. "We have a few hours to sleep before Brett, this community's leader, will want answers. Kaleb talked with him and satisfied him for now, but he's mad and we can't stay for long."

Jordan briefly explained the pacifist community's origin. It was created by a man Jordan used to know, but the man had been murdered by thugs the community helped.

Spencer blinked, mind whirling. "I'm confused. They let us come here?" "Ted did, but Brett doesn't like the fact we're gonna bring trouble the longer we stay." Jordan checked his watch. "I've gotta head out of here soon. George still needs me."

Spencer gulped. "So how long can the vics stay?"

"The vics can stay for a week and we'll move them, but Brett doesn't want all of us to stay." Kaleb scoffed. "He's freaked."

Spencer laughed weakly. "I imagine a pacifist would be with a whole armada of fighters within his walls."

Jordan shook his head. "I've been thinking..." He eyed Kaleb. "Did Brett give details on what happened?"

Kaleb sighed. "He didn't give me much. Why?"

"His dad was murdered... but I knew him. He wouldn't have offered shelter to anyone. Not unless he had a reason." Jordan sipped his coffee, rubbing his temple.

Kaleb crossed his thick arms across his chest. They were all still wearing bloodied, battered clothes, but they'd washed up best they could. "What's that mean?" "I don't know. I need to talk to Brett before I go." Jordan stood tiredly.

"Sleep," Kaleb said. "I'll call George and say you got hit on the job we supposedly took. He's in meetings now trying to watch the White House be taken over. He'll need help, but he can survive a few more hours."

"Help?" Spencer gulped. "He'll need us back soon? What could we do right now?"

"Anything the Union needed. Extra hands, firearms, who knows, but we need to get back to reality." Kaleb hesitated. "But we'll see, of course."

Spencer didn't like that. He didn't want to go fight the Civil War. He didn't want to follow George's orders. He wanted to stay on this job and see it through.

And why does Kaleb look so smug?

Jordan glanced at Kaleb. "Go get J. We'll head out in five hours."

Spencer slipped out of the room, heart hammering. He checked his messages. He needed answers. He needed to know if George needed him. Would he send him to a battlefield? To the White House to be shot down by Brian Jones—Kaleb had said Brian was the terrorist in the big house.

Spencer's hands shook. He had a message from George, *"Stay low, Anderson. I'll have the crews on duty, but you and Randy stay low."*

No explanation. No cause. Was it a trap? Did George know Spencer was a traitor? Was he sending someone to kill him? Or would someone already there at the community kill him—Jaxson? Kaleb?

I can't trust anyone.

Someone's gonna kill me. George knows I'm a traitor, and he wants me to disappear entirely. Just like Ed Brooks.

I'm gonna die.

Spencer struggled for breath, stumbling outside. *George knows. He knows. I'mdeadI'mdeadI'mdead. No! Randy!* He quickly dialed Randy's number, but Randy didn't pick up.

CHAPTER TWENTY-FIVE

January 6th, 2028

RENE' RAN TOWARD THE medic house, tackling Simon in a bear hug—or a rabbit hug, considering how short she was. "Si!"

The pacifist community was almost like a ghost town, though it was late at night. The Springtown civilians had faced a few mishaps on their ride out of Kentucky and to the Missouri woods. But they were all in one piece, and Simon was alive and in Rene's arms.

Simon held her tightly, sinking his face against her neck, fuming. "You shouldn't have come here, you shouldn't be —"

"Shut up," Rene' cut him off, hugging him tighter. She pulled away to cup his face in her hands and kiss him quickly. "I have a job too, Si. I want to help these people too."

Simon set his jaw, and then lifted his gaze to meet Mr. Fisher's expectant expression. "They're all inside, sir. I-I didn't know Spencer called—"

"We made our decisions," Mr. Fisher said, shaking his head. "These people needed help, and Rene' was coming whether I liked it or not, so I'm here, too." He headed inside the house, leaving Rene' and Simon alone in the dark.

Rene' squeezed Simon's hand. "Have you rested any? Will you rest while we take a turn helping?"

Simon groaned. "It's not safe out here, Rene'. I'm doing all of this so you'll be at home and you'll be safe—"

She kissed him again to shut him up.

It worked, and he wrapped his arms around her, pulling her against him. He was holding her again. All of his fears, doubts, and concerns melted away as he gripped her, his tense shoulders relaxing.

And she'd kissed him.

He fought a weak smile. Rene' was safe and she loved him, despite the chaos around them.

Maybe he couldn't protect her alone. But he wouldn't let her down again with God on his side. She deserved a long, beautiful life and he'd do whatever it took to ensure that.

Rene' pulled away, gulping. "We're partners, right? We fix things together. Let me help fix this. Then we'll go home." In the dark, with no electricity in the community and the moon offering little light, it was hard to make out Simon's scowl, but she sensed his frustration.

"Fine," he said. "God, help me, you don't listen ever, do you?""

"I listen." She smirked. "Sometimes."

He led her inside and her smile vanished. Bracing herself for whatever she faced, Rene' sent up a small prayer, asking God for strength.

As they made their way through the medic house, Rene' overheard voices from the kitchen, and she slowed. She recognized her father's voice, then Jordan's, and then Kaleb's.

As they passed the room, Rene' spotted two unfamiliar men speaking quietly, one with short dark hair and scars along his arms, the other younger and with shaggy brown hair. They both seemed urgent, as if trying to explain something to the others, but Rene' didn't know what.

"They're leaving soon. George needs them for some work before he flees the country," Simon whispered.

"What?" Rene's stomach twisted.

"C'mon, I'll update you on stuff," he said, pulling her toward the hallway. They slipped into a room where a few victims slept on pallets and cots assorted in the tiny room, a small battery-operated heater going in a corner.

Simon and Rene' checked the victims but they slept soundly, none of them badly injured or needing assistance. Simon turned to Rene', sighing. "A lot has happened, and I haven't had time to fill you in—"

"You can now." She touched his arm. "What's going on, Si? Why would Spencer call us over this—I mean, yeah, we can help, but Dad acted like something bigger was wrong."

"That's because there is more going on than just some rescues from domes," Simon mustered, keeping his voice calm, collected. "Rene', I've told you how we heard rumors that the government was taking people for lab experiments?"

"Yeah." She gulped. "You said it was just gossip."

"It's not. We destroyed two huge domes and we found a lot of proof, proof that the UN is creating genetically enhanced people—machines and hybrids and all sorts of stuff. They're using innocent people, Rene'. Aborted kids for lots of it, and people they catch from homeless caravans, even targeting small towns and taking the people there that can't fight." Simon hesitated, voice tightening. "We have proof the government is buying people. The fight domes and human trafficking rings are a part of something bigger. But... but there's something else you should know."

Sick to her stomach but steeling herself, Rene' asked calmly, "What?"

"Brian is the terrorist in the White House."

Rene' forced a breath. "He's what?"

"He's the one who took the White House, Rene'. He and his team, they went AWOL, and they're holding the White House and the President hostage. We think they assassinated Kaden. He's gonna, from what Kaleb says, hold it till the rebel presidents and soldiers get there to take over. They're going to win the war, Rene'." Simon held her arms, grip firm.

Rene' tensed, mind racing. "Brian did all of that? It's not a trap?""It isn't so far."

"S-so... does Dad know?"

"Kaleb might've told him."

"Oh," she said, fighting the lump in her throat. "And... and this job, why did Spencer call?"

"Um, well, this community is... strange."

"Strange?" she laughed bitterly. "A bunch of pacifists surviving a war? What's strange about that?"

"They know something, Rene'." He lowered his voice. "We all sense it. We can't keep the victims here. We have to move out, but some can't be transferred again for a while."

"What? What do they know?" Her blood went cold.

"We don't know." He explained how the previous leader and founder of the community had somehow managed to make the community fall off the face of the planet, until they, for some reason, allowed refugees inside the walls. "He was murdered, but these people won't say why or what happened after that. Dad thinks the killers hunted this place down on purpose."

"Why?" Rene' blinked.

Simon glanced toward the door. "Because the founder was a UN scientist. He might've known what the labs were cooking up and tried to make a run for it, make a new life. It was a bad plan and it sucked, but he did it. If someone knew that and wanted to kill him so he could never speak about what he saw..." he groaned, shaking his head quickly. "We're just forming theories, we don't know anything for sure. But Dad knew the guy, Mr. Black, before he vanished off the maps, and the people are all acting weird. They won't let any fighters or soldiers stay after tomorrow but the victims can stay."

"They're scared of you guys," Rene' scoffed.

"But Dad and Kaleb have to go to George, so we're trying to make a plan and nothing's working yet, so we thought Mr. Fisher could help us move the vics to Springtown. Only Spencer dove into that idea without telling us. Or so he said," he muttered. "Idiot. The labs are taking women and using them for experiments. You shouldn't be here, it's risky—""I'm glad he called. We can do that," Rene' said quickly. "Do you know anything else? About the labs and George running and the government?" Invisible hands clutched her heart, clamping down harder, harder, harder. A million questions tore at her head.

Simon hesitated a moment too long. "Rene', a lot is happening and honestly I don't understand it all, but we're not letting George, the UN, or any creepy freaks take our freedom again. We're going to work together as teams to stop the domes and the labs and the government... no matter what it takes. The evidence we have, we're gonna use it to wake up the nation the best we can, and stop these tests before it gets way out of hand. George didn't expect all this to happen, not really, so he's taking precautions."

Rene' nodded softly. "So the things you learned from these jobs is gonna help end the war?" she breathed.

Simon pulled her close. "More or less, yeah, we think so. We think we actually have a shot, Rene'. With Brian AWOL and on the Confeds' side, well, it might help, and West..." He trailed off.

"West?"

"He's trying too—we all are. You know about Hunter?"

"Yeah."

"We have a lot of good guys in the shadows doing good. We have to hold onto hope it'll work out if we keep fighting. That's what I have to do, Rene'." His voice wavered for a split second.

She held close, breathing in his strong scent of sweat, dried blood, and strong coffee. "I'm fighting with you Simon, but you have to let me fight by your side. I don't want to be left at home where it's safe."

He sighed tiredly. "You're not giving me much say in the matter."

A loud voice from the hall jerked them from their conversation and the door opened, Nate peeking his head in. "Si, Rene', we have a problem. Flannery is headed this way with his armada."

CHAPTER TWENTY-SIX

January 6th, 2028

WEST LED JOSH AND the woman through the snow-covered forest in silence, but the silence was shattered by the soft, distinct sound of a silenced gunshot. The heavy thud that followed made West jump into action. He grabbed the woman, shielding her with his body, and pushing her down behind a tree.

She screamed when Josh's body hit the snow. "Josh!"

West kept her head down, unholstering his gun as he hissed, "Stay down; shield the baby."

The bullet had come from the north, but if more men were hunting them, they could be surrounding them. In the snow and in the dark, it'd be hard to tell.

"Come on out, Sere!" A man's voice called. "Don't make me shoot the man you're with too!"

West eyed Josh's unmoving body in the snow. It'd been a headshot—quick and precise. This guy meant business. He wouldn't be expecting a Johnston, and if West had the element of surprise, he'd take it.

"I said come out, Serenity!" the man shouted. "I'm not playing games anymore. You remember what I told you."

The woman, Serenity, sobbed in the snow, staying low with the baby. West's anger flashed and he watched the woods, searching for any sign of movement.

"Who did you sweet-talk into helping you?" The man continued, voice tight with rage. "Some pimp?" He got closer to the small clearing, stepping over Josh's body and leveling his gun toward the trees where Serenity wept. "I said come out—"

West aimed and fired before the man could finish his sentence, his gun's laser doing the job before the man noticed. His body dropped and a man from the woods behind him swore, running toward his friend's body. West shot him down as the man fired wildly.

"Wait!" a third voice called sharply.

"If you value your life, get the hell out of here!" West shouted. "I'm not here to play."

A moment passed as the man—and whoever else was with him—registered the voice. West snarled, "It's

Johnston. Now run."

They didn't waste time. West watched as they scrambled through the snow and ran, leaving the two bodies behind. West waited a moment but figured that was as safe as they'd get—their leader was dead, and they were too cowardly to face a Johnston. He'd take it.

"Serenity?" West turned around.

The woman scrambled up from the snow, rushing to Josh's side. Sobbing, the baby bundled close against her, she grabbed Josh and spoke hysterically. She was fairly short and thin, even through the few layers of clothing, and her dirty blonde hair was tangled in a ponytail. Tears soaked her grimy face as she held her dead brother.

Something snapped inside West.

Something familiar.

He stepped over, jaw tight, and knelt beside her. Her body shook hard with sobs, her face torn with agony. West hesitated for a brief second before gripping her shoulders. When she didn't yank away and scream at him, West wrapped his arms around her and the baby, pulling her away from the body. She collapsed against him, body racking as she wept, her cries muffled. The baby whimpered and West held tight.

"We have to move, Serenity." He gulped hard. "I'll carry him, but we have to reach the road. Help will come. We have to go."

He didn't look at Josh's corpse. He couldn't. It reminded him of his past. It reminded him of his future too, how easily his life could shatter in the same, familiar way.

Serenity cried but let West help her to her feet. West pushed his memories and fears aside, putting the body over his shoulders. "Don't stop walking." He started off, voice tight. "The baby needs to get out of the cold Serenity, keep walking."

She didn't stop walking, steps staggered and weak, but she made it through with West in the lead. When they reached the road, West froze in his tracks, the corpse weighing heavy on his shoulders. A familiar old truck was parked on the side of the snowy road.

"Jack?" West called. "Jack!"

Jack ran over, dressed in warm, thick Carhartt's and waving his arms. "Come on! The truck is warm!"

"How..." West trailed off and carried the body to the bed of the truck. Jack helped Serenity and the baby into the truck's passenger door, then rushed to West. He had a body bag in his hands.

West set his jaw but helped put Josh's corpse into the black bag, not allowing himself to look at the man's freezing features.

Jack zipped it up, voice steady, "Get in the truck, West." His demeanor was calm and steady. All their lives, it was

Jack who was the solid rock, the unyielding shelter, the one who always knew how to help others.

West had left him. He'd tried to con his own father, and in the process had taken the role of the Johnston heir. Had he lost himself? Or had it all been a lie?

If I were strong, I wouldn't need Jack right now.

No, no, that's not how teams work. Teams don't make a man weak. They make him stronger.

Don't they?

"West," Jack repeated, nudging him. "Get in the cab." He shut the truck bed.

"I-I have to get to George." West shook his head.

"I'll take you and drop you off so you can walk back, then I'll get this girl someplace safe." Jack guided him to the cab. "I've got your back, West. It'll be all right."

But Jack was wrong. He knew every detail of what was going on—West kept him up to speed. How could he say such a thing when the world was crumbling?

Faith.

West crawled into the cab, dusting snow off into the floorboard with red, raw hands. *Jack has faith.*

I'm supposed to have faith.

Lord... I don't. But I'm trying to. He glanced at Serenity, who was warming the baby up in front of the heat. Tears still ran down her cheeks, but she didn't stop trying to warm the baby. West set his jaw, heart falling.

Jack got into the truck, shutting his door fast. He took off his coat, gloves, and hat. He extended his hands toward the child. "Here, let me help," he said. "My hands are warm. You two grab the blankets under the seats and take off your wet clothes; toss 'em on the floor."

Serenity hesitated but handed the baby over. Jack focused on tending to the baby, while West and Serenity stripped their top layers off quickly.

"Let's roll," Jack said, placing the baby back in Serenity's arms and driving toward the Johnston mansion.

CHAPTER TWENTY-SEVEN

January 6th, 2028

GIDEON GOT WORD FROM a contact that Flannery was spotted—three hours away from the area where the community was located, though the contact didn't know the last part. Gideon swore, keeping one hand on the wheel of his SUV but dialing Keegan with the other.

"Hello?"

"Coast?"

"Clear."

"I just got word that Flannery is three hours away from the community. I won't make it in time, Black. Especially not in time to set up defenses or convince them to run."

Keegan swore. "I—"

"I have a friend there. I was just told half an hour ago, but I've sent them word of what's going on. They should be able to handle things. I'm still headed over." Gideon cut him off, voice sharp.

"OK, I'll... I'll try to call Brett again."

"Again?""He won't listen to me," Keegan said with force. "He refuses to leave, and he's going to kick out the victims your guys brought.""Handle it, Black," Gideon snapped. "Now." He hung up and focused on the road.

Alex flinched, studying him. "We'll make it."

"Might've, if we hadn't gotten stopped by those rebel soldiers looking for supplies."

"We handled it."

Gideon forced a deep breath, rage rising. "You know who's in that community, Alex. We can't fail." If Gideon didn't stop Flannery, he'd kill Jordan and Kaleb's teams, including the innocent, like the Fishers and their men who'd gone to help.

Alex looked away, rubbing his temples with shaky hands. "I do. But God's got this covered." He dialed Percy, updating him. Percy and forty close members followed their trail.

Gideon didn't respond, focusing on driving the short cut, picturing what it'd feel like to kill Flannery nice and slow.

FLANNERY WAS APPROACHING WITH the Falcons, and the pacifist community refused to fight. Jordan and Kaleb had vanished, headed to George in the Northern states to try to balance the nation during the frenzy.

Spencer got scared often. He wasn't proud of the fact. Gideon, Alex, West, Jack—all the guys around him had it together no matter what. They were strong and steady.

But Spencer was scared as hell.

He just couldn't show it.

Mr. Fisher and the community's leader, Brett, were speaking in the med house's kitchen. Mr. Fisher was calm as a cucumber, but Brett lost his cool, snapping, "load up your people and leave!"

Spencer winced, anger flashing. "Don't talk to Fisher like—"

"We're working on moving our victims," Mr. Fisher said, unphased, his body language teetering on the edge of challenging. "But your community is at risk. I doubt we have a chance to fight, but you at least need to move out."

"And go where?" Brett growled. "We don't have anywhere to go. I've got too many people to just relocate, and there's nowhere in the USA to relocate to! It's just another suicide mission!"

Spencer set his jaw, frustration growing. He stood from the table wearily. "Talking about it isn't getting us anywhere. Flannery is coming closer. Mr. Fisher, I'll deal with Brett, you finish the loading."

"Brett, if we move out now, we can offer assistance, but if you'd rather face the Falcons alone, that's your choice. At least let your community make their choice too. They might not want to die." With that, the mayor of Springtown left the kitchen and went to help his family and friends with the evacuation.

Spencer gulped hard and turned to Brett, fists clenching. "What is your problem?"

"Get out of my face," Brett snapped, stepping past him. Spencer grabbed his arm and shoved him back.

"No. You're about to lose your entire community if you don't get out of here," Spencer said.

Brett was around his age, and just as tall, though Spencer had some fighting skills on his side that he doubted the pacifist would. Whoever said violence wasn't the eventual answer was wrong.

Brett glared, expression darkening. "If I run with you people, there will still be violence. You're all thugs. My father told me about your people—"

Spencer stepped closer, threatening, his patience diminished. "You say *people* like we're a bunch of freaks, but right now we're all you have, Brett. Hate us if you want, but I refuse to sit by and watch you get this community killed. There are kids here, Brett. They don't get to choose! Are you gonna sit by and let them be shot down?"

Brett's eyes narrowed and judging by his red face, Spencer had gone too far as usual. "You think I like this situation, Anderson? Don't think I don't know who your father was. My dad had a lot to say about him too—about all of you. I won't accept help from monsters!"

"It's monsters or all of your people in a ditch with their heads blown off!" Spencer snarled, temper flaring. "I've seen enough kids in ditches, Brett. I'm taking who wants to come and leaving. You wanna join us, fine."

"You're not taking anybody! That's kidnapping!"

"Stop me!" Spencer didn't budge. A part of him wanted the man to take a swing, but that obviously wouldn't happen.

"Keegan shouldn't have called Hochberg for help," Brett spat. "We can handle ourselves."

"Like how you handled those spies?" Spencer asked bitterly. "They got your dad killed. Honor his memory by saving the people he cared for."

Brett's green eyes flashed. "You have no idea what you're talking about, Anderson. What happened was unfortunate, but at least we offered sanctuary. Look what it got us. Why would I follow people who bring bloodshed wherever they go?""We are your only chance," Spencer said coolly. "And you know it. If we walk, those little kids... they'll be sold off like animals, Brett. Your women will be raped and your men will be killed—or worse. Stop fighting us."

Brett's jaw clenched hard, a vein in his forehead bulging.

Spencer pushed harder. "Why are you fighting what you know is true? Let's move while we still can and the rest can be decided later—when we're not dead. Deep down inside, you know you have to do this. All right?"Brett shoved past him, his body shuddering. "I don't have a choice."

Spencer followed, rushing to the others to help ready the victims, the crew mates left behind, and the pacifists staring at them with wide eyes as they stepped outside. He'd never would've dreamed a group of pacifists could've survived the Second Civil War, even if their leader had hidden them well and paid for protection, which is what Hochberg had told them via phone call just a short while prior.

Would they survive after this?

Spencer doubted it. People were born with the will to fight, the primal instinct to survive, no matter the cost. Pacifists, well, they went against human nature. They didn't survive wars. They'd be dead weight on the road while fleeing from the Falcons. If they got in a battle...

Spencer pushed the fear away, forcing himself to glance at a few young children cowering behind their parents near the trucks.

This is bad, Spencer thought. *But for the kids and victims, I won't go down without a fight.*

RENE' HELD A YOUNG teenage girl close, stroking her tangled black curls, whispering to her gently. The girl was shaking, sobs racking her frail body as the van bumped along the road. They'd only traveled for about thirty minutes, and the minutes ticked by at an agonizing pace.

Rene' had a bad feeling gnawing in her gut.

Gideon had called and said Flannery was about two hours out.

It had taken the group of over a hundred people a while to move out. At least sixty of the people were the pacifist members, though Rene' didn't have a solid number on them or their kids. The crew that had stayed behind, Jordan and some of Kaleb's men, totaling maybe fifty, Rene' really didn't know.

The trail they made on the road however, was a sight to see.

Pushing her fears and doubts aside, she focused on praying and speaking comforting words to the girl. The girl clung to her, silent as death.

Did we make it in time, Lord? Rene' chewed her lip, glancing over at the victims around her. Besides a few strangers and a teammate she recognized from Jordan's crew, the van was crowded with the rescue victims from the dome.

What if Flannery caught up with them? Could he?

She caught herself again, smoothing the girl's hair and taking a slow breath. Simon and Nate were driving a truck ahead of her. Lee and his group of boys were in another vehicle, helping tend some wounded. Her dad was leading the armada with some of Jordan's finest soldiers. They had trained men on their rear and in the middle of the trail of vehicles too. Why was she freaking out? Gideon and his group were headed their way too, ready for the hunt, desperate to kill Flannery and please George.

It would end all right.

Exhausted, Rene' closed her eyes and held the girl.

SPENCER GOT WORD FROM Mr. Fisher that help was on the way—two different sources of help. Gideon, of course, and Richard Johnston, the one and only brother to George.

"What?" Spencer blinked, almost dropping the phone.

"One of the dome rescues had Richard's contact and called him as soon as y'all got to the community, apparently. He's on his way, said he has a place of sanctuary we can hide in till the Falcons are handled," Mr. Fisher said calmly. "Just be ready."

"Yessir," Spencer answered, glancing over at the pacifists he was surrounded with. He hung up and took a slow breath, bringing up George's message again. *Please God, don't let him know I'm a traitor. Whatever he's talking about, please, I don't want to die.*

What did "stay low" mean, anyway? Spencer was technically off the map right now. George didn't know where he was, the gang didn't know where he was. He trusted the men he was with—Jordan's crew, Kaleb's crew, Gideon's group, and the people from Springtown. The pacifists weren't a threat. He'd be fine, right? No reason to be scared. He was as below-radar as he'd ever been, in a sense.

So why couldn't he fight the dread building in his chest?

Less than thirty minutes later, the trucks kept going, one long line of vehicles speeding down the highway— when the line changed direction. Spencer glanced out the window, watching as a few more armored trucks joined the parade. Richard Johnston really came? Why? He pushed his doubts aside and glanced at the driver, grinning. "We might just be saved."

CHAPTER TWENTY-EIGHT

January 6th, 2028

"WE HAVE CONTROL OF the White House, Johnston," Brian said calmly. "We need the Confederates here ASAP. I've got injured men and one dead."

"They're on their way; they're hurrying," West promised. "What's going on?""We took out the super soldiers," Brian said. "For the President and Speaker's sake, the Union isn't sending in more—yet."

"The hostages are safe?"

"Classified."

"The rebels are coming—just hold tight." West rubbed his aching head. He was in his mother's favorite spot, the cold wind howling outside of the SUV. He had the heaters overworking.

"I'm beginning to doubt this will work."

"Well don't," West snapped. "I can't explain it all, but this will work.""The rebels aren't the good guys here," Brian said. "There are good men in the Union too. One side might win, but no one truly wins. It's not going to work."

"More leaders are being assassinated, Jones, if we take out the President and George, we can win this. We can start over. We have foreign aid, we have soldiers from both sides who want to restore a constitutional federal republic. We have spies and we have supplies. If we're wise, we have a slim chance. That's all we need." He couldn't tell Brian about Cindy's actions, taking out officials, alerting the civilians of the truth. Every little action held immense reactions.

Brian scoffed. "With the millions of people safe and sound in government housing, fed their daily meals like sheep, blinded by the UN broadcasting? You're living a dream, West."

"The hell I am," West said sharply. "You have a wife and kids. You want them to live like that forever? Stop now. You're still fighting, so you have to understand this is our last chance to save our nation."

Brian hung up.

RENE' TEXTED SIMON AND Chloe for a few minutes, trying to stay awake. Chloe had hopped on the van with Gideon and a few of the victims, tending to the wounded but texted that she was fine. Simon explained what was going on to Rene' quickly—Richard Johnston was helping them to a ranch for safety.

Rene' closed her eyes again but caught herself. If she relaxed, she'd panic, her chest would tighten till she couldn't breathe, and she'd see the images—

The girl stirred beside her, and another girl had fallen asleep against Rene's shoulder. She focused back to where she was. She had a job to do, and she'd focus on it till it was finished.

Then she'd break.

As they drove on, Rene' prayed, but her prayers were cut short when the van lurched forward.

One of the soldiers with her swore. "Everyone, get down," he ordered.

The girls woke up, a few sobbing in fear. "What was that?" a woman asked shakily.

"Tire's blown." The soldier moved to the front, but the van suddenly slammed to a stop. They were jerked forward and a girl screamed. Rene' scrambled to push the victims down just as bullets pelted the sides of the vans. It was supposedly built to withstand bullets, but she didn't trust it.

The soldier reached the front of the van, and Rene' tried moving closer to him. "We have to keep going!"

The windshield busted through with bullets spraying the cab. Blood splattered from the front seat. Rene' froze as the soldier dropped hard, falling onto one of the victims.

He was one of the men not wearing a bulletproof vest.

Rene' swore. "Stay down! Everyone stay down!" She grabbed the radio, but it was static. One of the victims screamed uncontrollably, but they kept low as the bullets stopped hitting the van. Rene' held the girls low and pushed toward the front of the van, mind racing.

They had to keep moving—staying in one place was a death wish.

The windshield was gone, blood staining the cab, the two soldiers upfront hunched over dead. Rene' reached over the driver seat, staying below the dashboard so she didn't show through the hole that used to be glass. She yanked the driver's door open, panting. It took wrestling, but she unbuckled the soldier, shoving his body out the door.

Bullets hit the door and she cried out, steeling herself again. Once he hit the ground, she reached to slam the door but the girls screamed from the back again.

Rene' lifted her head, blood pouring from where the busted door glass had sliced her face.

The vehicles behind her had stopped, but the ones ahead kept going. Rene's van had been almost in the crew's center.

They're leaving us. They're leaving us! Panic flooded her chest as she tried to shut the door. *Keep moving. Drive!*

Gunshots echoed in the night. Men's voices flooded her ears and a bullet hit the van, inches from her head. One of the girls grabbed Rene' by her leg and shoved hard. "They're in here! Go! *Go*!"

The enemy's in the van?

Rene' tumbled out of the van, swearing. She unholstered her gun and ran to the back of the van. The truck behind her had flat tires, dead soldiers in the cab too, but another soldier had taken over. He opened the van, ordering the girls to move to the back of the trucks. More men joined him, and Rene' spotted Spencer running over.

"We gotta keep going!" Spencer ducked behind the van, grabbing one of the girls. "Run! Stay low!"

Rene' helped move the victims and the pacifists from the second truck toward the third truck behind the line. Already the crew members stuck behind the flatted vehicles were going around, bullets hitting the side, but they didn't get shot down.

A few bodies dropped as they ran. Rene' let go of the girl she was leading and ran back. One of the community members, a father and his wife, lay bleeding out, and the baby in the mother's arms looked dead. Rene' grabbed the baby—if it was still holding onto life, it needed a fighting chance at survival—but felt two large hands around her shoulders, yanking her back.

"Rene'! Run!" Spencer snapped. "Get to the truck, now!"

The mother cried out, reaching for the baby. Rene' hugged the bundle close and staggered back. As Spencer helped the woman to her feet, another bullet pierced the mother's head and she dropped.

Rene' screamed and Spencer lunged, dragging Rene' behind the trucks. "Move!"

Screams filled Rene's head. Screams and shouts. She followed Spencer but two more trucks had stopped on the road. Rene' breathed, "Spencer, they have to come back, w-we need help—"

"No turning back kid, we're on our own. Get to the truck that's armored," Spencer said, running to the trucks to unload the victims before they were all shot down. Soldiers picked up arms and built a small barricade around the disabled trucks and the trucks waiting to be overloaded with more passengers. Shots rang in the dark and Rene' occasionally heard a body drop onto the road.

Rene got the baby to the back of the truck and tried to see if she was breathing. The baby wasn't moving, pale-faced but not bleeding. Someone from the back of the truck snatched the child from her and a soldier slammed the doors, yelling for the driver to go. It tore off around the disabled vehicles and followed after the line of vehicles who couldn't turn back.

Dad, please, keep going.

The thought tore through her mind before she could rush to help the others move toward the next truck. The soldiers battled for them, their cover limited but doing something.

Lee and Dad, they were all ahead of us.

God, don't let them turn back, please.

But they would. For her, they'd turn back, even if it was the wrong thing to do.

Wouldn't they?

She prayed not as she helped a teenage boy into the back of a truck. As she watched the truck rush on, another realization struck her.

Simon is behind us somewhere too.

―――――

SIMON DIDN'T STOP MOVING but it didn't matter —they were losing. Most of the victims had been shot down. The soldiers were dwindling, and the backup trucks coming along were just getting shot down as they moved forward. So much for backup. The seasoned vets were getting hammered—they couldn't see their enemy, but the enemy saw them.

Simon kept low, trying to snipe some of the shooters. The men hid behind the trees, scattered on either side of the road, hidden by the night. He shot down three before he heard a loud engine from behind.

A large van rushed down the side of the highway, headlights glaring.

Simon didn't recognize the van as their own.

The ambush was working, and the enemy wasn't planning on taking all of them out either.

They were taking the living.

Simon ran, yelling for Rene', panic flooding his chest. She was loading up the last of the victims in a van but turned, eyes widening. "Si!" Spencer was at her side, shooting down an attacker.

"Get in!" He pushed her toward the truck, but the doors had been shut. The truck drove quickly for cover.

"What?" Rene' pulled away.

"They've got backup." He gestured to the van stopping on the side of the road. "They're taking the rest of us—we have to go!" He pulled her toward the next truck, but the gunfight raged on around them.

They were going to get shot.

More vans showed up. The people left in the road who were waiting for trucks to arrive, began screaming and fleeing.

No more trucks were coming. The rest had been stopped along the road too. The living would be rounded up or shot.

"Simon!" Rene' gasped.

Men jumped out of the vans and overtook the men shooting back. Simon cringed, watching the soldiers—Jordan's men, Kaleb's men, pacifists trying to fight back—fall.

"Rene'! Stop!" He grabbed her again, pulling her behind a truck. A few soldiers ran toward them. Simon shot one down, and Rene' shot the other in the chest, but the next instant, Simon felt something sharp stab his neck.

A dart.

"Rene'! Run!" Spencer fell hard onto the road.

Simon swore, blackness engulfing his vision as cries and shouts filled his head, pounding against his skull.

The ambush was over, and the enemies—whoever they were—had won. At least half of the rescue crew and victims were dead. Rene' and Spencer, had they made it?

Simon's senses darkened until he knew nothing besides the sound of someone crying. *Rene'.*

CHAPTER TWENTY-NINE

January 6th, 2028

"LOOK WHO FINALLY MADE it." Fernando eyed the monitors. Brian rolled his eyes, leading Amir and Bosch to meet the rebel President and Vice President at the White House. The outside of the White House was barren—Brian didn't allow anyone outside. The armada parked outside however, showed Brian just how much the rebel soldiers had on their side.

Humvees, a tank, and armored trucks, and enough soldiers to hold the White House for a good while.

If they lasted that long.

Brian rushed them all inside to safety, not trusting that the Union didn't have snipers waiting outside in hiding or some other trick of attack. President Larry calmly shook his hand, expression guarded. "We were told about the enhanced soldiers. We're sorry for your loss."

Brian ignored the pleasantries. "Wave two of the bastards are headed our way. You need to announce to the nation what the hell is going on, and we need to take them out."

President Larry frowned. "We're not announcing anything to the nation until the soldiers are killed, then we'll officially announce the terms of surrender.""Surrender?" Brian stared at him as they hurried down the halls.

"Yes."

"You're not killing the VP?""He's president now, and no, we won't kill him," Vice President Smith spoke up.

"He's an American traitor." Brian set his jaw. "He's sent countless soldiers to their deaths and refused to bring countless more home from camps. He sends men to the labs. He deserves to die too, just like Kaden."

"But you didn't kill him."

"I needed him as a hostage to make the government hold back."

"And now?" President Larry asked.

"I'll kill him myself once the surrender is made," Brian said simply. "We'll handle the SS."

"We will help," Smith said. "We have men to help and plenty of tools that might be worthwhile."

Brian said nothing in return, leading them to where the battles would continue. Within a few hours, if all went according to plan, the nation would have a new president, and the Second Civil War would be at an end.

As the soldiers, both Union and Confederate, readied for the attack, Brian got a call from Kaleb Savage. He stepped away from his crew, answering.

"Brian, I've got some news."

"Unless you've found a way to stop the second wave of super soldiers entering the White House, I've got work to do right now."

"Rene' was taken on a job in Missouri," Kaleb snapped. "The crew lost at least fifty vics and members, Rene' included."

Brian froze, blood running cold. "Who took her?"

"We're not entirely sure, but I've got some moles saying there's a good chance the survivors are being sold to the government." Kaleb didn't sound phased in the slightest. "If you want to argue that, save it. I'll prove you wrong."

Brian wouldn't argue. He'd watched innocent people be used before. But if those victims suffered, in the future, his family would be kept safe.

Not now.

"Where are they being taken to be sold? Union lab? Drop off?"

"We don't know. If you guys settle the soldiers and leave the mess with the rebels, I thought you'd want to come help us hunt, if we're still hunting by the time you're finished. I hear Bo Brewer and Nabeel Shahin are with you —use them and bring 'em back when you come."

"The UN has a new strand of tests," Brian forced out. "If we don't save them before they're sold—" They would break Rene'. He couldn't let that happen. Not again.

"We're going to handle it."

"You can't handle shit. You've got George to handle," Brian hissed. "You and Jordan are wrapped around his finger. One wrong move and he finds out about your secrets."

"He won't find anything out." Kaleb chuckled. "And his days are limited. Hold up your end." He hung up.

Brian shut his eyes briefly but Amir stepped closer, dark eyes heavy with concern. "Who was that?"

"Kaleb."

"What did he say?""Focus on the job," Brian said tightly.

"Don't give me that BS."

Brian hesitated and glanced to the others briefly, working his jaw. "Someone—we don't know who—just kidnapped a group of victims from a rescue op and my sister was taken too."

Amir fell quiet and then, "the same one as before?"

"Yeah. The same one I left behind last time." Brian didn't meet his gaze.

Amir nodded, large body straightening ever so slightly. "We finish this and go find her."

"It's not that simple—"

"But it is, Jones," Amir said firmly. "The job you have can wait for this. I'll make it."

CHAPTER THIRTY

January 7th, 2028

DURING THE COVER OF the night, the large group followed Richard Johnston to the safety of a Missouri ranch. In the middle of 500 acres set six large cabins, all within sight of one another from what Simon could tell. A few paddocks surrounded a large black barn, but Simon didn't spot any animals or people, though a truck was parked out front.

Richard had briefed the leaders as they reached the ranch and wasted no time in helping unload the community and the victims. Simon made a bee-line to the truck Mr. Fisher and Lee were in, heart in his throat.

They had lost over half of their own. Simon hadn't counted the victims lost or the crewmates lost. He only cared about one person—Rene'.

Mr. Fisher immediately gathered anyone willing to go hunting. Nate stuck close to Simon's side.

Many of Jordan's men prepped to leave and find the kidnapped, which totaled ten women and children, including Rene', and a few men. While some of the team members got the victims inside the cabins for safety and tending, the rest were high-strung, hungry for blood and action.

Simon ran to the trucks once everyone was inside and the rest were ready to run. His blood hadn't stopped boiling since the attack and he had one focus: save Rene'.

Any guilt or fear could be handled later. All that mattered was they found Rene' and the others in time.

Just as they cranked up to head out, a group of four armored trucks and a van, Richard ran outside. Mr. Fisher started to ignore the man but another soldier shouted at him.

"They're already here!" Richard shouted. "The Falcons are here!"

Simon swore darkly.

The soldiers didn't hesitate, forming a new plan that would keep the ranch safe and that would kill a good portion of the Falcons, but it was all white noise to Simon.

"We have to go," Simon snapped at Mr. Fisher as they got out of the trucks. "We need to move! We have to find them!"

"We will." Mr. Fisher grabbed his shoulder. "But we can't bring her home if we're dead." His eyes were pure fire, a dark expression on his face that Simon had never seen before.

Fear gripped Simon's chest, and he quickly followed Mr. Fisher toward the armored Humvee. Mr. Fisher shouted for Lee and his boys to stay back at the ranch and for once, Lee didn't argue, his pale face tightening as he led the boys inside a cabin.

Simon didn't look back after that. He held his AR-15 with white knuckles in the Humvee, listening to the engine, waiting till they stopped to hide in the woods. He'd shoot anyone who got in his way.

Once they stopped at their location, the vehicle hidden behind a large pile of dirt and trees, the men parted. More vehicles drove on, men with RPGs, fire launches, and grenades that would take the Falcons by surprise at the start of the acreage entry.

Simon kept low, breathing calm and steady, gun propped and ready to fire. He barely made out a familiar figure racing by his side—Brett. When had the man joined him? Rage burned in Brett's expression as he growled. Brett had lost a large portion of his people—had it been enough to shake him into action? Would he be their ally or would he slow them down?

Simon didn't let himself think. If he thought, he'd think about Rene' and about failing her and then he'd snap. He couldn't snap. Not yet.

I failed her again.

I was there and I failed her.

THE FALCONS LOCATED THE ranch at full-throttle. Gideon's men were only minutes too late.

Over a hundred gangsters, judging by the vehicles and men on foot, attacked the ranch at dawn. Gideon had gotten word that the victims were safe inside the ranch bunkers, and the only ones waiting for the onslaught were ready fighters.

They weren't ready enough.

Gideon's crew ambushed as quickly as possible, surrounding the Falcons and giving it all they had. The Humvees were bombed, Gideon's crew moving in after the vehicles were downed.

The Falcons dispersed almost immediately, a few vehicles tearing off down the road to reach the bunkers, the rest on foot running through the woods. A strange way of exposing themselves, until Gideon saw the fighters waiting in the woods. The Falcons were trying to take the defenses down, no matter the cost.

Gideon sped up and reached the woods, grabbing his semi-automatic and jumping out. Alex swore, "Gid! No!"

As usual, Gideon ignored him and ran into the danger zone. He shot down a few gangsters in the back and caught sight of Mr. Fisher, wrestling on the forest floor with a thug. Gideon shot the enemy down and ran over, yanking Mr. Fisher out of the line of fire behind a ditch. A large knife was stuck in Mr. Fisher's right arm, and he had a head wound pouring blood.

Gideon swore and spoke into his comm, staying over Mr. Fisher to shield him as the gunfight raged above them. "Percy, I need a medic to the—"

A body jumped into the ditch and shoved Gideon aside. Percy flashed a grin at Gideon, setting to work on Mr. Fisher's wounds, giving him a quick shot of morphine. "I've got him. Stay low."

Gideon pushed himself up. The enemies were all over, dropping like flies, but this was just the distraction. Some had gotten past the defenses and were headed to the cabins.

He took off but stopped short when a man dropped hard to his left, screaming, "Hochberg! Help me!"

Gideon swore and ducked, grabbing the man and pulling him behind a tree. "Hang on," he ordered, demanding for a medic over his comm. "Just hang on, Myer."

The man struggled for breath, clutching his bleeding stomach. The few bullet wounds were terminal—they both knew that. Gideon helped him hold the wounds, calm, keeping Myer's head shielded as another grenade went off someplace in the forest. The sounds of screams, shouts, gunfire, and the explosions were eerily distant to Gideon.

"Hang tight, Myer, help's coming," Gideon said into the man's ear. Myer clutched Gideon's hand but his grip slackened a moment later and he went limp in Gideon's grip. Gideon set his jaw, lowering him to the ground and closing his eyes. Sucking in a sharp breath, Gideon picked up his gun again and kept moving through the chaos.

He ran toward his truck again but Alex wasn't there. He climbed in, trying to get contact over the comms.

"I'm with the wounded," Alex responded quickly. "You and Percy lead without me." His voice was thick with emotion, and Gideon immediately wanted to ask who they'd just lost—but he decided against it. He alerted Percy and the man ran from the ditches, blood on his hands as he jumped into the truck.

"Fisher?" Gideon asked, driving through the chaos, slamming two thugs on the road and leaving them smeared on the churt.

"Stable and with the others."

Gideon focused on the road, bullets hitting the back of the truck but not penetrating. "Can you—"

Percy was already on it, speaking into the comms and telling the men to follow them toward the ranch. "The squirmish is just a distraction to dwindle numbers. We gotta reach the big guns going for the vics."

Almost immediately, during the choppy gunfire and small explosions of hand grenades, men began filing in after Gideon, their vehicles roaring to life as they followed. Gideon took off to the center of the fight, never looking back. The men left behind would have to cope and handle themselves.

Until Gideon stumbled upon Preston, holding Jacob's disfigured body in the middle of the forest floor. Oblivious to the ruckus around him, Preston sobbed and screamed like a child. Gideon swore and darted over, snatching Preston off Jacob's corpse. "Move!" he snarled.

Preston shoved him off. "No!"

"Keep going, kid." Gideon pushed him toward the trees. "Move!"

There'd be time to grieve later. They'd bury the bodies later.

Right now, Flannery was at the heart of the ranch and Gideon would kill him, no matter the cost.

SIMON SPAT BLOOD AND sat up, deafened by the blast of a grenade that had hit too close for comfort. Mr. Fisher was in a ditch just beyond the fight, and the thugs were shooting fast and all sporadic—when half reloaded, the other half took over.

Simon pushed on. Instead of a blinding rage, a terrifying calm took over, every move he made calculated and fast. He needed to find Rene' and they were in his damn way.

In the center of the pandemonium, Brett Black, the pacifist community's leader, was dragging a corpse away from the hell fire. Simon hesitated a brief moment, anger rising. *Let him die,* a part of him whispered. *He deserves it.*

Simon swore to himself before rushing over, covering Brett, killing a man who aimed at them from the road. Adrenaline surging through his blood, Simon gave one last shove and got Brett and the body behind the trees.

Brett dropped beside the corpse, sobbing. "Ted!"

Simon knelt, feeling for the man's pulse, but there wasn't one. He'd got caught in gunfire, the bullet wounds covering his chest, dark blood soaking his shirt. Simon steeled himself. "He's dead, Black. Keep moving. Kill the ones who did it." Refusing to look at the bloodied body of the kind man who'd helped the victims at the community, Simon left Brett and ran.

A Falcon member jumped out from the trees and tackled Simon to the forest floor. Simon yanked a knife from his sheath as the man shoved his gun toward Simon's head. The soft crunch of Simon's blade shoving through the thug's neck sent blood splattering over Simon's face. He snarled and shoved the corpse off, scrambling up.

"Si!" Nate's voice, ragged, hoarse.

Simon staggered and whirled around, ducking as a few shots went off nearby. "Nate?" He spotted his friend on the ground near a few corpses. "Nate!" He ran over, breath catching. Nate's clothes were singed like he'd been on fire. A long gash ran down his left cheek to his collarbone.

Nate groaned in pain, clutching his face, eyes dilated. He gripped Simon's coat.

Simon swore, grabbing Nate into his arms. "Hold on to me." He doubted Nate could hear him—he'd probably been too close to a blast, or in one. Simon pulled him over his shoulders and took off toward the ditch. It was the safest place he knew of, instead of the road where the fight was still raging.

But he needed a medic.

Simon hauled Nate into the ditch, breathing ragged. The ditch had a few fallen, a few wounded, and a man with wild red hair trying to tend to the severely injured. He glanced up at Nate and took over, shooting him with morphine and trying to stop the heavy bleeding. Nate passed out, head lolling against Simon's chest. Simon panicked but the medic snapped at him. "He'll be fine. Get back out there."

Simon leaned his brother against the dirt, hands flinching before he got to his feet. Nate would be fine. He had to be. Simon glanced at Mr. Fisher, who was a bit drugged up but gave a quick nod—it was all Simon needed.

With that, Simon rushed back into the fight, shooting down two Falcons before he got out of the ditch. He heard men's shouts—familiar shouts telling them to keep going.

Gideon's moving forward. The fight's moving toward the cabins.

Simon ran to find one of their trucks with others, hungry for blood.

CHAPTER THIRTY-ONE

January 7th, 2028

THUMP.

Thud.

Thump.

A small scuffle filled Rene's ears, followed by a pained cry.

Her throat burned. Had the scream been her own?

Darkness engulfed her, and no matter how hard she batted her eyes, it didn't leave. The sickening smell of blood and sweat filled her nostrils. Rene's throat tightened as she fought a cry of pain. Her heartbeat throbbed in her skull.

Sharp, stabbing pains burned through her body, stemming from her head, though her stomach seared with pain too.

"Don't move," a familiar voice whispered. "It's OK; just be still. You're hurt."

Spencer? Rene' lifted her head off the hard ground but immediately writhed in pain. "S-spencer…"

"Just take it easy, kid," Spencer said firmly, voice weak and ragged. "Stop moving around. The drug is pretty rough."

"W-what…"

"I'm not sure, but it'll wear off soon."

Rene' focused hard, making out Spencer's shape nearby and various other figures around her. Judging by the feeling of motion, they were in a moving vehicle— probably a van. Rene' sat up, and Spencer steadied her with a bruised hand. "H-how long have we been…?"

"Not sure. At least ten hours though." Spencer sighed. "You were out pretty hard. I think they overdosed you."

"Oh," Rene' mumbled, holding her temples, dried blood rubbing off. "Who…"

Spencer hesitated. "Just… rest."

"Who took us?"

The others flinched a little. Only a few were awake, women a few years older than Rene' with downcast eyes.

"From what I can tell, a dome trader. Kelsey, I think her name is, I've never heard of her, though. But her last name sounds familiar—I think it was on the list of traffickers we found at the last dome..." Spencer trailed off. "Rene'? Is something wrong?"

Rene's breathing grew strained like someone had her lungs in a vice. She struggled for air, vision blurring. "Kelsey?"

"Yeah?" Spencer frowned. "Rene', you look—"

"She's my sister," Rene' whispered. "Kelsey is my sister." The overwhelming sense of numbness wrapped around Rene'. Her head throbbed and her breathing was short, ragged.

Spencer paled, eyes widening in disbelief. "That... that woman... she... She doesn't look anything like you guys! She looks like a freak!"

"That's all you have to say about this?" Rene' forced.

He winced and wrapped a protective arm around her shoulders, pulling her against him. "I've got you covered, kid. They won't touch you. OK? Just stick close."

Rene' rubbed her face harder this time, trying to feel something. "Si... Dad..." Her heart crashed hard, a sob building in her throat. Had they made it? Were they someplace safe?

"They got away." Spencer sighed.

"But Si—"

"He's alive," Spencer cut in. "He has to be."

But Rene' had seen him fall...

She shuddered, closing her eyes and fighting a sob. Spencer held her close and she drifted off, nightmares plaguing her. Dreams about Kelsey and Brian and Jed— Dark dreams where Rene' could never escape, no matter how hard she tried.

BY MORNING, THE VANS were still on the run, leaving Missouri behind. There were two vans of victims, and Spencer counted about five trucks of thugs—the men who had wiped out Jordan and Kaleb's men, the pacifists who fought back, and innocent women and children like cattle.

Rage burned inside Spencer, and he focused his gaze on the floor. He'd been kidnapped before. Being captured was part of the job, or most often, the bitter end. Though Spencer had been raised to believe that capture was a sign of a weak soldier, he didn't believe it. Plenty of men had gone MIA, or been imprisoned, during many battles in histories—they were still dubbed heroes. Just because someone was taken didn't make them weak.

He glanced down at Rene'. She wasn't weak. She'd been fearless in her efforts to help get the kids and victims to safety. She'd saved lives.

Spencer didn't know her all that well, even though he'd saved her life once before. From what Simon said, she was pretty quiet, unless she was with her family, and then she was often goofy, doing whatever it took to make them laugh. Despite her small size, she really wasn't a weak person—and Spencer had failed to save her from this.

He set his jaw tightly. He'd grown up protecting Randy. Randy, the goofy kid constantly in trouble. Randy, the boy who'd been sent to the hospital at seven because of their father's drunken rage.

Spencer had spent his life as a protector, but he'd failed more than he liked to admit. This was one of those times he couldn't fix it easily, either. Escaping the mini militia of thugs would be near impossible, especially with all of the victims, and Rene' wouldn't leave any of them behind.

Another quality Spencer admired—honor. Or nobility. He didn't know the exact word for it, but Simon and Rene' had a whole lot of it.

Spencer wanted it too.

I'll get her back to her family and Simon no matter the cost. She deserves it. Simon rubbed his face weakly. *And Lord, help me do the same for these complete strangers. They deserve help, too.*

CHAPTER THIRTY-TWO

January 7th, 2028

GEORGE WATCHED THE BROADCAST on his office holographic television, sipping on whiskey and nursing painkillers. He had a headache from the devil. Cindy was napping in their room and George had sent West, looking as run-down as roadkill, to catch a few hours of sleep before things hit the fan.

Things had already hit the fan. The White House was still being held by terrorists. Kaleb and Jordan were on the hunt to assassinate a few rebel leaders headed for DC.

The past week had been nonstop chaos—the broadcastings and news anchors were being fed mixed intel. Most were paid off by the UN to report fallacies.

But a few were getting different intel and were loud about it. Independent persons, even conspiracy theorists hiding from the safety of their bomb shelters, spouted off the intel via radio, encrypted online messages, and more. Rallies were being held outside of civilian townships. Government-paid people were getting a strange taste of the war right outside their doors.

It was dangerous.

The USA had lost itself as soon as it allowed history to be erased and lies to become mantra. Without the upper-hand with the news, the UN would lose the people's trust and the ability to lead them at will. Most would ignore the truth anyway, but those who resisted would cause more hell.

Alone, this change of setting wasn't the drastic end of the war. But it would cause trouble for when George took over and reigned the US as his empire. People weren't hard to control if he maintained the ability to cage them up. With the people limited to their government housing, their acceptable jobs, they were seperated from the rebel townships and the real world of battles and deaths around them.

Once they saw that, they'd question just how peaceful their new democracy was.

George didn't need that. He rubbed his head and got another drink. His efforts to maintain control weren't without fruit, but the UN leaders were pushing back hard. He didn't need to stay involved just yet—as a ganglord, he was better at smooth-talking the angry officials and taking care of the bothersome pawn pieces in the shadows. Kaleb and Jordan were taking care of the dirty work. George could focus on the mental games.

The office door opened without a sound and George glanced over, sighing. "I changed the security code."

"Abracadabra." Guns locked it behind him and grabbed a bottle of beer from the mini bar. "The state of the nation is crumbling and you're drinking?"

George scoffed, gesturing to the television. "What's there to fight, Guns?"

"The armies are about to wipe each other out." Guns studied the broadcasting, sipping his beer. "Before long, all of the nation will see the lies they've been fed and more will rise up."

"I'm not afraid of civilians with no training." George shook his head. "I have men on that—hunting for the person giving the nation different intel. When they find him, he'll be dead."

"It'll be too late by then. You want your empire," Guns smiled softly. "You'll get it... but only if you let this work itself out."

"What?" George frowned. "If I let it play out—"

"The weak will be weeded out, the officials killed like cattle—someone's slaughtering them, and it isn't stopping. No matter what side wins, if you come back to save the day, and with all of your men... you'll have more power. More control. More resources."

"The UN won't agree with me leading just yet."

"They won't have a chance if you play it right."

"What are you talking about, Guns?" George snapped. "I'm too tired for games. You can't expect me to actually run now. The leaders are counting on my help, the UN needs me to do well to trust me—"

"You can maintain their trust while getting out of dodge," Guns said. "The men being killed... you don't think you're next?"

"Of course I'm expecting someone to assassinate me, but they won't get that close." George got another drink. "You know how prepared I am."

"I do." Guns followed and sat at the counter. "But I have an idea."

"Spit it out."

"We prepared for the worse and that's happening," Guns started. "What if we changed our approach? Instead of staying and fighting the rebels ourselves and offering aid to the UN, what if we escaped through a back door while remaining loyal to the rest?"

"How?" George frowned. "I already suggested I take my family and run to Canada but they refused."

"Cindy and West want to help," he agreed. "They want your empire to come."

"But we can't have that if we're dead," George said dryly. "What's your plan?"

Guns smiled. "The UN is creating the enhanced soldiers at a rapid speed. You can go to Canada and get out of dodge, and still maintain a look of control by allowing some men to stay behind and help the Union soldiers. The news is so distracted right now, George. You can make a clean break and no one would notice. You can tell the officials you have foreign affairs to handle in Canada—you can gain even more aid."

"You don't think I've thought about that option?"

"What's stopping you?"

"I'm too close to triumph to run now," George said. "Whoever is taking out the officials might hunt me too, but they've also benefited me. I have less people to fight to gain my control."

"As you said, can't do that if they take you out."

George chuckled. "I can handle the risk."

"But your gut said to run," Guns reminded him.

George ran a hand through his thick black hair, sighing. "It did."

"You've never ignored it before," Guns said. "And if I'm saying the same... I've never been wrong, either."

"The soldiers..." George hesitated. "I heard a rumor that the new President, Stu, had every intention of taking me out. I doubt he was behind the other officials' deaths, but he could very well be behind my own."

Guns nodded. "I heard the same. He likes you way less than President Kaden liked you. Only the rebels have the White House, George."

"Do you think the UN will keep this diplomatic?"

"No, there will be a bloodbath, but you don't have to be here for it. Let the officials and the UN wipe themselves out and destroy their army, then you can jump in as a hero to the nation. A touch different than your original plan but worth the shot."

"The original plan is hard to keep with Kaden dead." Kaden would've been easier to control and get rid of. The new President hated George, and George wasn't in the position to kill the man since he was held hostage. The terrorists were AWOL Union soldiers to top it off. Brian Jones himself led the militia.

Guns chuckled. "The nation is rioting, George. You need to make yourself scarce and come back with more fire power... and super soldiers."

George raised an eyebrow. "You're considering that?"

"Of course I am. You have a handful of good candidates for the enhancement."

"We'll see." George sighed. "For now... let's run."

He would take control of the US, after the leaders battled among themselves and lost it all together. He would come in as the hero and bestow a new nation unto West. He was unstoppable, with support from many foreign and domestic officials who didn't breathe a word about selling out for the Johnston empire.

George had enough money to own the nation. He just needed to let the weak weed themselves out a little longer. The plan's execution had changed, but the end goal was the same, and it was closer than ever.

CHAPTER THIRTY-THREE

January 8th, 2028

THE RANCH WAS IN flames. The fire lapped at the morning sky, scorching the cabins and flickering out from the windows. The Falcons, their deed finished, focused on shooting down anyone who escaped the cabins.

Before Gideon could reach the cabins though, their ugly flames were in sight, a Humvee pulled out in front of the road. Gideon swore as a man jumped out, shooting at the truck tires. Though the truck was armored, the tires were hit and the bullets must've been strong enough to get through.

Before Gideon could slam into the Humvee, Percy snatched the wheel and they ran off the road. Gideon pushed on the breaks and they skidded into some trees, the windshield busting. Gideon swore and grabbed his gun, shoving his door open.

But no bullets hit their truck. It was like the men had stopped attacking them.

Percy grabbed his shoulder, grip tight. "Gideon, stop."

"The cabins—" Gideon didn't look back, shoving against the door again, breathing hard.

"It's over, Gideon. I'm sorry."

Before Gideon could get out, a sharp needle pierced his neck. Gideon swung hard, mind racing, but Percy grabbed him by his shoulders and pinned him against the seat.

"I'm sorry," Percy repeated, eyes flashing. "It'll be OK." He held the side of Gideon's face, bloodied hand gentle. "I promise."

Whatever drug he'd used wasn't one Gideon was immune to. Darkness flooded his vision, and he couldn't move his limbs to fight back. Everything slipped away and darkness settled in.

THE FALCONS FLED AS soon as the cabins were up in flames, the truck and Humvee engines roaring as they tore down the churt road, almost as fast as they'd come. Alex ran from the woods, covered in blood—most of it wasn't his own—and breathing hard.

The growing flames stopped him in his tracks.

Richard Johnston and others were hurrying the victims out of the cabins, the kids' cries filling Alex's ears. He jerked into action, running over. He didn't see Gideon or Percy anywhere, but knowing them, they'd probably ran inside like reckless morons.

I can't go inside. Alex couldn't go inside, he'd freeze up. *But if they're in there...* He ran to a cabin where Richard was guiding a woman and child outside.

"Johnston!" Alex shouted. "Where's Gideon?"

Richard helped the two victims to the front yard. "I haven't seen him!" He ran back to help and Alex followed, insides churning.

Simon was carrying a man outside, pulling the body off the porch and into the yard. Simon's coat was lit in flames, and he staggered under the man's dead weight. Alex quickly tackled Simon to the ground, shoving him onto his back to extinguish the angry flames.

Simon groaned and got up, soot covering his face. "There's still people inside—"

"Is Gid in there?" Alex demanded.

Simon pulled himself up. "Gid was taken, Al." He spat blood from his mouth, lips busted. "I tried to stop it but couldn't. The Falcons took him and Percy." He pulled away and ran back inside one of the flaming cabins.

Something came over Alex, something that hadn't come over him since he was eighteen, back when a job had gone bad and he was the only person standing between Gideon and death.

Like a flip switched in his head, Alex got up. He ran toward the closest cabin, right on Simon's tail, and went inside. The smoke hit him hard, filling his nose, burning his eyes. He ignored the panic tugging at his mind.

Victims were rushing from the basement and crowding into the foyer and halls of the cabin. Judging by the forming crowd outside in the yard, most had been saved. The wounded that couldn't run out themselves had been brought up to the foyer and were crying and screaming for help in panicked states.

Alex fought for breath, pulling his bandana up around his nose. He grabbed an injured soldier, helping him stand. The man was twice Alex's size, but Alex pulled him toward the door, trying to steady him since his left leg was bandaged. Alex got him outside, sucking in deep breaths when they hit the yard. His lungs constricted, his mind begging him to stay outside and find some other way to help, anything to stay away from the fire.

He sat the man down and ran back inside. They were running out of time.

Smoke filled the halls and nearly blinded Alex. So much smoke. The heat sent sweat pouring down his back.

God, help us.

A man grabbed his arm—Brett Black, covered in blood but not his own. He snarled, "hurry!"

Alex picked up a woman cowering in the foyer, her cries barely reaching his hearing over the shouts and the roars of the growing fires. He held her tight, rushing back outside and coughing hard. Once she was with the others, Alex looked back, tears running as his eyes stung. Other men raced out of the cabin, their shouts filling the air. "That's everyone! Stay out!"

Brett carried a man out into the grass, panting as he tumbled beside Alex.

Alex shuddered, glancing toward the large crowd of people standing, sitting, or laying in the yard, a safe distance from the burning cabins. He fought a sob. It looked like everyone had gotten out alive—but what if some hadn't? What if they left someone behind? What if —

Simon pushed through the crowd. "We have to get the wounded from the forest. Now!" He shouted to the soldiers, dashing toward a truck.

In the same instant, Richard took over and restored order in the chaos, instructing the able-bodied to load up the wounded so they could head out.

Alex stumbled over, gripping Richard's arm, fighting for his voice to stay steady. "Sir?"

Richard turned and studied him, his body already in motion, and his eyes flashing at being stopped. He looked like an older version of West, but with short-cropped hair and a pair of glasses that rested on a sharp nose. "What?"

"Gideon is gone. The Falcons took him, Simon said—"

"Once everyone is safe and rolling out, we'll search for those taken, Thompson." He pulled away, leading wounded to the trucks quickly.

Alex stood there, breathing hard and coughing, his legs swaying. He watched the cabins burn for a moment, mind crumbling. *Gideon is gone. Rene' and Spencer and the victims are gone. We lost over half of our own.*

Mr. Fisher! He blinked hard, the smoke, the giant flames, the people moving toward the trucks snapping out of focus. Brett headed over to the truck and Alex started after them. "I'm coming!"

BY THE TIME THE remaining survivors and soldiers were loaded up, the numbers were lower than Simon would have dreamed. Jordan's men and Kaleb's men were dwindled in numbers, but they led the evacuation alongside Richard. The team was headed for Kentucky and wouldn't stop till they reached the outskirts of Springtown, which on a good drive, would take at least eight hours, if they weren't stopped by enemies or a caravan.

Simon sat with Mr. Fisher and Nate in the back of a med van. Nate was sleeping soundly, stable, though drugged up on painkillers. Though they'd given him enough painkillers to numb the pain and sleep, Mr. Fisher refused to sleep.

"We'll find her, sir," Simon said tightly.

"We need to find her now," Mr. Fisher snapped. "I'm not going anywhere."

Simon pulled his phone and called Richard. Before the man could speak, Simon spoke coldly. "Either let the vans stop so Mr. Fisher, some of our own, Lee and his boys, and myself can get off and find Rene', or I will stop this van myself." For emphasis, he cocked his pistol so the snap could be heard over the phone. He eyed the driver of the van.

Richard paused for a moment, then said, "you saw Gideon and Percy taken?"

"Yeah. Dragged into one of the Falcon's trucks before they ran."

"You're going after the team who took your friend?"

"Rene'," Simon snapped. "Of course we are, but we need to go now—"

"I've got intel on who took her, boy, but we will stop." Richard hung up and a few minutes later, the driver got a text and slowed to a stop on the side of the road. Simon jumped up, helping Mr. Fisher sit.

The back of the van opened and Richard offered a hand to Mr. Fisher. "We'll take a small group," he said. "I'm not going, but someone will be along to help soon." The rest of the line of vehicles pushed on down the road, only a few stopped alongside the curb, allowing for men to get off, including Chloe, Rene's friend. Brett and a group of his men from the pacifist community had tagged along and hadn't left Mr. Fisher's lead.

"Who took my daughter?" Mr. Fisher didn't accept Richard's help, standing alone as Simon followed him out of the van.

Richard's dark eyes narrowed and he shut the back of the van. "Kelsey, the daughter you and your wife fostered years ago. She left Springtown and she went into the trafficking rings, Fisher." He waved a hand and the last of the trucks moved out, except one.

Mr. Fisher paled but he didn't hesitate, "I-I knew about what she went into but I... I didn't know it was like this." His voice was controlled, eerie.

Simon fought a shudder, rage building. Rene' had told him about Kelsey, but nothing more than she'd been her sister and Rene' hoped she made it, despite the abuse Kelsey had put them all through.

And now Kelsey had taken her. Simon gritted his teeth.

"She's got a big crew," Richard said tightly. "She's taking the victims to a New Jersey lab for DNA testings that are future generation level tech." He gestured for a few men who came over, all wearing casual street clothes but strapped with guns—military ops. Simon blinked. "Where—"

"These men will help you," Richard said. "They had to meet us here. I'm sorry for the delay. They know the rough area ahead. All intel from here on out will come from them and some other contacts; it'll make sense soon. I have to go."

Lee rushed over with his small team, hugging Mr. Fisher tightly. "Dad!"

Mr. Fisher held him close, glancing at Richard, his worn face heavy. "Thank you." He turned to the man and Simon stepped over, anger pushing him.

Richard nodded, voice firm. "You'll find them." He got into the remaining vehicle and it started off after the others, the light of the day fading into a soft dusk.

A cool breeze hit Simon's face and he turned to the others. "Let's go!" he snapped.

The men, and Chloe, loaded up into the two waiting armored trucks. Simon stuck close to Lee and his boys. Questions piled inside his head—where in New Jersey was Rene' being taken? Who would help them find them?

He turned to the driver, voice low. "Who's meeting us?" he asked.

"We don't have a name, kid. But according to Rich, he's the same guy who talked Thomas Flannery down and made him run."

"What?"

"Flannery was just sold off," the soldier said. "He would've done a lot worse than take Hochberg if this anon hadn't stepped in."

Simon gulped down the lump in his throat. "But this anon knows where Rene' will be? How can we find them?"

The passenger, a large, buff soldier with a cross tattoo on his neck, scowled at Simon. "Kid, we have to find the victims before they reach NJ. We know the route the traffickers usually take. We'll hit it up first. The best thing you can do right now is sit down and let us do the groundwork. You'll save your girl."

Simon's anger flashed but he sat down, pulling out his phone. He tried texting Rene' but she didn't answer. He tried Spencer's number too but got no response.

Rage ran through his body like fire and he held his face in his hands, struggling for breath. *I let her down. She's going to get hurt. God, why did this happen? How could I fail her again?*

A firm hand gripped his shoulder. Simon jerked, looking into the face of Lee. Lee was pale, his face streaked with dried blood, but he held Simon's shoulder with a comforting grip. "She's strong. She'll be fine. We'll get her back. Just hold on."

Simon breathed in sharply, straightening. "You guys OK?" he asked the boys.

Lee's small team was obviously shaken up, with wide eyes and ashen faces, but Lee's Mexican friend, Mo, offered a smirk. "Rene' will probably have those guys beat before we even get there."

Lee smiled weakly, eyes hollow. "Yeah. I'm sure."

Simon pulled it together for their sake and tried holding onto the truth that God was in control—even when Simon wasn't. But it wasn't comforting like it should've been.

CHAPTER THIRTY-FOUR

January 8th, 2028

RENE' LICKED METALLIC-TASTING BLOOD from her lips, vision fuzzy. A man shouted and the van doors opened, a few victims gasping. Rene' gripped Spencer's arm without thinking, sitting up, pain flaring in her skull, but she ignored it.

A thug shoved the doors wide and snapped at the prisoners. "Move. Get out!" He yanked a girl out by her arm and she froze up, stumbling out.

Rene' snarled and got up quickly. "Don't touch them!"

Spencer yanked her back before a thug could strike her. "Easy, pal," Spencer said, voice calm.

The victims got out, a few of them collapsing from exhaustion and fear, but Spencer helped them carefully.

They were escorted in the dark of the night, the moon hidden by thick clouds, across a small lawn and toward a large suburban house. The area was abandoned and ransacked.

Rene' didn't know what state they were in, or how long they'd been driving, though it must've been at least a day. She'd been out cold for most of it.

She staggered over a rock in the path and a thug dragged her up the porch steps. Spencer snapped at him but another thug stepped behind them, chuckling. "They're just stir-crazy," he said. "Don't be too rough yet."

The other thug scoffed and led the victims inside the front door. Rene' glanced around, heart in her throat, but she hadn't seen Kelsey once since being taken. Maybe they'd been wrong, maybe Kelsey wasn't involved.

The suburban home was large and meticulously clean, the bright lights making Rene' wince. A man came from the hall, smiling. "Nice lot, Rex."

The first thug, the tall, broad one with the crow tattoos on his left arm, eyed Rene'. "Split them like we talked about?" he asked the stranger.

"Of course," the man smiled, accent insanely thick and Russian.

Rex grabbed Rene' by her arms, holding them behind her and pushing her toward the hall. Rene' immediately slammed her right elbow against his groin. It caught him off guard, but he twisted his body in time to block most of the blow. "Nice try, kid."

The Russian laughed and took Spencer by his cuffed hands. "Come along, then. We have work to do."

The other thug calmly led the other victims down the other hall, and Rene' tasted bile in her throat. They separated her and Spencer from the others—why?

The Russian led Spencer toward a door and led him inside a basement, holding Spencer's bound wrists as if expecting an attack. Rene' set her quivering jaw and let the thug guide her in too.

The room was large, with chains drilled into the floor by metal pieces. The hardwood floor was clean, but the white-wash walls made Rene' cringe.

"What? We don't get a bed?" Spencer sighed. "A cot? Do the other vics get a cot?"

The Russian chuckled softly, "Ah, humorous, just like your father."

Spencer's eyes flashed and he eyed the man. "What the hell did you just say?"

"You heard me, Anderson." The Russian led him over. "Take those chains and put them on."

Spencer didn't move. "What are you going to do to us?" he demanded. "Why the separation?"

The thug pushed Rene', picking up the chains and locking them around her ankles. Rene' winced, "Hey—"

The Russian snapped the chains onto Spencer's wrists, undoing the previous binds. "Because you two are uniquely valuable to our cause," he said. "Now, rest for a few hours—we move early." He led the thug outside of the room and the door locked behind them.

Rene' shuddered, a lump in her throat growing. "You OK?" she asked Spencer. They'd both escaped the ambush with only a few scratches, no major wounds, but the drugs had caused plenty of pain. It was only now wearing off.

Spencer pulled at the chains against his wrists, growling. "Fine."

"What was that guy talking about your dad for?" Rene' asked.

"I don't know." His voice was tight. "But it can't be anything good."

She winced. "Are you OK, Spencer?"

Rage burned in his eyes, and he worked his jaw as if holding something back. Rene' didn't know much about Spencer—he'd helped save her from being killed when she was kidnapped the first time. Besides that, she knew he was a loudmouth and a hothead in George's group, but one of George's finest workers.

She'd never stopped and wondered why or how that last detail came to be.

"Listen, Rene', no matter what happens, you need to watch out for yourself." He held her gaze, eyes narrow, heavy with... rage, but sadness too.

Rene' shook her head. "No."

"If you get the chance to run—"

"I'm not running," she snapped. "I can't leave you guys and besides, if either of us could escape and get help, you'd survive better than me. You'd have to go." She refused to abandon him or the other rescues. They deserved freedom, too.

Spencer fumed, but before he could open his mouth, the door opened. Rene' tensed, bracing herself for whatever would happen next.

But it didn't help.

Kelsey flashed a bright smile, pearly whites contrasting against her dark purple lipstick. "Hello, doll! It's been a long time." She wore tight-fit black clothes, her long blonde hair tied up in a ponytail. While she looked older, it wasn't by much.

Rene' froze, blood running cold. This couldn't be happening. *Nonono. Not her.*

Kelsey brushed Rene's tangled brown hair from her face, raising one eyebrow. "What, you didn't miss me? Didn't the town think I was dead? Except Dad, of course."

Rene's heart climbed into her throat, mind going numb. "Dad?"

"Yes, Dad." Kelsey smiled. "He didn't tell you?"

Rene' opened her mouth, voice tight, "Tell me what?" Realizing Kelsey's hand was still on her face, Rene' acted on instinct. She slapped Kelsey hard.

"Oh!" Kelsey stepped back, clutching her cheek. Her brown eyes flashed. "You little b—"

Spencer stepped closer, intervening. "Hands off!"

Kelsey set her pointed jaw, turning. "This isn't about you right now, Anderson."

"You have me in the same room," he snapped. "It's my business now."

Rene' licked her lip, studying Kelsey closely and bracing herself for a blow. *She's worse than she ever was. She'd have to be, wouldn't she? She's trafficking kids.*

And Dad knew?

Kelsey rolled her eyes and smiled at Rene'. "It's not personal, OK, love? But we're running out of bodies and you seemed the easiest option. Don't worry, you'll live."

Rene' held her head high, smirking. "I know I will. What about the others?"

"Same fate as you," Kelsey said cheekily.

"Spence?"

"Oh, you're on a nickname basis now?" Kelsey clicked her tongue. "Well, he obviously can't bear children, but he has a purpose here too. No worries!"

Spencer scowled. "Then back off and leave Rene' alone."

Kelsey eyed him and flashed another smile, batting her eyelashes. "I'd watch your tone with me, dear."

Spencer didn't react and glared at her. Kelsey turned, opening the door again, voice airy. "I'd best let Rex get to work here." She smiled. "Have fun, dears!" She slipped out of the room and a man stepped in after—Rex. He shut the door and a shudder ran up Rene's spine.

Rex sat a small black case on the small table near the door. "You guys tired yet?" He pulled a needle from the case and filled it, watching the dosage closely.

Spencer eyed the needle and grinned. "Just getting started, Clark."

Rex's eyes narrowed as he stepped over, a vein in his neck bulging ever so slightly. "You won't be so quick for a fight before long." He smirked.

Rene' jutted her chin when he approached her, readying the needle. She waited till he was close enough and shot a quick kick to his left knee-cap, but he yanked back, missing the blow. As Rene' jumped back, he swung, shoving the needle deep into Rene's neck. She snarled in pain, the sharp throb shooting panic through her chest.

Spencer swore. "Don't touch her!" He yanked against the chains, grabbing for Rex but he couldn't reach.

Rex pulled the needle away and laughed, eyes boring holes into Rene's. "How's that feel?" he asked. "Still feel like fighting?"

"If you have a bone to pick with me, Rex, deal with me. Don't bring a kid into it," Spencer snapped, pulling on the chains again slowly, his exterior surprisingly calm for someone with white knuckles and gashes forming on their wrists.

Rene' gulped hard but her lungs tightened, like giant claws sank deeper and deeper into her chest. Her skull throbbed as if it might explode and her knees buckled. She dropped to the floor and winced hard, catching herself on her left arm. Rex's laughter filled her ears.

Spencer's voice flooded in again. "We can talk like adults, Rex. C'mon, man. This isn't about the kid."

Rex's voice came short, angry. "No. This is about you. And you're going to tell me everything I want to know. Not tonight, but soon. I'll use the girl and whatever else it takes to get an answer, Anderson, and don't think I haven't gotten my hands on Randy, too."

Rene' leaned against the wall, panting as her head throbbed, her eyelids closing. Fear gripped her—she couldn't sleep. She couldn't sleep when she was bound and that freak was about to hurt her. *Stay awake, focus, don't break*. She pulled in a breath.

"What did you do to Randy?" Spencer asked, voice hard—scared? Rene' couldn't hear him right. A shout followed and the clanking of chains, followed by the door shutting and the click of the lock.

Rex had left but Rene' fought sleep, tears swelling. *Don't panic, breathe.*

Breathe.

She couldn't.

Breathe.

Her lungs grew smaller, smaller, smaller.

Her head pounded, as if it'd grown twice in size, pushing against her skull.

Breathe! "Rene'," Spencer's voice plunged into the darkness surrounding her. "Rene', sleep. It's fine. I've got you."

"No!"

"Sleep." He repeated. "It'll be OK, kid. We're gonna be OK. They'll come."

They'll come.

A sob choked Rene'. *Simon, Dad, Lee, they'd all come, they'll find us and save us. God, let them be OK. Don't let them get hurt.*

Rene' clamped her eyes shut as pain filled her chest. *God, don't let me die.*

CHAPTER THIRTY-FIVE

January 8th, 2028

WEST SAT IN THE large log cabin, staring at a steaming cup of coffee on the table beside a holographic laptop that he was using to watch the US news in live time. George hadn't wasted any time in flying his family to their secure home in Alberta, Canada.

West gritted his teeth, watching the live videos of civilians attacking US officials' homes. A group of rebels and civilians had even stormed the Capitol, the live feed blacking out when the watchers got too close.

The rebels would be shot down. Any civilian who dared lift a hand against the corrupt government would be silenced, their blood staining the stone steps of the Capitol and the news never getting a whiff of it.

West listened to the videos anyway. The people screamed and shouted, chanting, "hang Stuart Landry!" Their angered and broken cries rang in West's ears. He couldn't get them out. Every time a video ended to black, his heart twisted.

How many lives would be lost at the officials' homes? At the Capitol? Word had it from some sources the outbreak was only beginning.

How many civilians had decided to stand up after Cindy's keen intel breakthrough? Would their courage matter, or would they end up smeared against roads with cops standing over them with batons and guns?

"West?" George's voice came from the grand kitchen's doorway. Cindy had Southern charm-esque extravagant taste, and it showed in every house they possessed.

West sighed softly. "Hey, Dad." He straightened, erasing any sign of weakness.

George sat beside him, squeezing his shoulder as he eyed the videos. "Why do you watch that? We get intel sent straight to us. There's no need to watch it."

West shrugged. "Just might pick something else up that's useful."George's eyes narrowed. "You sympathize with these rebels?"

"No." West frowned. "They're asking for death, I know that."

"But still, you grieve over something. What?"

West watched a video for a moment. Young people and old people pushed onward together, battling and shoving against the cops, people dropping from mace and rubber bullets like flies. It was something out of a horror show. So why wasn't he ill from the sight of it? He was used to it, sure. He'd grown up in a horror film.

But this was different.

"I don't know, George. I don't. I see these people beg for death, but don't we beg for this too? We live in constant expectation that we'll be assassinated at any moment," West said. "We're hunted, just as these people are. What makes us different from them? We're just as controlled as they are, aren't we?"

George, instead of bristling or shouting or slapping West like a disobedient child, smiled. "Ah. I see."

"You do?" West tensed.

George reached over, pouring himself a cup of black coffee. "I've been where you are, son."

West waited, unsure how to approach his father's strange exterior. George was never understanding.

"I was young," George said with a chuckle. "And my father was as tough as I am, though I'd say he was far more harsh and strict. I allowed you to part ways, West. I did not stop you from running with the other boys and trying your hand at being normal. What did you find through your experimentation?"

"It wasn't worth it," West answered tiredly. "I always came back to you. I can't run from who I am." These answers were drilled into his very being, but that didn't make them true, did it? He'd tried to be honorable his whole life. He had done good deeds with Jack and the others, all the while hoping those actions would erase who he was—a Johnston. Still, he hadn't run from who he was. He couldn't.

"You have done me proud," George said. "We are a different breed, West. Our legacy, our DNA, it is strong and sacred. But we are still human." A long sigh escaped him. "For now at least we are limited by our physical minds and bodies. If all goes well in technological advancements, perhaps this will not always be so. But it is how it is now, and we still face the grievances that not every person we care for can be allowed life."

West blinked. "I'm not sure I follow, Father." Bile rose in his throat.

"You are grieving." George gestured to the laptop. "Because millions of people have risen up and made it painfully obvious how pathetic and weak they are." He sipped his coffee. "You have grown up aware that the government has complete power over the media and over every single detail the American people have been exposed to, yes?"

"Of course," West said. "You taught me to be smarter than the government and the sheep."

"And you have." George beamed. "You understand the steps the government has taken for an Orwell-like world government, and you understand the psychological state of the world citizens, as well as the plan for our future."

"I do." West chewed his lip.

"Then you grieve for opportunities lost." He nodded in agreement to his own statement. "How many have died for a reckless, fool's cause? Countless and countless more will die shortly. When the super soldiers help the US regain control, the UN will continue the plan for a one world order. You will reign, West. If not the UN's empire, then the empire of the Johnston's here in your homeland. But you must not allow pity for the sheep to cloud your lion's view."

West steeled himself, as usual, and nodded. "Yes, Father. Do not doubt me—I am not doubting our empire."

George hugged him, strong arms tightening around West's shoulders in a strong embrace. "I do not doubt you, son. You have proven yourself worthy. Now, let's sleep. We have work to do in the morning."

CHAPTER THIRTY-SIX

January 9th, 2028

THE DRUGS EASED THE pain in Nate's body, but it did nothing to ease the storm in his mind. By the time the survivors reached Springtown, they were a measly number compared to how they'd started out—a handful of pacifists, a group of survivors from the dome, and wounded thugs from Jordan and Kaleb's men.

They'd survived hell, but at what cost? How many dead had been left behind? How many kids had been burnt up in the attacks? How many families waited in homes for their fathers and brothers to return in vain?

Nate rubbed his aching head and watched the victims be herded into the Springtown buildings. The hospital was overfilled, so people were moving some wounded into the courthouse and some closed shops on mainstreet. The children were ushered to families to sleep and get medical attention.

The bodies were loaded into truck beds to be properly buried in a cemetery at the edge of the town.

Nate texted Simon again without receiving any response. The Fisher men—Mr. Fisher, Lee and his friends, and Howie—had gone off into the battle alone. Even Brett and his pacifist friends had joined the fight, but Nate had been left behind as a wounded.

Anger burned within his chest. He'd be useless in a fight, but he shouldn't be here, sitting around helpless. His body insisted he rest, but his head wouldn't slow down. *I have to help. I have to save my friends.*

Rene' was a good woman. She didn't deserve any of this.

Spencer was a pain in the ass, but he didn't deserve to be strung up and killed. Nate shuddered, remembering the state Simon had been in only weeks earlier at the ruthless hands of Flannery.

Gideon wasn't exactly a good guy either, but he wasn't all that bad. And the survivors the group had taken deserved safety and protection.

Nate had to do something. He had to help.

Pushing himself off the cot, he climbed out of the truck weakly, vision blurring. The wound across his neck and down his torso was bandaged and he didn't think it'd been that deep, just a lot of blood loss.

The world spun and the asphalt grew strangely close—before two strong hands grabbed him from behind.

"Easy, man." A young man—EZ, the boy Reese had been after—held him upright. "You lost a lotta blood. The transfusion didn't magically fix you."

Nate struggled for breath, legs giving out again. "I need to help."

"Can't help if you're dead." EZ sighed. "Come on, a Mrs. Fisher is here waiting to take you home."

Home.

The Fisher farm.

But I didn't deserve to be the one home right now. Everyone but me deserves to be home.

Nate shoved EZ off and braced himself against the truck. *I'll be damned if I act weak in front of Mrs. Fisher.* "Where's Reese?"

"He's helping get wounded inside," he answered tightly. "Why?"

"I need someone to take me to the group. We have to find the others." Nate wouldn't expect EZ to understand —he'd spent his whole life as a rogue without friends or family, judging by what Nate knew.

"You can't, Nate. They left you behind for a reason; you'd slow them down." EZ frowned.

Breathing ragged, Nate looked around again. The last of the injured were moved inside, the trucks almost empty, all of the women and children in safe homes getting attention. A heavy atmosphere hung over the town—every single civilian knew where their mayor was, and that the rest of the Fisher family might not make it back.

What would Springtown do without Mr. Fisher? His son-in-law? His friends? Lee and his group? Rene'?

They needed them.

I need them.

"Go inside, Nate," EZ repeated. Nate took a weak step and caught sight of Mrs. Fisher making her way through the frenzy. Nate tensed, heart dropping to his feet. What would she think of him? Would she be angry? He deserved that.

Mrs. Fisher stepped over, pale. "Nate, you should be resting!" She pulled him into a gentle hug. "Come on, let's get you home; Terri's waiting." Nate froze up but quickly pulled away. "I-I'm still bloody—"

"We'll get you cleaned up," she said, waving a man over. Nate scowled. He didn't want anyone treating him like a child.

"I'm fine, they took care of me."

Mrs. Fisher gave him a cutting frown. "You're coming home."

"But—"

"Don't *but* me, Nathan."

Nate bit his tongue and followed her, legs shaky, EZ still keeping a grip on his arm. He knew better than to argue with Mrs. Fisher. But he still felt worthless.

I've gotta fight. Anger burned in his chest and his stomach twisted. *I should be out there!*

He was led to a truck and got in before passing out.

CHAPTER THIRTY-SEVEN

January 9th, 2028

SPENCER COULDN'T GET OUT of the chains. He'd been captured before and gotten out of stupid chains before—but not this time. They'd stripped him of every weapon and pick he had. Overcome with guilt and rage, he sat there on the floor, blood trickling from his left leg. He'd stood for as long as he could until Rex's last beating, which wiped him of all energy. He couldn't feel his left leg.

"C'mon, Anderson," Rex said. "You don't wanna face Royal. Tell me what I need to know before I keep going on the girl."

"Don't touch her." Spencer spat up some blood.

"You're not leaving me much choice. Royal doesn't like girls, but he won't hesitate to rape her if you don't talk,"

Rex snapped. His temper was flaring, patience worn thin from the past three hours of beatings and mental tactics.

Spencer stared at him, fighting for breath. "Royal?" The name finally hit his consciousness. "What?"

Rex smirked and raised one eyebrow. "Oh, you didn't know?" he jested. "Your trusted ally is a two-faced bitch."

Spencer set his jaw, catching himself quickly. Mind game. Just another mind game. *They don't have Randy. They haven't killed West. Royal isn't a traitor. Stop believing the lies. Hold it together.* He had kept his head about him thus far, he wouldn't crack now.

Rex sighed. "It's not the end of the world, Spence. Tell me what I need to know. Where's Anderson? What intel did he leave with you?"

"I'm telling you the truth—I don't know anything." Spencer snarled and coughed again, pain flooding his chest. "Just let Rene' go. I don't know shit. I would've told you by now if I did, Clark!" A lie, but Spencer wasn't a bad liar when his life depended on it.

Sometimes.

"Bull," Rex said tightly. "He kept you and Randy informed. And he's not dead, so shove it and tell me where he is."

He picked up a knife from the small table, jaw quivering with rage. He'd always been fast to blow his fuse, more so than Spencer and Bo combined. He'd been fun to tease but a good friend too.

Or so Spencer had thought.

He'd never been good at reading people's true intentions, but Randy was.

"Rex, Dad didn't tell us anything. He hated us, remember? You know that. Just let us go! If I'd have ever told you anything about what happened, I would've told you when we were friends!" He gritted his teeth. "But that was a lie too, wasn't it? Just another con? Another job? For this?" Spencer tossed his head toward the door in a brash gesture. "You're working for some slimy bitch who doesn't know what she's getting herself into!"

"We know what we're into, Anderson, and you know it's bigger than what the world thinks. So tell me where your dad is so we can finish this. You want the war to end, don't you? Then rat out one of the scumbags who started it!" Rex held the knife ready against Rene's left thigh, though she didn't wake from her pained slumber.

Spencer forced a breath, rage blinding him. "If I could, I would! I'd sell Dad out in a second! You don't think I would keep that kid safe, moron?"

Rex pushed the knife down with even pressure, cutting through Rene's jeans and straight into flesh. Blood seeped into the fabric, but Rene' didn't even wake.

Claws clamped down on Spencer's heart and a choked sound escaped him. He pulled it together quickly, remembering that he was on a job and he had to focus. "Don't, Rex. You know I'm telling the truth."

"Would Hochberg know?" Rex smiled, that damned sly smile of his that had gotten all of the girls into bed and had gotten all of the boys into fist fights.

"How would I know if Gideon knew about Dad?" Spencer rolled his eyes. "Just, get the knife off her, Rex. This isn't you. You're a creep but you're not—"

"We'll have to take this to the big guns, then." Rex tossed the knife into his pocket, still fuming, but his smirk remained. He stepped over. "I tried, Spencer. Don't say I didn't try giving you two the easy way out. Kelsey might say this isn't personal but it is to us. Isn't it, old pal?" He slapped Spencer lightly, then again, hard enough to make Spencer sway.

Hold it together.

Work the job.

"If I knew, I would've told you—or if you think I know, then I obviously don't care about the girl enough to talk. So why the grand gestures, Rex? Where's the electrocution? Or the game of Twenty Questions? You're wimping out on me. Kelsey won't be happy when she finds out you haven't gotten your answers yet," Spencer said, voice casual. "What's holding you back?"

Rex flashed a grin and straightened. "For starters, we're not allowed to get the girl pregnant. And second, well, Royal didn't want me to mess you up too bad. Said he has something in mind." He headed for the door, yawning. "I did warn you, Anderson." With that, he left the room and locked the door.

Spencer cast one weary glance toward the table, but Rex hadn't left anything to be used as a means to escaping. Spencer groaned in pain and leaned back against the wall.

Hours ticked by. The pale dawn light started creeping into the window, past the blinds, beckoning Spencer to close his eyes.

He forced his eyes open. "Rene'?" he whispered, but it wasn't any use. She was out good, the cut on her leg still bleeding. Spencer couldn't reach her to stop the bleeding or to shake her awake.

We're hopeless.

How did this happen? Was this what George warned me about? If George knew someone was after me and Randy, and he warned us—no, he wouldn't send help. Who will come? Randy? West and Jack won't. And if Rex isn't bluffing, and they have Hochberg... no, they couldn't have Gideon. Focus, Spencer! Help, whoever that is, will come. Mr. Fisher, at least, will come for Rene'. Then I can help get her home.

He couldn't grasp onto hope, no matter how he tried. Before he could try to rest, the door opened again and a large, buff man came over and pulled Spencer up, undoing his chains. Another man pulled Rene' from the room, and they were led down the hall. Rene' woke weakly, staggering, disoriented expression paling.

They were dragged into a bathroom. The tub was full of clear water and Rex waited nearby, expression tight. "I asked nicely, Spencer."

Spencer's gut wrenched. Rex pulled up a small holographic pad and faced Rene', lifting the screen. "Spencer, tell me what I need to know, or this will be little miss mayor's girl's fate."

The video was a short compilation of clips—clips of women in labs, some pregnant, some screaming in pain, and some images of dead victims, all in flashing precession. Rene' paled and stepped back, but the man held her tight by her wrists.

"Don't touch her!" Spencer hissed. "Just let her go, Rex! I'll talk!"

"Don't talk," Rene' forced.

Rex laughed and took Rene', forcing her into the tub as she struggled hard. "Don't talk?" he asked. "You're just asking for some trouble."

"Rex!" Spencer jerked hard, but a few more guards rushed in and pulled him back.

"Is your future not scary enough?" Rex grabbed Rene' by her long hair and shoved her head down into the water

Spencer jerked hard, every fiber of his being screaming. "Rex! Let her go! I'll talk! Dad was part of the war!"

Rex held Rene's head into the water. She splashed and struggled weakly, frigid water hitting Spencer. He kept fighting. "Dad left! That's all I know!"

Rex let Rene' come up for air. She gasped and sputtered, pushing her arms out against the tub wall. Her body racked with sobs, desperate for air. Rex grinned at Spencer. "Not good enough, Spence." He yanked Rene' off balance and plunged her head back into the water.

Spencer's arms were behind him but he jerked himself sideways, grabbing the gun off the guard to his right. He fired the gun into the man's groin, unable to make another shot. The second guard yanked Spencer back, but Spencer kicked out and broke the man's left knee. The third guard immediately disarmed Spencer but he slammed his head into the man's face, blood spurting from the thug's nose. "Let her go, Rex!" he roared.

More thugs came in and slammed Spencer against the floor, pinning him prostrate. The man with the gunshot wound kept screaming at the top of his lungs in agony.

Rex pulled Rene' from the water, sighing. "You two just insist on making things hard, don't you?" He tossed Rene' at a man, fuming. "Let's roll out, guys."

Rene' gasped and coughed up water, shaking like a leaf in the wind. They pulled her out of the room, water pouring from her clothes, and the other thugs dragged Spencer up. "Don't fight again," a thug warned. "Or we'll take it out on the girl."

Spencer glanced at the man still screaming from his wound. More men came and helped the man out. Spencer spat on them as they passed.

If I fight again, she suffers.

If I tell the truth, she suffers.

How do I win this?

We could run. But another part of him refused. That was the coward's way out. He wouldn't follow his dad's footsteps anymore.

CHAPTER THIRTY-EIGHT

January 8th, 2028

"WE USED TO BE an unstoppable force, the three of us," Kaleb mused, focusing on the road before him. His armored truck hadn't failed him yet, and it better not now.

"Did Hunter ever come outta hiding?" Jeremy asked, shuffling through some files on Kaleb's phone.

"Recently, yeah."

"How'd the kids take it?"

"Not sure," Kaleb said, sighing. "It's been... busy."

"You can catch me up later." Jeremy smirked. "So, where is the big guy?"

"He ran to Canada."

"West and Cindy, too?"

"Yeah."

"So the kid really tried to take this on himself, huh?" Jeremy sighed softly, rubbing a temple as he kept reading the files. He'd been in the domes for years, only grabbing hints and rumors of the state of the world and political affairs. For a man like Jeremy, the forced arrogance had been challenging.

"Yeah, he did. I'm not sure what it is about these kids but..."

"They learned from the best." Jeremy's voice was dry.

"We weren't that bad. Hunter and I always stuck together, and when you came along, Jordan joined, too. We were a team. These kids... they just rush into things blindly, trying to keep each other safe by leaving each other behind." Kaleb scowled.

"Hm." Jeremy raised an eyebrow. "SO you don't remember the times you got yourself in trouble—alone?"

"Shut up."

"You haven't changed a bit." Jeremy chuckled wearily. "How's Nate? I saw he got wounded."

"He'll recover. He'd recover faster if he rested, but he'll no doubt be on board to hunt down Gideon and the others." Kaleb shook his head. "I worry about him, J. It got worse after you left."

"Tell me later." Jeremy cut him off, as if knowing it didn't need to be discussed yet. "After we hit George, where are we going next?"

Kaleb gave him a coy smirk. "You know where we're going next."

"And then?" Jeremy's face was hard as stone. He'd always been an ace at hiding any emotion or feeling behind an unreadable expression.

"I'm in the mood to kill some officials and the Union president, but we'll decide after the news gets back how the rebels did."

"Think we'll get a chance to take out super soldiers?" Jeremy mused wryly.

"Always was a dream of yours." Kaleb rolled his eyes.

"SEALs have to have a new challenge every once and awhile."

"You survived in a dome for years, that wasn't enough to set you for life?"

Jeremy made a face. "What do you think?"

Kaleb sped up on the highway, grunting. "Stick with us, J. It'll be worse than old times."

"Is Hunter coming with?"

"Hunter's probably already there."

"Did he dismantle the web?"

"Not yet, but he has someone else on that. We're not as tech savvy as we used to be. Times changed."

"I know."

"It changed even more so in the past few years," Kaleb warned.

"Can people still marry sex dolls?"

"Sex bots, and yeah." Kaleb made a face.

Jeremy sighed. "I should've stayed in the dome."

"I'm starting to wish you had—you won't shut up.""The best company I had for years were kids, a man who would strike at his own shadow, and a rat I named Herb. Give me a break," Jeremy snapped.

"Would you give me one right now?"

Jeremy huffed. "Sure, that's what friends do."

"Then I'll ease off."

Jeremy paused for a long moment. "Have any of them got a girl yet?"

"Just Si." Kaleb frowned. "Why?"

Jeremy glanced out the window, his answer absent. "Just wondering."

"Don't worry. This has to end sometime. They'll have futures." Kaleb steeled himself, holding onto that truth with everything in him.

"You didn't used to be this optimistic."

"It's not optimism. I just won't let anything else happen to them."

Jeremy reached over and roughly slapped Kaleb's shoulder. "That makes all of us, cowboy."

"Don't call me that.""Texan?"

"Go back to sleep, J. This is gonna be a long drive."

CHAPTER THIRTY-NINE

January 8th, 2028

"IT IS ON THIS day, January 8th, 2028, that I announce the Union's official surrender to the Confederate Army, and I will give my seat in the Oval Office to President Larry Simmons. This surrender is made in hopes that Larry will unite the states once again and bring the UN that we love dearly." The Union President spoke calmly, voice passionate and controlled, in front of the live recorder for the whole world to see.

Stu didn't dare move or say a falsehood—he was under the aim of a gun from across the room, courtesy of Brian's finest soldiers.

But something more had happened. Hunter had paid the president off himself with more cash than Brian ever thought the president would settle for. "He doesn't want to die and he knows we'd kill him if we don't get our way," Hunter had said.

Apparently, politicians were more ball-less and greedy than Brian imagined. This man was supposed to be the president and protect the nation and fight for justice—and he had surrendered over the cause he'd fought so long for. And why? For cash? His life?

Brian set his jaw harder and watched, waiting beside Lavi as the previous President stepped down. He told the citizens of the US to depart from their rioting and burning, return home, and obey the new command. "It will bring us peace," Stu continued. "Your husbands and sons can come home. We will come out of this brother's war stronger and more united than ever. God bless you, and God bless this nation."

The feed cut out, and Fernando finished handling the tech side of the situation, whistling. "Not bad, President."

"Traitors," Stu seethed, his calm, pristine exterior flashing red with a snarl. "You work for the government and this is how you turn on us?"

"We work for the people," Lavi corrected, his accent hinted with amusement. "Not you."

Stu opened his mouth to speak but President Larry cut him off easily. "Thank you, Stu. I understand this was not easy to do, but we both want peace, and this is truly the only way to end the war without the slaughter of half the nation's population. Isn't that a win?" He smiled, every word eerily proper.

"The only reason I surrendered is because we are not prepared if Russia attacks, and I'd rather you and your damn hicks take the fall and the death count," Stu hissed. "You can't run this nation—it despises you. When the UN turns on you and Russia jumps in for power, the Union won't save you."

"You're right." President Larry chuckled. "It won't because it won't exist anymore. See, Stuart, the thing about us good ol' country boys is that we're not scared of a fight if it's for the right reasons. You just sold your nation out to save your life. I know good Union men, men who proudly serve their government and their cause with good hearts. We don't agree on everything, but we don't cut each other's throats, either. And you betrayed those men."

Brain stepped over and grabbed Stu's arms, cuffing him with military grade tech cuffs. "That's enough, sir. Let's go."

Bosch took over and led the previous President out of the small office. Once they were gone, President Larry turned to Brian and Vice President Smith. "The troops are moving in. We don't have much time. The citizens are angry and we need to calm them down—and we need to send backup to the—"

"I have it covered." Brian held up a hand. "Some platoons are going AWOL. Lavi got word before Stu went live—soldiers are leaving like we did. They'll be there to help, sir. Some of us still want a republic. The battle isn't just yours."

"The Union commanders and leaders won't back down this easily. Not without one last fight. As we speak, both sides are raging."

"We'll handle them."

"Then let's get to it," President Larry said, leading them out.

IN THE NIGHT, THE soldiers came again, a large fleet of super enhanced men marching through the underground tunnels. President Larry ordered a group of his men to ready defenses, but Brian led his men first. Their plans to end the raging battles were cut to a cruel stop.

"We'll take the brunt," he said. "You boys be ready for the rest."

The thugs, Bo and Nabeel, followed like dogs. An eager grin plastered on his face, Bo said, "We're going into the tunnels?"

"If we have to." Brian hesitated. Who was he kidding? At the rate they'd gone before, none of them would make it through the night.

The supersoldiers weren't as badass as the debriefings had said—they were worse. They were re-equipped to take over the very structure they'd been hard-wired to defend. The White House had been ready to take the soldiers out if they turned, and the scientists had readied the soldiers for those defenses, rendering the House defenseless.

Brian and his crew were the rebel's last chance. If they lost the fight till more rebel soldiers came, the enhanced fighters would win.

The group readied in the underground, the same streamline of defenses prepared as before. The bombs were ready to roll—even some laser technology Brian hoped the soldiers weren't equipped to withstand. Besides Bo's incessant babbling, they loaded guns in silence. .

But the attack hit them faster than they'd calculated.

"The cams are out." Lavi's voice came urgently over the comms. "I can't see the halls, General."

The lights immediately went out and Bo swore. "I thought we had control over the damn house?"

Brian cocked his gun and turned on his headlamp, voice tight. "We did. They must've found a way to kick us off."

The door to the underground unsealed and opened, leaving the White House vulnerable to the super soldiers. Bosch swore. "How'd they get back on?"

"I've lost control over the defenses. Don't enter the tunnels—the defenses are theirs," Lavi piped up sharply. "Just focus on taking the soldiers out," Brian ordered. "We can take them by hand."

They couldn't, but they wouldn't go down without a fight.

The soldiers flooded the halls, their footsteps almost silent on the tunnel floors, immediately firing at the opening. The rebel soldiers stood their ground at first, firing the first row of super soldiers down like flies, but it was dozens of enhanced soldiers against a group of exhausted men.

We have to do better. Brian fired a soldier down and darted for the door that led upstairs. "Lead them in!" he snapped through the comms. "We can pick them off upstairs. If we stay in this room, we're dead!"

The rebel soldiers held fast, one man arguing. "If they reach the top floors, they'll kill the president!"

And then he dropped as a super soldier's bullet pierced his skull.

"General, there's more enhanced coming on the White House grounds." Lavi's voice broke through the chaos of men's shouts and gunfire. "We're surrounded."

Brian growled and shoved Fernando toward the door. "Everyone move back!"

Bo dropped beside him, screaming in agony as a large round ripped through his leg. With the firepower the enemy had, Brian's men would be beaten senseless.

"Move out!"

Nabeel snatched Bo up and tossed him over his shoulders like a sack of potatoes, fending off the soldiers with his AR-15 at the same time. Brian's crew moved backwards for the door, some of the falling, but all of them shooting like champs.

A gunshot went off in his comm, sharp and distinct from the chaos around him. "Lavi?" he snapped, pulling a fallen comrade from the ruckus. The super soldiers advanced despite the crew's attempt at retreat.

No response.

"Shut the door!" a rebel screamed. "We'll hold them off!" About seven rebel soldiers remained at the opening of the tunnels, somehow withstanding the enemy's force —and willing to die there, protecting their president.

"Shit!" Pulling the man into the hall, Brian turned and slammed the second door shut, leaving the rebels to their fate.

"They're on the grounds, Brian. We need—" Fernando began, but Brian cut him off. His crew and a few wide-eyed rebel soldiers tensed when screams and cries rang out from the door they'd just enclosed.

"We can't let them reach the president," Brian snarled. "We start phase two!" If fire launchers, RPGs, and gunfire didn't stop the enemy from all sides... Brian would have to find something that did and fast. But if they were surrounded from all sides and had few numbers to begin with...

We'll have to assault our way out. It's a slim chance. It's all we have.

The crew shared his realization no doubt, but obeyed orders and moved out, toward the top floor. Nabeel carried Bo like a ragdoll, but Bo was out cold. Besides that, no wounded were dragged along—no one else had made it and were left behind.

Lavi's comm snapped to life, "Sir, they're breaking through defenses on top floors."

"Get the Presidents and get ready for a retreat," Brian snapped. "We'll fight 'em off as long as possible, but they have the upper ground. We'll abort."

Their last chance to win the war and they'd just lost it.

CHAPTER FORTY

January 8th, 2028

"HEY, GIDEON," A SOFT voice came from nearby, right beside Gideon's left ear. Gideon's blood ran cold, and he jerked upright but something tight restrained him. "Easy, Gid, take it easy."

The voice. The truck. The attack. The crash.

Percy.

Gideon snarled and lifted his head that felt heavy—he'd been drugged. Hadn't he? A hand gently smoothed his hair back and sweat trickled down Gideon's back. His vision blurred but Percy stood beside him, a smirk on his pale face. "There you are," he said gently. "Don't fight the constraints, it won't do you any good and we have work to do."

Gideon's breathing hitched. Pain throbbed from the back of his spine upward. "Percy, what are you doing?" He kept his tone even. He was in control of himself if nothing else. He wouldn't lose that control.

Percy's smile brightened. "Working the job, Gid. You know I've always been good at it. Better than anyone else besides you."

Gideon gritted his teeth and snatched against the binds holding him, each limb tied to a post of a small bed. "What part of the job is this?" Gideon didn't have any clothes on so he didn't have anything on him to break free with.

"The fun one." Percy smiled. "I need some answers, Gid. When you give them to me, you, Rene', and Spencer can all go home. The victims will too, but only if you tell me more."

"You were good, Percy, but I still know when you're lying." Gideon didn't look away, anger rising. "You lied to us. Why?"

Percy's smile flickered. "I lied to protect you. All of you."

"How?" Gideon snapped. "By torturing me for intel?" He didn't dare ask what this was about. Not yet. A part of him expected to wake up in a cold sweat in bed with Alex down the hall and Noah up too late roaming the halls. His nightmares were something he could fight and handle.

This was real.

"I'm not going to torture you." Percy's expression hardened. "I know that's basically useless. The only thing that might make you talk would closely kill you, considering the lack of medic supplies or docs we have here."

"Where are we?"

"I'm not gonna hurt you like that. You wouldn't break, and I need answers. I'm trying to help, Gid. If you care about the others, about the war, help me."

"You're going to have to explain what the hell you're doing, Percy. You took me out and kidnapped me. I don't trust you right now."

Percy sat on the edge of the bed with a sigh. "Remember when we were teenagers, Gid? Before the world went to hell, you told me that you'd fight with me."

"I said I'd fight with my friends," Gideon said tightly. "And I have."

"No," Percy said. "You've played god."

Gideon studied him without a word.

"You've led your band of merry men to every disaster you could find. You've had us in hodunk freaking nowhere —for what? For Springtown? For those pacifists? All these years, you manage to keep George in the dark and still cause chaos. It's what I love about you," he smiled. "But I know there's more to it."

"There's really not." Gideon's mind spun, but he controlled his reaction.

"You're looking for someone," Percy said. "Maybe not consciously, but I think you're after someone. More importantly though, is the fact you've fooled George while still being one of his right hands." Percy laughed. "I've watched you do it for years. Helped you do it, too. It's been thrilling, Gid. The game of cat and mouse we've played. The risks we've taken together—"

"What is this about, Percy?" Gideon cut in, voice cold.

"Well, the war is ending." Percy gestured with his hands. "And the new states will need someone to run them."

"You?" Gideon asked. The pain in his lower back throbbed steadily but he ignored it.

"Us." Percy grinned. "Think about it, Gid. Years of working, years of being the bad guys, we can take this easily. We take out the rest of the leaders and we purge the nation of the weak."

Gideon swallowed the bile in his throat, stomach twisting. *He can't be serious. This isn't him. This can't be him.* But Gideon knew it was, and no amount of good memories could change the fact Percy had betrayed them. The faster Gideon could work through the denial, the better for everyone. "All right... Then why do you have me tied up for intel?"

"Kelsey." Percy sighed heavily. "She doesn't know what I want for us."

"What does *she* want from me?"

"Intel on your family and the gang, all the info you have on George. George has a pretty penny on his head right now. We want it. If the world knows we took out one of the most hated leaders in the US, we'll be set," he said firmly. "You'll end one legacy for yourself, Gid, and we can start a new one."

The bile rose again. "We can't trust Kelsey, Percy." *Work the job. They have Spencer, Rene', and the survivors. Work the damn job.*

Percy sighed, shaking his head. "She won't be a problem. I have her under control. She's greedy, not controlling anymore."

"So she's letting you run this gig?"

Percy leaned forward slightly. "I learned from the best." He winked.

"You always were obsessed with trickery." Gideon didn't budge.

A laugh escaped Percy and his expression darkened. "What, skinshifting? You remember that from when we were kids?"

"A little." Mostly because it'd scared Gideon. He hadn't liked fiction as a teenager. Percy's myths and folklore had ruined it for him.

"It amazes me how humankind will cling to the idea of changing skin, as if we can't already." Percy leaned back and gestured at himself. "We both played a good part, Gideon. The noble shadow in the dark and the dutiful servant by his side. But it's over now. Tell me what you know about George, your family, and the war, and we can start over together. You know things I don't and we need that knowledge." Despite his ludicrous claims, Percy's tone was gentle, genuine.

He had lost his goddamn mind.

Gideon licked his lips, glancing at the door. "I can't do that without knowing the others will be released immediately after. I'll stay with you, Percy. But the others have to go."

Percy's eyes lit up. "You'll—"

"But let me see the others," Gideon said.

"I can't." Percy smoothed his black hair back with a tattooed hand. "Just tell me what we need to know before Kelsey gets impatient. She's hard to cool down when she gets going."

Gideon set his jaw and considered his options: tell the whole truth about things, tell the half truth, or say nothing.

The latter was his default option, though if they had Rene' and Spencer, they'd no doubt use them against Gideon. Both had been tortured enough, though Spencer could handle it more. Knowing Kelsey's MO with her use of getting what she wanted no matter the cost, Gideon figured they'd use Rene' to get to Gideon, and he'd still have to talk and spare her, or keep silent and watch her get raped.

"I know what you're thinking." Percy sighed. "And I don't want anyone else to get hurt any more than you do. So please, talk to me."

Pain throbbed and seared from Gideon's back and his vision went muddled again. "I can't, Percy. Not without knowing they're safe."

"You can't take my word?"

"Not this time, Percy." The words almost choked him.

"Don't get upset. You know you're enjoying this, too. You're a blind man, Gideon. You're living a life that will only be destroyed. I'm the only one trying to open your eyes. I'm giving you a future." Percy's voice tightened. "It's taken all this to get your attention. That's not my fault."

"I can't tell you everything, Percy." Gideon snapped coldly.

"Why not? I've done all of this, Gideon. I've balanced keeping your lives protected and giving Flannery what he wants. I can handle running the US with you—I just need what you have. Talk to me." Percy set his jaw, vein in his forehead throbbing.

"You..." Gideon paused. The attacks, the jet bomb, Flannery always getting out in time... "It was all you?"

"Most of it. Not all." Percy smirked. "So talk, Gideon. If we combine what we know, no secrets allowed, we can fix this war."

"No." The word grated Gideon's heart. He knew this fight wouldn't last. He knew someone would get hurt if he kept quiet.

But he couldn't help the enemy.

Not yet.

"Then I'll have to make you scream a little." Percy's voice fell heavy, rough. "Just a little..." He moved closer and Gideon couldn't push him off, the drug finally setting in, immobilizing his bruised body.

CHAPTER FORTY-ONE

January 8th, 2028

"WE'RE GETTING CLOSER," SIMON said tightly. "But they keep moving." He rubbed the back of his neck, watching the world fly past. Mr. Fisher had taken a turn driving so the soldiers could get some rest, but the vehicle wasn't going fast enough to suit Simon.

Mr. Fisher, eerily silent, didn't respond. His phone rang and he reached to answer it, but froze when he did. "Who is this?"

Simon leaned up, eyes narrowing. Was it the kidnappers? Kelsey? No, Mr. Fisher would recognize her voice.

"Where?" Mr. Fisher asked quickly. "Are you sure?"

Simon listened but couldn't hear the voice on the other end. His heart pounded in his chest, hopes lifting ever so slightly. Every update he'd gotten so far had been good, but not what he wanted: the whole crew of soldiers and survivors, those remaining after the attacks, had reached Springtown with Richard. Doctor Vince had joined them to help, and Ty had texted that he too was there as aid.Good news, all of it, that their mission was mildly successful, but not the news he wanted.

"Thank you; we're on our way." Mr. Fisher hung up.

"Who was that?"

"Travis." Mr. Fisher focused on driving, voice sharp.

"Travis?" Simon blinked.

The rogue had stopped them once before, when they'd brought Rene' home from Jed's clutches. That kidnapping had been Gideon and West's fault. But this one? This one was Simon's.

"He says he knows where the group is going, a different lead since the soldiers stopped getting updates.""Their friends are probably busy in battles right now," Simon said bitterly. "Let's trust Travis. He wouldn't lie. Dad trusts him." Simon was desperate for a lead that got him closer to Rene' and the others. Their rescue team was large but moved fast enough to make good progress, but Simon's patience was nonexistent.

"I'll change routes. Text the others and message Randy the details." He wasn't going to ask the soldiers permission and showed a small soft side for Randy, who'd raced to join the team on their expedition. Randy had sounded crushed on the phone last time he called and Mr. Fisher was probably trying to offer the loner some help. "Travis says the group had grown."

Simon frowned deeply. "You think... do you think that's where Gideon was taken?" They'd gotten word he'd vanished with Percy shortly after it happened but Simon hadn't allowed himself to think of it.

Mr. Fisher's expression grew hard as iron. "It's possible."

"But he's..." Simon rubbed his temples. "Taking Rene' and the survivors I understand, they can be used in the labs, but Spence? Gideon? They're men. Why would the trafficking ring want them?" Every time he allowed himself to voice a question burning in his mind, he'd wished he hadn't.

"I don't know, son, but we'll find them. We'll fix this." A long pause, and Mr. Fisher's cold voice added, "Vengeance is the Lord's and He's not finished with this. Neither are we."

Simon nodded, texting the others and giving Randy a short call. Mr. Fisher gave him the new route and he put it into the GPS for better guidance. Even as he worked, the image of Rene' curled up in pain the first time they'd helped her back to freedom burned in his head. The questions flooded his mind but he slammed the walls backup. No time for emotions. He'd save her and then deal with them later.

"Mr. Fisher?" he asked, forcing his voice steady.

"What?"

"I can take a turn driving, sir."

"Later," he said. "AJ and his team are headed this way— with extra arms and ammo. Help me make sure that Brett and his boys get their share, all right? They won't be any help unarmed."

They probably wouldn't be helpful with arms, since they'd never practiced and had only fought for the first time the night of the ambush, but Simon didn't say so. "Yessir."

Simon watched the world go by in a blur, chest tightening. By accident, the thought popped into his head, *what if the world hadn't changed the way it did? What if I'd met Rene' in a normal nation? I could take her out to expensive restaurants and concerts. We could talk for hours on end. I could buy her whatever she wanted—I'd have a normal job and Dad would still be rich, I guess, so I could earn enough to give her a nice house and animals and—*he stopped, heart heavy and sinking lower. *I failed her. I failed her after I promised this wouldn't happen. How can*

I try to stay with her after this? Mr. Fisher won't say it but I know he thinks the same. She'd be better off without me. Maybe I am just a gangster's son. Maybe even God can't change me.

CHAPTER FORTY-TWO

January 9th, 2028

THE WEE HOURS OF the morning were George's favorite. So much could be done in those hours, while the nation lay sleeping soundly in their beds, accepting their caged fate as noble freedom. It had been a long career, and George finally had tastes of the fruit he reaped—it would only get better. He would rule the nation and pass it to West. West could continue the Johnston Empire and conquer Canada, Mexico—

A knock on the office door jerked George from his fond reveries. "Who is it?"

"Dad, I need you." West's choked voice, hard as stone but near broken.

George opened the door quickly and helped West in, gently lowering him on the thick-padded desk chair. "Easy son, it's all right."

Sweat rolled down West's temple and neck, his face pale and twisted in pain. His ragged breaths made George's blood run cold. "West, what hurts?" He steadied him.

"I-I can't breathe," West forced, clutching George's arm, grip firm but weak. George smoothed his tangled hair back, opening his desk drawer and pulling out a small box. West struggled and gasped, eyes dark with agony. George unlocked the case and withdrew a vial and needle from a locked box.

"Hold on, son, this should help." George filled the needle with the correct dosage for a man of West's large size before capping the vial again. The specific drugs for the Test side effects had been used once and it was too precious to waste—but George had waited long enough.

"Here." He injected the fluid into the vein in West's arm, jaw tight. Had George waited too long? The side effects could have already wreaked havoc on West's body. If he was weak, he couldn't lead—

West groaned in pain, a cry escaping him as he crumbled. George caught him. "You have to tell me where—"

"Everywhere," West gasped. "I-I can't move my legs, Dad."

Anger flared in George's chest. "Why didn't you tell me the episodes were this bad?" he demanded. "I could have helped sooner, boy!"

But the pain flooding his son's face gripped him, and George gently wrapped his arms around West, smoothing his hair back. "Just breathe. I'll hold you up, just focus on breathing."

West coughed hard, breathing ragged, panicked. It wasn't like West to panic. George gripped him firmly, "You have to calm down, West," he said firmly. "Don't panic. You're safe."

"I think my heart," West gasped, "my heart is giving out, Dad. Oh, God—" he clutched George's arm tighter, growing paler.

George grasped him by his face, words sharp. "Enough of that. Breathe. Focus on me. Take a breath. Your heart is fine!"

West forced a shaky breath, face full of terror. George had seen the pathetic display of pain before, but not often. The first time, West had been ten, and following one of George's strict beatings, the boy had fallen into a horrible panic attack which he got scolded for.

"Strong men never panic, even in pain," George reminded West, wiping sweat from West's face. "Remember? Now breathe."

West dragged in another breath, clamping his eyes shut briefly.

"I know it hurts but focus on breathing. Focus on me." George kissed his forehead. "It's all right, boy."

West leaned against him. It took a few minutes for the medication to take a hold of him but his breathing mellowed out and his body grew slack. George rubbed his back, sighing. "There you are. It's all right. Can you move yet?"

West groaned again, pain lacing his words, "S-sorta." His legs trembled. George patted his back. West shuddered softly, "I'm sorry, Dad. I'm so sorry."

George squeezed West's shoulders gently when the door to the office opened. George sighed. "Cindy, I've got—" He froze mid-sentence, heart lurching to his throat.

Hunter and Kaleb Savage stepped into the room with another man behind them, all clad in black with masks on that they lowered upon entrance. Kaleb gave a small smirk. "Miss us? We finished the jobs you gave, figured we needed a little meeting. A recap, if you will."

George's anger flared. They were the best of the best—if they wanted to get past his security, they would've, even if he'd strived to keep that from happening again. "What is there to discuss?" he asked. "I gave you enough work for at least a week with the state of the nation the way it is."

Hunter closed the door and stepped over, expression unreadable but his eyes glinted. "Yeah. You gave us plenty of work. Orders to kill soldiers while they slept in camps. Orders to loot more towns so the labs have more bodies to mess with—gave me a list of men to kill."

"Did you take care of it, as you say?" George released his grip on West. "There's plenty more to take care of—"

"And yet, here you are, safe and sound in your cabin." Kaleb came over but the third man kept his mask on. George tried but couldn't recognize the stranger. "Like a little rat." Kaleb's eyes narrowed. "While we get killed for your empire."

George cocked his head. "You two are speaking strangely, Kaleb. I'd watch what I say. The war is challenging everyone and tension is high, but there's no need to allow emotion to cloud your judgement."

Hunter laughed. "Our judgement has been clouded for decades, George. We've been blind men." He glanced back at the others. "But now, we see. Not just that…"

"We're doing something about it," Kaleb said firmly. "Your cabin is on lockdown, we have men outside, and you know the best part about this ambush, George?" A smile cracked his lips.

George scowled. "What are you thinking—"

"Cindy let us in," Kaleb said softly. "Opened the front door up and let us waltz in."

George's heart hammered in his throat. He forced a calm breath, immediately chastening himself for allowing a brief moment of response. "That's very funny."

"And I distracted you." West's voice came, soft yet firm, and he lifted his head and stood from the chair. A pained expression fell over him. "I'm sorry, Dad. I love you. But this can't go on."

Rage filled George's chest and blinded his vision. He reached for the top desk drawer, but Hunter grabbed him by his arm and threw him back against the wall. A picture frame rammed against George's back, and a few frames clattered to the floor, the glasses shattering.

"What the hell?" he snarled. "West, this is your Empire! You can have everything. You can lead the people—you can lead them to prosperity. Isn't that what you want?"

"No," West said, meeting his father's gaze. "I don't want your legacy. I want freedom—for me and for the world."

George swung hard at West, but Hunter blocked his path and laughed.

George hissed, "you still need me. I'm leading this game; you need the information I have to end the war! I have too much power for you to kill me now!" His voice rose with unbridled rage.

"Ah, that's where you're wrong," Kaleb opened the mini bar cabinets and pulled out a whiskey and a shot glass. "Good men don't hesitate to pull the trigger." He eyed the masked man. "So, see, George, we'll get our info. We'll end the war. The way God intended—without the aid of the enemy." He filled the glass and sat it onto the desk, smiling. "And you'll die the way God intended too, with one last drink and for just a few of the men you wronged to watch. Scared?"

"I'm your master," George said, voice trembling. "You can't do this. I've done everything to help you people, to help this nation, the only way I could—the only way it deserves. How am I the monster?"

THE HINT OF DOUBT slammed West's heart as soon as he saw his father's fear. He'd never seen George scared in his life. *He's scared of dying.* For a split moment, a part of West begged, *give in, stop this, don't let him die. He's your father!*

But the other part immediately cut the fear down.

He is not your father.

He's murdered hundreds. He's tortured innocent people. He ruined Hunter's life and he caused Rene's torture. He killed Ed and the others. He hurt my family.

He needs to die. He has to. Even if it hurts.

Jesus, help me.

"Take the drink, George," Hunter said. "We have a lot of work we have to get to, after all."

George's hands shook and he clenched them, knuckles white. "No. I refuse to die like this. I've saved this nation from a fate worse than war. All my decades in government and the gangs, and you think I'm the monster? You're a fool, each of you!" He faced West, red with rage. "Tell them to back down, West. Now."

West stepped closer. "You've killed my friends, George. You've smothered every dream I've had." A pause, a breath. "You're going to die here if it's the last thing I do."

Hunter cut into the tension with a chuckle, "But first, we're waiting for a friend of ours."

George didn't lift a hand against West again but faced Kaleb and Hunter. "You will be hunted," he said coldly. "You three and West—when word reaches the masses and my men that I am dead, you will each die for this."

The words clawed into West's chest, but he let them and smiled in response. George was afraid, after the years of reigning with terror, he had a taste of his own poison. It wouldn't be enough—he deserved more, but perhaps God would take care of the rest.

George reached into his coat for his phone but West stopped him, whispering into George's ear. "If you love me and Mom, you won't fight."

George's eyes flickered but he yanked free, hand dropping. He stared at West as if he'd spoken in tongues. West's resolve strengthened as he looked into the eyes of the man who had abused him, lied to him, and killed his friends.

Footsteps sounded from the hall. George's face fell blank when Guns walked into the office with a small whistle. "Hello, George. You took my advice and ran; I'm sorry it hasn't worked out as neatly as I explained." His eyes shone.

A vein in George's neck bulged, and his face grew eerily pale. "So it's been you?"

"Me. Cindy. West. Gideon. A small handful of us with many, many helpers." Guns glanced at the three men behind him now, his hand clasping George's shoulder. "We lost a few. It took effort on Kaleb and my parts when you killed Robert, but the plan was what he died for, so we honored that."

West looked away briefly, chest aching at the mention of his friend who George had executed by Kaleb himself.

"Robert's blood is on Kaleb's hands," George said darkly. "I'm not the monster here! You know that Guns, better than anyone. Don't do this. You need me."

Guns raised his eyebrow. "Have a fun time explaining yourself in hell." He patted George one last time on the back, stepping back.

The masked man stepped past Hunter and Kaleb, unholstering a small pistol. George's eyes flickered. The man pulled his mask off, a cold, small smirk on his face.

"You should have left my boy alone, George." He leveled the gun.

After they registered the look of pure horror on George Johnston's face and the flash of fear in his eyes, Jeremy pulled the trigger.

Blood splattered against the picture frames clinging to the wall. George's body crumpled with a resounding thump, but West hardly heard it. Hot blood burned his face—George's blood.

His father's blood.

West stepped closer, legs shaking. The lethal shot to the head closed the last chapter of West's old life. A man feared by all with an unstoppable empire lay dead.

Just like that.

West's body froze. He couldn't move, his head heavy like every part of his body shut down. Strong hands gripped his shoulders, and he sank against Hunter weakly, shuddering.

"It's over," Hunter said. "Richard's on his way. We have a lot to do, boy. Are you able to go?"

West jerked a nod but no words left him. *My father is dead.*

God, it's over and it's only beginning... but You made it happen.

Jeremy holstered his gun and turned away. "Don't let Cindy see the body, K. You've got five minutes to get rid of it and we head out."

West steeled himself, his insides shattering for only a moment. He clasped Hunter's shoulder. The drug George gave him still kept him steady, but his exhaustion and his episode had not been faked, though originally the distraction was supposed to be feigned.

"I'm fine," he said softly. "Kaleb, I'll help, just, let me be with him for a minute. Please."

The men exchanged dubious glances but left the room quickly. West forced a breath and knelt beside George's body. Blood pooled from his distorted head and stained the dark wood floors. West shut his eyelids, the image of the hollow eyes stuck in his mind forever, and rummaged in his father's pockets. He took his phone, wallet, the watch from Richard and George's father, and a small case of cards and keys. West pocketed everything he found off his father's body, mind blank, all emotion subsided.

Until he finished and was left alone in the room with the body of the man he'd loved.

West licked his chapped lips, taking George's hands tightly and kissing them. "I love you, George. I'm sorry it had to be this way." Despite his love, West couldn't pray mercy for the man. Not after all he'd done.

But the love he had was nonetheless real and raw and burning.

He got up, leaving the room, steps firm. He wouldn't fall, no matter the poison his father had put into him. West would fix his father's sins. No matter the cost.

CHAPTER FORTY-THREE

January 9th, 2028

SPENCER COULDN'T TELL RENE' what was going on—not in full—but he couldn't let her be scared either. Judging by her hollow eyes and weak breathing, the drugs had tortured her plenty. How much more could she take? What if Rex got physical with her? She couldn't take more —Spencer wouldn't allow it.

Maybe he did need to tell Rex everything.

Or at least some of what he knew.

The van bounced along, stopping a few times, making a beeline for what Spencer assumed was the north. Kelsey was a trafficker, and that meant the survivors, Rene', and Spencer, were the traffickees. *Traffickees? Was that a word?*

He sighed. Nothing besides that made much sense. Rex mentioned something about the crew not being allowed to get Rene' pregnant—a weird detail to note. Rex also said something about Percy having something special in mind, but he had probably been messing with Spencer's head. What he'd said about Percy wasn't true, just like them finding and killing Randy was another lie trying to break Spencer's psyche. He wouldn't allow their instilled fears to trigger him.

I wish Rene' would run. He glanced down. Still and quiet, Rene' leaned against his shoulder. She slept restlessly and every now and then, Spencer felt her flinch or tense up. The drugs should wear off again soon, but if they just gave her more, Rene' wouldn't be alert the whole time. Spencer set his jaw, pushing away anger. She might be out of it but she was still scared. He'd kill all of them for that.

The van stopped a few hours later, the survivors lifting their heads wearily. Spencer gently reassured them to stay calm and quiet, that help would come. He shook Rene' and she jerked, groaning.

"We're stopping for the night," Spencer whispered, helping her sit up. She rubbed her eyes and steeled herself with a nod.

The van door opened and a few men led the survivors out. Dusk engulfed the world, traces of yellow and orange in the sky's horizon, but darkness would fall soon. Spencer glanced around, unable to identify where they were besides in the middle of some old middle-class suburb. His mind briefly wandered. *We grew up someplace similar. We lived in a nice little neighborhood and made friends with normal kids and grilled hotdogs on the Fourth of July. The whole time, no one knew who my dad was. No one knew what he was helping the government do.*

A thug hit him. "Keep moving."

Spencer turned away from his memories and followed the other survivors inside a large house with white vinyl and brown brick siding. As the thugs led the survivors up the stairs, one took Rene' toward another hall. Spencer was pulled toward the stairs, and he shoved the man off. "Hey!" he called to the man dragging Rene'.

The man glanced over, snarling. In that brief moment, Rene' whirled and bit down on the man's neck with all her might, drawing blood. The man shrieked and jerked her off. Another thug ran over and snatched Rene' back but Spencer dropped his guard, rushing over. "Let her go! Let her fucking go!"

The thug slapped Rene' hard and snapped at Spencer, something in Spanish, while the injured man fled to the hall, probably to stop his bleeding. Spencer lunged, grabbing the thug by the neck and wrestling him off Rene'. While he had the thug against the wall, Rene' grabbed the man's gun from his side and cocked it.

Spencer swore and knocked the man out. Two more guards rushed over but Rene' shot them both down, one a kill shot to the chest and the next a sloppier shot to the man's collarbone as he reached for her. Both bodies hit the floor, blood pouring and staining the wood floors. Shouts and yells came from all over the house, outside—Spencer grabbed Rene's arm. "Let me see the—"

"So, this is the kid that you guys went through all that effort to save all those times? This is the girl Ed died to save?" a familiar voice mused from behind them.

Rene' whirled, leveling her gun at Percy's head. Spencer froze at her side.

Percy smiled, raising his eyebrows. "Remember me? I fought for Springtown, each and every time."

Rene' didn't budge, gun aimed for a clean head shot, her hand shaking only slightly, and Spencer blamed that on the drugs, not her unwillingness to kill.

"I'm impressed, Rene'. I think you have a big future ahead of you. And I'm sure it felt good to shed some blood, but the rumble is over now, both of you."

Rene' studied him, voice quiet. "Do you have Gideon?"

"Gid? He's here." Percy's eyes narrowed. "Now, drop the gun and kick it away. We have work to do."

Spencer touched Rene's shoulder, firm, comforting. Reassurance burned his tongue but he didn't dare comfort her. The less they all thought he cared about her, the better. Right? Did it even matter anymore?

"Did you plan all of this?" Rene' asked, still unyielding.

Percy laughed softly. "Most of it, yes, I did. Now drop the gun, unless you'd like Gideon to pay for your disobedience."

Spencer's stomach twisted and flipped. Royal had betrayed them—all along? For years, then? And none of them knew? He set his jaw and squeezed Rene's shoulder. Rene' drew a slow breath, shoulders relaxing, and clicked the gun on safety before dropping it. She kicked it over to one of the thugs waiting closeby.

Percy stepped over. "Gideon was right to save you. I take back my doubts I had at the time." His smile grew thin. "I'm sorry for this trouble, Fisher, but it will be worth it. You'll see." He glanced up at Spencer, his eyes flickering with... something Spencer couldn't identify. Something strange. Guilt? Anger?

Spencer had never been good at reading emotions. Or identifying them.

"Spence," Percy said softly. "I think we should talk alone." He told a few guards to take Rene' to her room and gestured Spencer over.

Spencer met Rene's gaze, nodding softly, but her eyes grew hollow again. Once they were gone, Spencer turned back, glaring at Percy. "What—"

"Have you given Rex his answers?"

"Tell me what the hell is going on! What kind of game is this, Percy? You'd better be playing our side and this better be some game—"

"It will make sense soon," Percy snapped. "Now shut up." He led Spencer to another room down the hall and shoved him in, closing the door behind himself.

"What are you thinking?" Spencer fought the rage building in his chest like a volcano.

"I'm thinking clearly," he said. "Unlike all of you all of these years. I will keep each of you safe but you have to do as I say."

Spencer set his jaw. "Like what?"

"You need to tell us everything you know about Anderson."

"Why?"

"Because he's a key token right now and the Union surrendered the war." Percy frowned. "We need to end this for good Spencer, and allowing the rebels to win is something we can't do."

"What does my dad have to do with this?"

"I think he's the man standing between the Union's triumph and surrender."

"I don't understand, if they've already surrendered—"

"Tell Rex what you know, Spencer. We're running out of time to play games. We'll reach the lab soon, and you'll have a lot worse to deal with if you keep fighting," Percy said tightly.

"What?" Spencer's heart dropped. "A lab? Why—"

"Are you going to tell Rex?" Percy demanded.

Spencer was quiet. Why was he trying to keep quiet? He didn't care about his dad. But if he told what he knew, and they got his dad on their team, he'd just hurt his own team. He couldn't aid the enemy, no matter what. "No. Where's Gideon?"

Percy sighed heavily. "Why can't you make this easy?" He calmly locked Spencer to the chains on the floor, then opened the door again. "You have an hour to reconsider, Anderson. After that, you'll have to make a choice." He slammed the door behind him. The click of the lock made Spencer's rage boil over.

He forced a few breaths but those didn't erase his anger. He would not aid the enemy. But if Percy and Rex made him choose...

They'd use Rene' as leverage.

Was helping his side worth the pain Rene' would go through if he kept silent?

Was being loyal to his team worth Rene' being raped? Killed? Cut open?

Nonono.

It's not worth it.

I'm not Gideon. I'm not West. I'm not that dedicated to this goddamn cause. I won't let her die.

He caught himself. Rene' would want him to aid their side. She'd fight too. If they didn't kill her flat out, she'd probably survive what happened, but it'd still be torture, if they took that route and not a bullet to the head. She might want to be a hero but Spencer only had one mission —get every survivor home alive.

But he'd be a traitor. If anyone found out he'd talked, would they kill him for treason? Or would they agree he'd done the right thing and protected Rene'?

Spencer gritted his teeth, steeling himself for what came next. He'd get their attention, tell them what he knew about his dad—which wasn't much—and then pray they kept their word. They wouldn't of course, but at least he'd done what he could.

A soft creaking sound came from behind the wall beside him. He cringed. He didn't know where they'd taken Rene'. Was that her? Was someone hurting her?

Spencer listened for a minute longer and then slammed a fist against the thin wall, fuming. It didn't stop the sound, and he started shouting for Rene'.

No response.

Footsteps fell outside his door. Spencer tensed, waiting. The footsteps stopped and a voice followed, desperate and masculine. Spencer moved as close to the door as he could, listening closely.

"Please stop, Percy. Please. He said he'll stay. Please stop hurting him," the voice pleaded.

Spencer scowled. He knew that voice.

Didn't he?

Who are they talking about? What's Percy doing? It wasn't Rene' at least.

A soft sound followed, like a slap, and then Percy's sharp voice. "I've waited long enough—we both have. I've got everything under control, Preston. I love him and he loves me."

Preston is here? Spencer tensed, pulse ringing in his ears. *Who are they talking about?*

"But—"

"But what?" Percy snapped.

A pause, and the voice dropped low enough so Spencer couldn't hear.

"I don't know what you think love is, Preston, but get over it. This is what it looks like. I'm doing this for him, for all of us. Don't doubt that. Now go watch the kids."

Footsteps followed again. Spencer gulped, calling, "Percy!"

Silence.

"Percy—"

The door unlocked and opened. Percy stepped in, expression dark. He only had on a pair of jeans, his tattooed torso and arms exposed. "What?" he growled.

Spencer stared. "What the hell are you doing?"

"If you're not going to tell me about Anderson—"

"I will! I will!" Spencer said quickly. "I will now. Right now."

Percy cocked his head. "Good. I'll send Rex in." He turned.

"Wait," Spencer said quickly. "Percy, what are you doing?"

Percy laughed. "You know what I'm doing."

"But... but who?"

Percy's smile vanished and he left the room. A few minutes later, Rex came in with a phone, grinning wide. "All right, let's get this over with. Tell me what you know about your dad. Every detail."

Spencer licked his lips, stepping back. "Is Percy with Gideon?"

Rex frowned. "Are you gonna talk or not?"

"OK, fine." Spencer caught his breath. He closed his eyes and told Rex some of what he knew—a few important bits and some minor notes. If it wasn't enough, everyone else would pay. If it was enough, everyone else would pay anyway.

But what else could he do?

GIDEON WAITED TILL PERCY fell asleep beside him before moving. The key to the cuffs were in Percy's jeans, but Gideon couldn't reach them on the floor. He rolled over, pain flaring through his back, but still couldn't find a way to reach the keys.

Rage burned every fiber in his being, and he fought the urge to go berserk. Losing his temper wouldn't get him free. It would only wake Percy and blow Gideon's cover. Right now, the con was the only thing keeping things civil. If Percy got his bloody heart broken, it was game over for everyone.

I have to get the others home. I have to.

But how?

Gideon stared at the ceiling, jaw clenched. Barely across the room lay his only means of escape, and he couldn't reach it.

Of all the situations he'd escaped in his life, he wouldn't have thought a pair of cuffs and a traitor would be his final challenge.

Percy stirred in his sleep and Gideon tensed. The other option was murder Percy in his sleep, but that'd only anger the others and potentially get the survivors harmed during the aftermath. Besides, Gideon's hatred for the man didn't outweigh Percy's usefulness or knowledge, and they'd need that later if Gideon could keep him alive.

Killing him was preferable, but not yet.

After about two hours, Percy woke up with a small jerk and sat up. "Why are you still awake?"

"Can't sleep." Gideon didn't look at him.

"Well, you'll be able to rest soon." Percy sighed. "We're about halfway to New York."

"Good." Gideon kept his tone even. Worked the con. Didn't let any doubts in his mind remain. "I'm sorry, Percy. If you had told me what you felt... I wouldn't have done all of this. I would've listened. We could've been together sooner." He sat up tiredly.

Percy smiled. "That's behind us now. I knew you, Gideon, better than you knew yourself. That's why I waited."

"Was it worth the wait?"

Percy laughed. "You were always worth something. Now go to sleep. We need to head out at four."

Gideon didn't fall asleep, but Percy did, leaving Gideon alone with his plan. Gideon tore it apart, putting it together a million different ways, but it all ended the same. He needed Percy's trust until help arrived and they could kill the enemies without losing any innocent lives.

Preston would make things difficult—he was the only person on the enemy side Gideon might save. The boy was lost and had been in love with a boy who'd died defending the survivors on the way to safety. He'd turned, yes, but he was broken. Alex would want Preston to be given mercy so Gideon would try.

But Percy would get no mercy.

He should never have betrayed us.

CHAPTER FORTY-FOUR

January 10th, 2028

THE SUPER SOLDIERS REIGNED hell over the White House.

Brian's crew ran toward the exit where the presidents waited. The Speaker, along with other hostages, had been left locked in a safe room—but the Vice President of the Union was being taken along for the ride.

Gunshots echoed in the corridors, but the team didn't look back. Rebel soldiers had made their choice—die fighting to cover their leader's six.

Brian wouldn't allow those deaths to be in vain.

The enhanced men poured into the White House all at once, a strategy familiar to Brian, but he wasn't giving up.

They'd shot their way up to the top floor and they'd shoot their way out.

"We retreat," Brian said, glancing at President Larry and Smith. "We make a run for the Humvees. We'll cover your asses, just don't stop, got it?"

The men nodded solemnly, a strange glint in their eyes. Leaving their men behind didn't come naturally; Brian had seen their handiwork on the field. No man left behind was more than a motto to most soldiers.

But it'd be left behind this time.

"Fernando, Amir, cover the douche." He didn't look toward the Union VP, who shook in his shoes, face pale as a ghost.

"Move!" Brian led them out of the building and toward the grounds. A group of enemy soldiers awaited, cut down by Fernando and Lavi's quick fire.

Before the enemies dropped, Bosch dropped to Brian's left, blood splattering from a bullet piercing his skull. Brian pushed on and shot down a few more soldiers, clearing the way for the presidents.

Fernando swore and hauled the Union VP toward the Humvees. The enhanced soldiers hadn't gotten a chance to kill their escape rides, but that's where they were heading.

A swarm of the bastards rushed over, shooting rapidly at their targets. Lavi kept by Brian's side and didn't cease fire, her marksmanship stellar, as always.

But no amount of bullets would get them out of this one. They'd be slaughtered if they kept fighting.

"Run!" Brian shouted. "Move out!"

They reached the Humvees and piled in, the presidents pushed into the vehicles first, then the Union VP. The rebel soldiers readied the vehicles and started out quickly toward the road, shouts dying down. A few fell hard as the enhanced men shot them down during their retreat.

How many had they lost?

Brain didn't look back and shoved Lavi and Fernando to the vehicles, heart hammering in his ears. "It's not over!" he warned.

The driver slammed on the gas, following the others, but the super soldiers didn't stop shooting at them—where were their lasers? Surely they had something to stop their retreat?

A soft rumbling sound shook the earth and grew louder.

A chopper.

"Look!" Fernando panted, gesturing out the window. "What the hell is that?"

Brain craned his neck, swearing as he watched the Black Hawk move over the White House. A large white skull had been painted on the left side and gunmen hung out, taking fire at the enhanced soldiers below.

"Back up," Brian breathed. "They're too late. Lavi, call them off."

"Call them off?" Lavi paused on the comms.

"It's over, Lavi. We'll come back but it'll be a bloodbath now." And then, "do not question my orders."

The image of Bosch's body lying on the asphalt filled his mind, and Davy in the woods... those had been under his order as well.

He shook doubts aside. They had no place in situations like this. Options oftentimes were shit, but they still worked. You had to trust instincts and proven theories.

Anyone accustomed to war would know better than to take this battle on in the shape and numbers Brian's men were in.

But they'd come back for the White House. After all, they had the Union VP. That had to mean something.

The gunners in the Black Hawk shot the soldiers down like flies. It still wouldn't be enough, but the distraction gave Brian's crew and the Confederates time to retreat. Their trail of vehicles tore down the road, and Lavi routed them to a Confederate HQ as Larry instructed.

Brian kept a watchful eye, adrenaline pounding through his veins. The dangers were never over. But they'd made it.

Somehow, some of them had made it.

But we lost most of us.

Brian could help end this war—the final fight wore on even after surrender. The nation would have to rebuild. He'd be a part of that.

———————

AT DAWN, BRIAN STOOD outside of the Confederate HQ camp, smoking a cigarette outside of the meeting tent.

He took a slow breath, Fernando and Lavi's words all ringing in his head. His crew had been willing to go and save Rene'. But he couldn't bring himself to take such a risk.

Not now.

They had to regain control of the White House—if President Larry insisted, perhaps the man had another plan. Someone had to keep the riots and battles in check too, and the Union men in charge now weren't doing anything about it.

If the super soldiers were released again, his crew had the skills to wipe them out. Without Brian and his team, the rebels didn't stand a chance.

Brian dialed a number and waited as it rang.

"Hello?" came his father's sharp voice.

Brian hadn't heard his voice in years. How many years had it been? At least six. Eight? He forced a breath. "Have you found Rene'?" A pathetic question but he couldn't take it back now.

A pause, then a snarl, "What the hell do you want, Brian? Are you coming to help search for her?"

"The rebels have hope, Burl. Just keep doing what you've all been doing and keep your alliances—you'll need them when the nation rebuilds stronger than before."

"Don't avoid the question," Mr. Fisher snapped, tone ice.

"You have to understand," Brian said firmly. "I'm doing all of this to keep you all safe. It's my job. I'm doing it."

"If you cared, you'd be searching for your sister." Mr. Fisher hung up.

Brian clenched his jaw and chucked the phone against the frozen ground.

A light knock came from the doorway. "We're ready to plan, boss," Fernando said, raising one eyebrow. "I take it that the call didn't go well."

"They hate me." Brian growled. "I'm doing all of this to make them safe, and they still hate me. They blame me for what happened, but it was Rene's own fault for being stupid."

Fernando sighed. "Well, if you left my little sister behind, I'd hate you too, sir."

Brian shot him a look, but Fernando held up his hands. "Hey, we're off duty, and if you wanna make me eat my words, fire me."

Brian stormed past him and headed to the meeting room. "Is everyone ready?" he asked, ignoring the previous disaster.

Family could wait. The nation's future couldn't.

"Yeah, ready for the next phase." Fernando eyed him, keeping up with his fast pace. "You can be pissed all you want, Brian, but you know they're right. You should—"

"Not now, Fernando."

"Then when? There won't be a next time to play the hero, Jones. Rene' is going to die and you know it." Fernando grabbed his shoulder roughly and pinned him against the wall, eyes flashing. "Put your ego down for one second and face that. We could leave after the meeting and —"

"I swore an oath! We all did! We might've broken it and gone off the rails, but that doesn't mean I'm leaving behind my duties," Brian cut him off.

"We are aiding the rebels. We are keeping control of the battles in this nation. We're restoring order from the chaos. The nation doesn't stop just because Rene' is dying. Do you understand?" Brian asked sharply, breathing growing ragged.

Fernando's eyes narrowed. "Fine." But something flickered in his eyes. He'd do what he wanted to do later. Let him—Brian had work to do for his nation. Everyone would suffer if he tried to save only one person. He had lost too many comrades to throw their sacrifices away now. He'd keep his family safe, even if it made him look like the villain.

CHAPTER FORTY-FIVE

January 11th, 2028

THE GROUP STOPPED THAT night at a large warehouse. Rene' couldn't make out her surroundings in the dark as the survivors were escorted into the building, but she figured it was nowhere good.

They were going further north—she didn't know their destination but any place north couldn't be a good sign. She figured they would sell the survivors. She'd be sold and used like an object, just like millions of girls before her.

The thugs led them inside and split them all, as usual. Spencer was led down a hall with Gideon. The remaining survivors were taken upstairs. Rex led Rene' to a room down the hall, locking her inside. Rene' shuddered, though the chilly warehouse was the least of her concerns.

The survivors were all unharmed so far, but Rex's strange words hung in her mind.

What truly awaited them all at the end of this trek?

A trafficking ring? Some politicians who wanted a victim to violate without strings attached? Or something worse, like the labs Simon told her about?

Simon. Her heart dropped, and she wiped at the tears that sprang to her weary eyes. Even if Kelsey planned on selling them all to the labs for research and experiments, it wouldn't happen. Simon and Dad, all of the others, they'd save them. They would come. No matter what.

Though she prayed help came, she also almost wished it wouldn't. After all, they could get hurt, someone could get killed. Percy's jab stung her spirit. *Ed died because of me. Does someone else have to die just because I'm a fool, God?*

And as she'd come to expect these last months, God didn't answer, but Rene' didn't let that break her. Instead, she pushed away the thought of Simon, and his kind words, and his crushing big hugs, and—

Tears ran down her cheeks. Rene' sank against the wall, hugging her knees. *I have to be strong,* she scolded herself. *I have to save these survivors and Spencer.*

But I can't, God.

Can I?

She focused on her weak breathing. The drugs had worn off and they hadn't jabbed her again, but exhaustion coursed through her very bones. Her eyes drooped. *I can't run or escape without the others... I can't outwit them or out fight them...*

The door opened and a light voice filled the room, "I've been so busy!" Kelsey chuckled, shutting the door behind her. "I'm sorry, love. Where were we?"

Rene' glared at her, standing quickly. Kelsey didn't wear any sort of weapon that Rene' saw. *But I can still kill her.*

Rene's throat tightened. Where had that thought come from?

Kelsey smiled. "We're almost there, don't worry. This miserable trip will end. How do you feel?" Her narrow eyes cut right through Rene'.

"Fine." Rene' smirked. "I feel better than you look."

Kelsey rolled her eyes. "You haven't changed much."

"Actually, I have." Rene' shrugged.

"I hear you have a boyfriend?""Husband," Rene' corrected simply.

"I don't see a ring on your dainty little hand," Kelsey bit.

Rene' smiled, voice cold, "I don't see one on yours, either. Are you still with douchebag?"

Kelsey's cheeks reddened and her eyes glinted, a dangerous warning that Rene' faced plenty of times before. "Simon won't have a chance at finding you, I'm afraid. Their little expedition was stalled this evening. A few were killed." She smirked. "We'll see, hm?"

Questions flooded Rene's mind and almost slipped out, but she caught herself. If this was a game, she wouldn't play. Spencer warned her before that they'd try these sort of mind games.

"They'd be believable," he'd said. "But don't believe them.

Then again, he'd been wrong about Percy being a traitor.

What if someone did die? What if Dad... or Lee... or Simon...

No! Be stronger than that!

"We'll have plenty of time to catch up," Kelsey said softly. "For now though, we still need information from the pretty boys. Come with me." She turned, opening the door before pausing. "Oh, and I don't have to remind you that any attempt at fighting or fleeing will be the last this time, do I? There's one brat upstairs I don't mind killing, if you were to try something stupid."

Rene' clenched her jaw. "Wouldn't dream of it." She pushed the fresh memories from her mind. She'd killed men just the night before. It hadn't been the first time she'd killed, but it was the most personal and up close that she'd ever killed.

Somehow, though, a numbness encased the memories, as if she knew she ought to feel something about it. But only satisfaction settled in her gut.

She followed Kelsey down the hall and into the second room. Percy stood sentry at the door across from Gideon and Spencer, who were both stripped to their boxers and kneeling on the floor. They both had their hands chained behind their backs, the chains drilled to the floor. This warehouse was the least clean of all the stops thus far—blood stains covered the wall behind them. Gideon didn't look at her but Spencer paled, a nauseous expression crossing his face.

Rene' tensed, eyeing Kelsey. "What is this?"

Kelsey smiled and stepped back against the door. "Percy? It's all up to you now. I'll be in the other room." She slipped out.

Coward, Rene' fumed. Percy rested a gentle hand on Rene's right shoulder. "Spencer, you have a lot of explaining to do." His smile softened. "Rex failed but I won't. I got Gideon to talk, after all."

Rene' cringed and moved away but Percy held tighter, continuing, "So, starting with Spence, let's set the record straight. From the top." He smiled.

Spencer growled. "I already told you what I knew. I told Rex everything, just like I said I would!"

"But that wasn't the complete truth." Percy sighed. "If you can't answer me, Spencer, then you choose if Rene' lives or if Gideon lives. Understand me?"

Spencer paled and his eyes flashed. "I told you what I know!" He yanked against the chains. "I told you everything I know!"

Percy raised his eyebrows. "You didn't and you know it. *I* know it. There's no way that's all the man told you." He pulled a pistol from his waist. "Now, get talking or I choose for you."

Rene' couldn't breathe. By Percy's tone and the coldness in his eyes, he wasn't bluffing. She doubted Percy would shoot Gideon either, so that left her the loser.

Her heart hammered in her chest like a wild horse. *I don't want to die.* And then, *but Spencer can't help these people.* "It's OK, Spence," she choked. That was all she forced out.

Spencer's eyes went wide. "No—"

Percy sighed softly. "Spencer, are you willing to save a nation over your friend?"

Gideon met Rene's gaze, eyes narrow yet reassuring. Rene' clamped her jaw tightly, fighting a sob and a scream all at once. Numbness engulfed her and she shivered. *Why isn't Gideon afraid?*

Spencer looked between the gun and Rene'. Rene's stomach twisted but she squared her shoulders. "It's fine,

Spence. Please." The others deserved to live—not her. Her family, her friends, Simon—they were the ones who deserved life, not her. She could do what Ed had done. She could let go if it meant others would live. Maybe Brian had the right idea about letting her go to save the nation.

I don't want to die.

But that's OK, Lord.

Please, be with me.

"No," Spencer said softly, meeting Percy's gaze. His voice grew firmer, "No. The answer to that question is no. I'll tell you everything."

"Start talking, then." Percy smiled and holstered the gun.

Hot tears ran down Rene's cheeks. She stood silent, breathing shallow, still expecting a bullet any moment.

Spencer talked, filling the ear-ringing silence in her head, drawing her back into reality. Spencer didn't shut up till the story was out in full: his father had helped fund the war, building the tension between the nation's two parties for years as a politician and a ganglord, hiring hitmen occasionally to get his way. He had also helped fund and investigate research for the American laboratories— research for the genetic enhancements. Anderson had been close friends to George years ago before Anderson had gone off grid entirely.

None of it made much sense. If he was so valuable, why did he sound boring? Lots of men had helped research those studies and plenty were involved in politics and gang matters.

Percy lifted a hand, stopping Spencer's intricate ramble. He turned to Gideon. "Any of this a lie?"

"No," Gideon said. "He's telling the truth." He leaned back, shoulders sagging. "Keep going, Spencer."

Spencer's Adam's apple bobbed. His eyes heavy with fear and pain, his cool, con-artist exterior completely gone, he went on. "He ran years ago, Percy, and hasn't contacted either of us since all of that. I don't know where he went. Out of the country, probably." He sucked in a breath. Waiting. Watching.

Rene' bit her lip hard. Would Percy snap and kill her anyway? Had Spencer's attempt at saving her been a failure?

Percy patted Spencer on the shoulder, smiling wearily. "Much better, Spence." He glanced at Gideon. "You two stay here. I have some questions for Rene'."

Rene' tensed at the gleam in his eyes. She'd seen it before. Throat going dry, she stepped back instinctively.

"What would you want from her?" Spencer asked, eyes narrowing.

Percy laughed and led Rene' toward the door. Rene' gasped, shooting her palm up into Percy's nose with all her might. Her old sensei would've been proud of the fluid movement and how well it did the job.

Rene' ducked, avoiding Percy's grab, yanking his pistol off his side. Percy growled and clamped a hand around Rene's throat, slamming her against the wall with ease.

"Get off her!" Spencer shouted.

"Percy, stop," Gideon spoke up calmly.

But it was all too late. Rene' clutched the gun, moved it up against Percy's chest, his face inches from hers. He snatched the gun before she could get a finger on the trigger.

"Percy!" Gideon snapped.

Percy brought the gun up and Rene' cried out, shielding her head in vain. The butt of the gun hit her skull and she fell into nothingness.

SPENCER SCREAMED, YANKING AGAINST the chains. "Percy! Percy, stop!" Blood poured from the wound on Rene's head, her body falling limp in Percy's grasp. "Percy!" Panic flooded Spencer and his stomach twisted. "Please!"

Percy lifted the gun again but held it there. He huffed and dropped Rene's body to the floor. "I'm sorry, Gid, I..." he blinked. "I thought she... she was someone else."

He shuddered but holstered the gun. Turning, he pulled a key and undid Gideon's chains. "Help her."

Gideon quickly scooped Rene' into his arms and ran out of the room, shouting for a first aid kit. Spencer tugged harder. "Percy, let me out! Let me go to her! I did what you said!" His eyes burned. A blow like that could've killed her.

God, don't let her die. Don't let her die, please!

Percy licked his lips and left the room, slamming the door behind him. Spencer crumpled, his rage growing till he couldn't hold it in and it burst from every pore of his body. "Let her go! Let me go to her!" he yelled.

It wouldn't help. Kelsey and Percy had their wicked plan and nothing would stop them.

The image of Rene's limp, bloody form made Spencer wrench. He coughed, tugging against the chains, harder, harder, till blood seeped from the gashes he created. *God, please! Listen to me! I know You don't have to but she deserves to live! Listen! Please! Take me. Not Rene'. Don't take the kid!*

Panic and rage whirling in his chest like a tsunami, a sob escaped him. He hadn't protected her. He'd failed them all —Rene', Randy, Kaleb, everyone. His friends had counted on him and he'd betrayed them. If Rene' died, what then?

No. I can't think like that.

He snarled, pushing the pain away, deep down inside where it couldn't take any of his time. He needed the rage only.

I'll kill Percy and Kelsey. No matter what it takes.

Rene' would be all right, and the people who did this would die. Spencer was good at his job. He wouldn't fail this time.

CHAPTER FORTY-SIX

January 11th, 2028

GIDEON STOPPED RENE'S HEAD wound from bleeding further, bandaging her carefully. She wouldn't wake and her pulse was weak, no doubt due to exhaustion, dehydration, drugs, and the head wound all combined. He set his jaw once finished, pulling her close. Percy watched, eyebrows furrowed in concern. "Is she all right?"

"She needs medical attention." Gideon stood up from the floor and lifted Rene' off the couch. "Let's start with a bed?"

Percy nodded, leading him upstairs. "I am sorry, Gid. I acted off instinct. I didn't mean—"

"I know, it's fine," Gideon said. "She's tough."

"Spencer told us everything." Percy changed the subject. "We can finish this."

"Are you sure that was a bluff? Do you really plan on putting a bullet in my head that easily?" Gideon teased dryly.

Percy led him into a small room with a cot. Gideon lay Rene' down and covered her with a scratchy blanket at the end of the cot. Rene' still didn't stir.

Percy grabbed Gideon's arm. "You know that was just so Spencer would talk!"

Gideon chuckled. "I know. Relax."

"Don't joke like that." Percy frowned. "We have to work the job, right?"

"And it's going well," Gideon said. He stepped away from Rene' and glanced at the blood on his hands. "Just don't do that again. Spencer gets violent, Percy, you know that."

"I'll stay away from him." Percy nodded, pulling Gideon into the hall. "Come on. Let's get some shut eye."

Gideon set his jaw, following, pushing all anger and aversion aside. He had a con. Maintain Percy's trust till help comes and then kill everyone. "Mind if we just sleep tonight?"

"Sure." Percy laughed. "There'll be plenty of time for fun later."

"Where's Preston?" Gideon shut the bedroom door behind them, locking it. The room was small, but had a mattress on the floor, at least. The window was boarded up but a draft made Gideon cringe.

"He's got guard duty for Spencer till 12." Percy sighed. "We're almost there. It'll pay off, Gideon. I'll show you."

Gideon sat down on the bed, grunting in pain. "Yeah. I know."

"I'm sorry it didn't turn out how you wanted," Percy said quietly, staring out a crack in the boards against the window.

"Huh?"

"You wanted to save everyone and fool George... You wanted the US to be free and united again. None of that will happen. But... but the UN gaining control, Gideon, it won't be so bad. You and I can be free. Just watch. We'll be two of the very few who are smart enough to survive in a new, better world." He turned and offered a weak smile. "It's better this way. With Anderson aiding the officials and leaders too, the Union can triumph. And the nation will need men like us. That's what you wanted."

I wanted freedom. I wanted peace. I wanted to do my part. "Yeah," he lied. "It is."

"Are you angry I lied?" Percy asked.

"No, I understand why you did. I wouldn't have heard anything you said before, I was blind." Gideon lay flat on his back.

Percy sighed, relief flooding his voice. "I thought you'd be angry."

"I'm not."

"I love you," Percy whispered, sitting on the mattress. "More than anyone, more than anything. I'll prove it to you."

Gideon glanced over, words hollow. "You already have."

When Percy fell asleep, Gideon lay awake. He thought of Flannery, and Gideon's failed mission to kill the man for all he had done to Alex and innocent lives. Now, Gideon failed to guard the others and had to pay for the mistake of trusting Percy as a brother.

He'd fix his mistakes or all he'd fought for since he was a teen was lost for good.

And if George found out that Gidon had betrayed him and done all of this... Gideon closed his eyes. It was not over. He would not think of defeat.

Alex would hold onto hope.

He gritted his teeth, his brother's voice flooding his head. How many times had Alex voiced his dreams about a future? His faith never yielded. His dreams never died.

I have to make it out of this, I have to save everyone, for Alex. I can't let him get hurt again.

Gideon allowed himself one small, last prayer, a verse from the Bible he'd remembered years and years ago. *"And I will execute great vengeance upon them with furious rebukes; and they shall know that I [am] the LORD, when I shall lay my vengeance upon them."*

CHAPTER FORTY-SEVEN

January 12th, 2028

SIMON KEPT AN EYE on the clock, driving as fast as the back road would allow him. The large crew hadn't stopped for long since starting out. Since Travis had sent the new coordinates, a sense of determined rage had engulfed the atmosphere—there was nothing but moving forward.

No memories, no doubts, nothing but the mission ahead.

Dawn peeked its face over the world before him. Simon set his jaw and focused on the route the GPS gave him.

The men in the back stirred. Lee slept soundly for the first time since they'd started out. Mo was on his phone texting, his haggard expression paining Simon. Mr. Fisher slept beside Lee, and the other soldiers were quiet and resting while they could. Every vehicle followed Simon's lead and he followed Travis, who led half a mile ahead.

A message beeped through. Travis said, "*reroute first left turn .2 miles ahead ASAP. Tangos ahead.*"

Simon swore and barely made the turn, checking in his rearview mirror, but the others all made the quick change, as well. He called Travis, heart hammering. Travis didn't pick up. "Mr. Fisher!"

Mr. Fisher jerked upright. "What?" He pushed himself toward the front of the van, movements stiff and sore.

"Travis gave me a different route; he ran into trouble."

Mr. Fisher frowned. "He's a big boy, he'll handle it. Keep going."

Simon kept the new route for about ten minutes before Travis called. Mr. Fisher answered on speakerphone. "Travis?"

"Fisher, we got a caravan of Union soldiers surrounding us," Travis snapped. "They're tryna guard the roads and loot supplies. You guys can out race 'em but—"

"Where are you?" Mr. Fisher demanded.

"Still fighting," he said shortly. "Wanted to warn y'all. I'll send boys back if I can. These soldiers shouldn't be too hard—" A bang followed, cutting the connection.

Simon swore. "What do we do, Dad?"

"Keep moving," Mr. Fisher said. He ordered Mo, "get that drone going out of Brett's truck, now! We need to see what's going on around us!"

Mo swore and obeyed, using a controller from a supply box he leaned against, accessing the drone in the truck behind them. Simon set his jaw and sped up, pushing the van as hard as he could without risking the van's mobility. Mo got the drone running, mumbling under his breath.

"Well? Can you see anything?" Mr. Fisher asked firmly.

"Uhh, yessir. Some Humvees, uh, actually, look! There's a camp! Right up ahead, it looks like a camp of Union guys." Mo groaned. "That's not good, is it?"

"No," Mr. Fisher glanced at Simon. "Go back, now."

"Go back?" Simon growled. "We can't waste time finding another route! We can push through and fight them off. Travis said it wouldn't be hard!" "Go back!" Mr. Fisher thundered. "We can't afford any more losses."

Simon swore, but he flashed his lights and slowed, making a rather sharp turn and fleeing back the way they came. "If Travis is down—"

"We keep moving. Reroute this." Mr. Fisher took the GPS and gave it to Mo. By this time, Lee and a few others were awake, watching quietly. Mo rerouted them and handed it back, but Simon didn't look at him.

"We'll make it," Mo said softly. "W-we just lose a few hours."

A few hours didn't make a lifetime of difference. But Simon set his jaw and sped in silence.

God, let her live.

Let us reach them.

Let me kill whoever touched her.

EPILOGUE

January 12th, 2028

"THE THREE OF US together again, just like old times," Kaleb mused, watching the world pass them as Hunter drove them deeper into the USA. They'd passed plenty of caravans, customs, and whatnot, so far without a scratch.

Jeremy cast him a frown. "Have you checked on Richard?"

"Yeah, all of the survivors made it to Springtown." Kaleb nodded.

Hunter spoke up, "We can focus on the job, Jeremy. Everything else is covered for now." The White House was out of Confederate control, the battles raging throughout the nation would be extinguished—or flamed

—soon enough with or without the trio's help, and the Second Civil War had officially been declared a surrender.

Only, it wouldn't stop there. That's why they needed the whole team back.

Jeremy forced a slow breath. The storm had only just begun, but he didn't care about any other duty than the one before him—save his son.

I'm coming, Gideon. Just hang on. One more time.

He pulled up his phone and dialed his father. "Guns, listen, we might be a little late. Can you send backup ahead of us, and see if a mole in the labs can buy us some time, too? I'm not so much worried about the boys as I am Rene' and the victims getting impregnated."

"Already taken care of. But you'd better hurry," Guns said sharply. "I'm not God."

"I couldn't tell. Buying Flannery off all those times muddled my vision of you." Jeremy rolled his eyes and hung up. He took a breath and studied Hunter and Kaleb, a steadfast resolve overcoming him.

Train for war and fight to win. If there had ever been a time for warriors to rise up, it was now.

TO BE CONTINUED...

THANKS FOR READING THE MERCENARY'S DECEPTION!

The story continues in The Blood Republic!

If you'd like to support the book, please review it on Amazon and share the word about it on social media!

If you want to get the inside scoop on my new releases, sign up for my newsletter on my website!

Acknowledgments

As always, without God, this book would not have been possible. This publication was difficult. Writing the novel was pretty easy, since it was the book I had in mind when I started the whole series. But publication? Trial after trial, error after error, so the Lord is to thank for getting this book into your hands.

Thanks to my parents, for supporting my writing and editing career. Thanks for the hugs and surprise root beers.

Thanks to my siblings and nieces, for listening to me talk about the characters, what new torture method I researched that day, and for taking me on adventures to relax when I worked too much. You guys all rock.

Thanks to my friends, for being amazing and encouraging.

Thanks to Caleb, for helping me figure out how to create a pacifist community and destroy it.

Thanks to you, reader, for picking this novel up and giving it a chance. I hope it was worth it. Now, go forth and be bold.

AUTHOR BIO

Angela R. Watts is the bestselling author of The Infidel Books and the Remnant Trilogy. She's been writing stories since she was little, and when she's not writing, she's probably drawing or working with her amazing editorial clients. You can join her newsletter or connect with her on social media.

https://angelarwatts.com/

Printed in Great Britain
by Amazon